LOST IN TRANSLATION

AUDREY DAVIS

For my Family
And in memory of our dear friends Kevin Harty and Ann Breadie
who left us far too soon. So many happy memories of time spent
together in Switzerland. Always in our hearts ♥ ♥

CHAPTER 1

'MUMMY, WHY ARE YOU DRIVING SO SLOW?'

Charlotte gritted her teeth, gripped the steering wheel so tightly her knuckles whitened, and resisted the urge to turn around. 'Mummy is driving *slowly* because she's not used to driving on the wrong side of the road.' OK, technically it was the right side of the road in many countries, but until two days ago she'd only driven in the UK. Normally she wouldn't be acting like the grammar police, but today's first solo school run in Switzerland had her nerves jangling louder than the cowbells of the small herd inhabiting a field next to their rented house.

'Are we going to be late?' Robson, her youngest, was a stickler for punctuality. He'd learned to tell the time with incredible speed, and would sit, lunchbox and book bag ready, waiting to leave for primary school long before the appointed hour. Meanwhile, his older brother, Alastair, would remain glued to the TV, shoeless and lost in a world of cartoons. Charlotte fell somewhere in between. Either super-organised, with everything laid out the night before, or in a state of panic because a jotter couldn't be located and she'd poked herself in the eye with the mascara wand.

'No, darling. Almost there. Just—'

As she approached the sharp left turn into the school grounds, a swanky red sports car emerged; a large, open-topped beast which took a right and seemed to aim for Charlotte's humble VW Polo. Oblivious to the queue of cars behind her, she swerved to avoid a collision. A hideous scraping sound ensued, accompanied by screeches of alarm from the back seat. Letting rip with a very rude word, Charlotte tried to beep her horn at the flash bastard. But she still wasn't familiar with the car and merely set the windscreen wipers in motion.

'Are you OK, Mummy?' Alastair had already undone his seat belt and tapped Charlotte on the shoulder. Cursing again under her breath, she glowered at the sports-car driver. He didn't even glance her way, speeding off along the narrow road at full throttle.

'I'm fine, sweetheart.' Aware of an ominous crunching noise, Charlotte crawled through the gates and praised the gods above that there was a free parking spot. The previous times she'd done the school run — with husband Dom in the driver's seat — the parking area had resembled a dodgem track. One populated with people carriers, 4 X 4s and sporty numbers bearing personalised number plates. Oh, and with clusters of well-groomed men and women chatting and gesticulating as if they were at an upmarket garden party.

'We need to hurry!' Robson scrambled out of the car, followed by Alastair. Charlotte sucked in a deep breath and followed suit. They stood on the right-hand side of the Polo, surveying the damage. Most of the plastic strip running the full length of the car had been torn off, and deep gouges marred the silver paintwork.

'Oops! Looks like someone came a cropper with the wall

of doom.' Charlotte looked up to see her new 'friend' (if someone you'd known a handful of days could be called that), standing beside them. For a moment, her brain addled by the incident, she struggled to recall the other mother's name.

'He's a dickhead,' said Robson casually. 'In a fancy red car.' Charlotte gulped, aware he was parroting her outburst at the point of collision.

'I can probably guess who, although there are a few male candidates vying for that title!' Her friend — damn it, was it Sue, Sarah, or something else beginning with S? — laughed. 'Right, troops, let's get you into class before Miss Andrews sends out a search party.'

Together they made their way up to the quaint chalet that housed the school's junior department. Another woman called out. 'Sadie!' OK, close but not on the button.

'Coffee after we dump the darlings?' Sadie nudged her two girls toward their teacher. Robson sprinted ahead of them, Alastair trailing behind.

'Erm, wait a minute.' Charlotte hurried to Alastair's side. 'What's that in your hand?'

With a puzzled frown, her eldest looked down. Unfurling his small fingers, he revealed the slim TV remote control. Silently he handed it over, and Charlotte tucked it into her handbag.

'What are they like?' Sadie stood next to her, tapping furiously on her phone. 'My Miranda once took a box of chocolate liqueurs into class, because it was someone's birthday and yours truly burnt the brownies.'

'Did they get to eat them?' Charlotte imagined a bunch of seven-year-olds fighting over the Cointreau and Grand Marnier-filled treats, lessons descending into chaos as the alcohol kicked in.

'Nah,' replied Sadie. 'Miss Andrews confiscated them. I

should have asked for them back, but I figured that as she deals with that rabble daily, her need was greater than mine.'

As the last of the year groups disappeared inside the building, Charlotte walked back to her car. Sadie deftly removed the flapping plastic, opened the door and tossed it in the back seat. 'Right, no real harm done. Why don't you hop in and follow me to the café? A few of us meet at Le Petit Train a couple of times a week.'

Gingerly, Charlotte got behind the wheel. Her instinct was to drive home, throw herself face down on the bed and sob until Dom got home from work. However, as his new job meant he rarely left the office before seven, that meant she'd be sobbing for the next eleven hours. Charlotte had a long list of jobs to do, but as most involved exercising her rudimentary French, a caffeine fix and a sugar-laden treat seemed very appealing. Starting the car, she set off in Sadie's wake, wishing for the hundredth time that she was back in her familiar suburban enclave of England.

CHAPTER 2

'IT'S NOT THE END OF THE WORLD, CHARLOTTE.' DOM emerged from the en-suite bathroom, vigorously attacking his gum line with a strand of dental floss. He paused, looked at his wife huddled up under the duvet, and sighed. 'It's only a car, we'll deal with it. Why don't you come downstairs? We can have a glass of wine and admire the view.'

Bugger the view. Charlotte knew she was being overly dramatic, but she couldn't imagine calling this place home. Yes, their rented house offered spectacular views across the lake towards the Alps, but it all felt so alien. Coffee with Sadie and a few others had been pleasant, but they were all old hands, already comfortable with the driving, the language and the shopping. Oh my God, the shopping. Used to the delights of Tesco, Waitrose and the friendly butcher and deli near her previous home, Charlotte nearly had a meltdown when she encountered the village supermarket. Basic didn't cover it. The freezer cabinet was marginally bigger than the freezer she'd had at home in the UK, and everything closed early. And forget shopping on a Sunday. Those lovely impromptu barbecues they'd had in the past when the forecast brought sunshine instead of cloud were now ancient history. Virtually everything closed on the Sabbath, apart from the boulangeries (how much bread could these people eat?), petrol stations and churches. Even their local restaurant, a ten-minute downhill walk away (and a vertiginous climb back up), closed its doors the entire weekend.

'I don't want wine,' Charlotte said. 'I want to go home.'

The truth was, Charlotte hadn't wanted to leave the UK in the first place. She'd sobbed for days when Dom announced the job transfer, always careful to repair her make-up and paint on a smiling face when the boys were around. Robson and Alastair had taken it in their stride, as young children do. They'd barely glanced backwards on their last day at the village school, bragging to their friends that they'd soon be learning to ski and eating chocolate in vast quantities. Charlotte stood trembling on the perimeter of the playground, afraid to catch the eye of another mum or dad. A gruff 'good luck' from perpetually grumpy single dad Jasper broke down her defences. The poor man was probably still recovering from the shoulder-soaking she'd given him.

'You need to give it more time.' Dom perched on the edge of the bed, irritation seeping through his words. 'You've already made friends, haven't you? And the boys are happy. You've got to pull yourself together, Charlotte. Don't transfer your misery to them.'

Charlotte slid further under the duvet, hissing 'twat' under her breath. Juvenile, but Dom's failure to accept her struggle wasn't a recent phenomenon. The heady days of romance a decade ago were a distant memory. Yes, having two children in rapid succession wasn't the wisest move. Particularly when Charlotte had no family close by to help, and Dom's parents — a two-hour drive away — viewed babysitting as something that should be paid for. Their adored only son was always welcomed with open arms, although Dom found their devotion suffocating. They merely tolerated Charlotte and the boys; not that she ever relished visiting them. She still shuddered at memories of Robson vomiting all over her mother-in-law Jean's new cream linen sofa, and Alastair leaving a trail of soggy biscuit crumbs through the immaculately carpeted hallway. Jean took to following the boys around with a dustpan and brush and a can of stain remover.

'Why don't we throw a party?' Dom's eyes glittered at the prospect. Charlotte rolled hers so hard she felt dizzy. Parties — at least, *hosting* them — were up there with smear tests and ironing bedlinen on her list of things to avoid. Not that she was a terrible cook, or anti-social, but she just found the whole business of shopping/prepping/attempting to keep up with the conversation while listening out for the boys and the oven timer exhausting. Dom would work the room like a presidential hopeful, oozing bonhomie and topping up drinks after a mere sip or two. The only thing Charlotte oozed was sweat, as she fretted whether the soufflés would rise or the beef turn out tougher than a cowboy's crotch.

'And who do we invite, exactly?' she asked.

'That woman you keep talking about, Sophie or something.' Dom was as crap at names as she was. And Charlotte didn't *keep* talking about her. She'd briefly mentioned the get-together at Le Petit Train, attended by two other school mums.

Alicia, a former ballet dancer, kept her feet permanently in first position, and quickly established that Charlotte didn't fit into the mega-rich bracket. 'A three-bed rental, hmm?' she'd drawled when discussing homes.

'Alicia lives in a lakeside mansion with an infinity pool and hot-and-cold running staff,' whispered Sadie. 'She likes to mingle with the poor people from time to time, to main-

tain her superiority complex. Oh, and her actual name is
Agnes Blenkinsop. I caught a glimpse of her passport one
day. Well, I sneaked it out of her Hermes bag when she
wasn't looking.'

The other mum at the gathering barely said a word. She
stirred her milky coffee in endless circles, occasionally
taking a sip. Sadie introduced her as Pamela, mother of ten-
year-old twins Rebecca and Elspeth. They were in the year
above Alastair, both pin-thin with milky-white complexions
and hair in matching pigtails. Extracting information from
Pamela was like squeezing the last dregs out of the tooth-
paste tube. She restricted her answers to: 'Yes', 'No' and 'Not
sure, really', the latter in response to Charlotte asking if she
liked it here. It was down to Sadie again to fill in the details.

'She's been here since the twins were babies,' she revealed,
when Pamela disappeared to the ladies. 'Hired a nanny after
a few weeks: a pretty Croatian girl who took her job very
seriously. So much so that she decided to tend to Pamela's
husband's needs too. And I don't mean ironing his business
shirts.'

Deciding that a glass of wine might be a good idea, Charlotte propelled herself out of bed, shrugged on her dressing
gown and headed downstairs. All was quiet in the boys'
bedroom, and she resisted the urge to have a peek.

'So, shall we throw a party?' Dom followed Charlotte into
the kitchen. She unscrewed the cap of a bottle of red and
reached for two glasses. The satisfying glug of the liquid
soothed her edginess, and she took a swig. Dom tutted —
failing to say 'cheers' was a sin in his book — and pulled a
face when he took a toothpaste-flavoured mouthful.

'Let me think about it.' Charlotte needed time to get her
head around the idea. At some point she'd chat to Sadie and
see if one or two of the other mums she was on nodding
terms with at school might be interested in coming. Pamela

too, and her cheating husband. They were still together, the Croatian nanny sent packing when the affair came to light.

Charlotte wandered over to the large lounge window and watched as the sun set, a kaleidoscope of colours decorating the sky. Dom came up behind her, wrapping his arms around her waist. She welcomed his embrace and snuggled into his familiar, strong arms. And yet... There'd been a time, not long before the move to Switzerland, when she'd suspected something was amiss in their marriage. Or rather, someone else. As day gave way to night, Charlotte's thoughts drifted back to their life in England, and how they ended up being here...

CHAPTER 3

Six Months Earlier

'CHARLOTTE! WE'VE RUN OUT OF BUTTER!'

On her hands and knees in the boys' bedroom, trying to locate a vital piece of Lego under the bed, Charlotte blew out an exasperated breath. That dislodged an unhealthy wodge of tumbleweed, also known as a dust ball. No matter how often she dragged the vacuum cleaner around the house, the dust multiplied and accumulated in corners and under furniture.

Dom had been on at her to get a cleaner since the boys were little, but Charlotte wasn't keen. She'd quit her job as a medical receptionist when Robson turned one, Dom insistent that they didn't need her 'meagre' salary. His words, not hers. Charlotte had enjoyed the daily interaction with the patients: even the miserable ones, and the hypochondriacs convinced that every minor twinge signalled their imminent demise. Plus, most of her friends who had cleaners spent a good hour cleaning their homes beforehand, lest the hired help thought they were lazy bitches.

Harrumphing down the stairs, picking fluff off her black jeans, Charlotte mentally ran through her to-do list for the day. Gym at eleven, lunch with best friend Ruth immediately after, then errands to run, including dropping off a pile of Dom's suits at the dry cleaners. She'd done a large grocery shop the day before, and could have sworn she'd picked up a tub of spreadable butter. Mind you, the so-called 'mummy brain' experienced in the months after the boys' births seemed to have lingered throughout her thirties.

'You know I can't stand toast without butter,' grumbled Dom, fiddling with the coffee machine, which was playing up. Instead of a steady stream of fragrant liquid, it dribbled pathetically. He ran his fingers through his thick, dark hair, still damp from the shower.

Charlotte flipped the kettle switch — instant was her drink of choice — and pulled open the fridge door. 'Ta-dah!' Moving aside a four-pack of yoghurt and a carton of eggs, she produced the butter with a magician's flourish.

'Well, how am I supposed to find it if it's hidden?' Dom flicked off the lid and peeled back the foil, before popping two slices of bread in the toaster.

Charlotte bit back a reply. Too often these days the tiniest things triggered major arguments. Only last week Dom had complained his favourite shirt wasn't ironed, and her suggestion that he did it himself hadn't ended well. He'd huffed his way into the utility room, spent a good fifteen minutes figuring out how to switch the iron on, then burned a hole in the front of the shirt. They'd argued bitterly about everything from who dealt with the household bills (Dom) to who took the brunt of responsibility for the boys (Charlotte). It was like a never-ending tennis match, the pair of them permanently stuck at deuce. But wasn't that the case with most marriages?

'Don't forget we have the boys' school concert tonight at seven.' Charlotte made her coffee and passed Dom his cup from the machine, which had spluttered its way to a conclusion. Neither Alastair nor Robson were natural performers. Both preferred to stay out of the limelight, hiding (like the butter) behind the more flamboyant class members. For one night only they were part of a production of *Joseph and His Amazing Technicolour Dreamcoat*, albeit a scaled-down version. Charlotte had attended the dress rehearsal, her heart contracting at the sight of her two little darlings shuffling awkwardly, mouthing the lyrics she'd practised with them while Dom had shut himself in the study.

'I'll be there. Might be a few minutes late, depending on my last meeting.' Her husband drained his coffee cup, grabbed his office bag, and pecked Charlotte on the cheek. 'If it drags on, I'll text you.'

'Please try.' Her plea wafted towards the door, drowned out by the sound of Dom crunching across the gravel driveway and firing up his Audi Quattro.

And he *did* try. Like so many dads and mums shackled to interminable conference calls, their lives dictated by emails that had to be read, reports that needed to be filed, conversations that couldn't wait. None of them willing to acknowledge that their children's lives were happening with or without their presence. Charlotte painstakingly kept photo albums charting special occasions, family holidays and other memorable events. Dom liked to film important moments, either on his phone or his camcorder, when he remembered to bring it with him.

Sometimes, when she was alone, Charlotte would watch snippets of the boys when they were babies and toddlers. Those infectious gurgles and toothless grins. Those wobbly first steps, Alastair heavily reliant on a wooden trolley filled with coloured bricks to keep him upright. They were still young, but each passing birthday reminded her they wouldn't be her little boys forever. And that her fortieth birthday was just around the corner.

* * *

'DON'T TELL me you're still obsessing about the big four-oh?' Ruth, who'd jogged past that milestone with barely a backward glance, nudged her friend. 'You're only as old as the man you feel, which is why I fondle thirty-somethings.'

Charlotte giggled. Ruth always made her feel better, even if she had perfect grooming down to a T. Today's ensemble was black skinny leggings with a faux leather strip down the side, and a lacy white blouse that would scream 'early twentieth-century grandmother' on anyone else. Charlotte was still in her gym gear, sweaty hair piled up in a haphazard knot and make-up conspicuous by its absence. She'd left her change of clothes and toiletries by the front door, distracted by her ringing mobile. Dumping Dom's suits on the passenger seat of the car, she'd answered it.

'Good morning, Mrs Egerton! How are you today?' Charlotte had grimaced at the chirpy tone of her dentist's receptionist. The suitably named Angelica was a lovely girl, but her saccharine-sweet demeanour and ever-present gleaming smile made Charlotte's fillings ache. And the reminder that she was due a session in the hygienist's chair tomorrow filled her with horror.

'I'm not obsessing over it.' Charlotte scowled at Ruth. 'I'm just ignoring it in the hope it'll go away.' *Like the hygienist appointment, and the layer of flab that's taken up residence around my middle.*

Charlotte tugged down her Lycra gym top and eyed her

quinoa, lentil and feta salad. Two mouthfuls and she could feel her nose twitching, and her eyes drifting to Ruth's lasagne with a side of garlic bread. The woman ate like a horse, but kept the svelte physique of a well-exercised thoroughbred. Probably all that amazing sex with much younger men.

Anyway, she and Dom still had sex. Of course they did. Just … not very often. When was the last time? Ah yes, the night of Robson's seventh birthday, after their home had been invaded by a swarm of six- and seven-year-olds dressed in Disney costumes and intent on wreaking havoc. All her carefully planned party games for the garden had been for nothing when the heavens opened and they took over the lounge, kitchen and adjoining playroom.

An impromptu round of pin the tail on the donkey ended when Robson's classmate Lewis decided it would be funny to stick the pin in the arm of little Lucy-May. After mopping up the tears (and droplets of blood), Charlotte stuck on some music and encouraged the marauding minions to fill their boots with sandwiches, sausage rolls and a selection of home-made ice cream. Bad move. They used the scoops as catapults, sending dollops of vanilla, salted caramel and raspberry ripple arcing through the air. Only Charlotte screeching like a banshee on uppers halted the bedlam. The tiny terrors gazed in awe, mid-throw, as Dom strode into the room and restored order. She'd gladly succumbed to his advances that night, partly as a thank-you but also because she needed to let off steam and seek sleep as fast as humanly possible.

'What do you want to do for your fortieth?' asked Ruth, wiping up the remaining meat sauce with a wodge of bread.

Charlotte speared a cube of feta and shrugged. 'Dom's been talking about a family holiday somewhere. Florida or

Hawaii. Or maybe Centre Parcs. He's got a lot going on at work, so it's hard to plan in advance.'

'Whatever you decide, make sure it's all about you,' cautioned Ruth. 'You run yourself ragged looking after your family. Although that's easy for me to say, as a sad singleton.' Their server — who looked barely in his twenties — approached, and Ruth's eyelashes fluttered at warp speed. 'Two lattes, please,' she murmured huskily, using what Charlotte called her 'porn queen' voice.

Twenty minutes later, Charlotte returned to her car and drove the short distance to the dry cleaner's. Thanks to the distraction of the phone call, she'd forgotten to do her usual check through Dom's suit pockets for stray coins, parking tickets and other detritus. Finding a parking spot immediately outside, she pulled the bundle on to her lap and began searching. Two fifty-pence coins, a folded-up fiver and a crumpled scrap of paper with 'milk, bread and six sausages (butcher ones, not crap from the supermarket)' scrawled on it.

Charlotte reached into the last pocket, the satin-lined inner one of Dom's favourite charcoal-grey suit jacket, and felt something stiff. Gently she gave it a tug, and a business card fell into the footwell. Bending down, she retrieved it, instantly recognising the company logo. Design For Life: Dom's employer for the past five years. His rise through the managerial ranks was a source of great pride, and the reason they could afford their current lifestyle. About to toss it aside, Charlotte glanced at the back. She felt her stomach roil as she read the message written in sparkly silver pen: *To the future. Written in the stars. Gros Bisous xx*

CHAPTER 4

Parents and grandparents packed the school hall, wedged into the rigid plastic chairs that induced bottom numbness within minutes. Excited boasts of 'My Adam has totally aced his Elvis as Pharaoh routine!' and 'Wait till you see Jess in the costume I made!' vied with grumblings from a few, put out that their progeny had been demoted to sheep or onlookers. Charlotte felt numb too, but in a different part of her anatomy. Her heart felt frozen, and icy tendrils of fear clawed at her insides. Only five minutes until curtain up, and there was no sign of Dom. Anger at his non-appearance vied with the other emotions. No message either, although she'd switched her phone to silent following a stern warning by the headmaster.

As the lights dimmed and the curtains parted in clunky fashion, Dom slipped through the doors. Charlotte raised her hand and moved her jacket from the chair she'd reserved for her husband. *Her husband.* Father of the two little boys now visible — but only just — at the back of the stage. Ignoring Dom's hushed apology, she tried to catch either Alastair or Robson's eye, but they were staring straight ahead. The opening bars of music struck up, the narrator — an impossibly poised and heavily made-up thirteen-year-old girl — taking centre stage. After a few irate shushes, the audience settled down to enjoy the show.

* * *

'THE BOYS DID PRETTY WELL, didn't they?' Charlotte and Dom stood together in the school foyer, each clutching a plastic cup of tepid wine.

'Sure, if you can call shuffling from side to side and looking like a couple of rabbits caught in headlights "doing well".' Dom downed his drink and glanced around for a refill.

The tears she'd fought back since discovering the business card threatened to overwhelm Charlotte. Why did he have to be so mean? She was no tiger mum, but criticism of her boys cut her to the quick. When Alastair's teacher called her in to have a chat about his progress, she'd listened in disbelief to her description of him as 'immature for his age.' He'd just turned nine, for Christ's sake! She'd stormed home in a rage and let rip at Dom, who hadn't sided with the teacher. Then again, he hadn't exactly disagreed with her assessment, simply suggesting that both boys join the local rugby team. Luckily he hadn't used the expression 'man up', as Charlotte had been dicing carrots with a lethally sharp knife at the time.

'It's just not their thing, OK? At least they took part, which is what really matters.' Charlotte wished she could have a refill too, but Dom had knocked back his second glass of wine and a third was on the cards. They'd arrived separately, and common sense dictated she would drive them all home and leave his car until the morning.

'Mummy! Can we go home now and have hot chocolate with sprinkles?' Robson bowled into Charlotte's legs, the

remains of his greasepaint smearing her white jeans. Alastair
lolloped behind, deep in conversation with the narrator who
towered above him. Alannah Jones was the pin-up girl for
the pre-teens, still flailing around in a muddle of pre-pubes-
cent hormones and emotions they didn't know how to
express. The younger ones, like Alastair, basked in her attention. With two little sisters, Alannah knew how to captivate
an audience both on and off the stage, regardless of age.

'Great job, Alannah!' Charlotte knew her voice was
unnaturally high. Like the boys', before theirs eventually
broke, along with their hearts or those of the girls they might
meet. Or boys, of course. She'd chatted to Dom once about
how he'd react if either of the boys were gay. He'd laughed
and told her to stop dwelling on stuff that hadn't happened.
Probably wouldn't happen, was the unspoken subtext. Charlotte knew she'd love her boys unconditionally, unless they
turned out to be serial killers. That might prove more challenging. All Charlotte really wanted was a simple life. Not
that life was ever simple. One minute she'd been blithely
going about her day-to-day business, the next a small
rectangular card had thrown her entire existence off-kilter.

'Thanks, Mrs Egerton.' Charlotte realised Alannah was
staring at her, her perfectly smooth brow creased in puzzle-
ment. The boys were now waiting impatiently by her side,
costume bags packed. Dom herded them to the door, shaking
hands or nodding at other fathers he knew vaguely.

'Right, better be off.' Charlotte dug out her car keys, her
fingers touching the business card she'd rammed into the
small interior compartment of her bag. She'd contemplated
tearing it up, pretending she'd never seen it, but the words
remained etched on her mind. Part of her wanted to toss it in
Dom's face and demand an explanation. Another, larger part
knew he'd find a way to wriggle out of it.

Charlotte had never suspected him of cheating before,

but now her brain flipped through innocuous incidents, aborted phone calls when she entered a room, late nights at the office and their dwindling sex life. Round and round it went, like a washing machine on spin cycle, until she wanted to bang her head against a wall.

* * *

CHARLOTTE REMAINED quiet throughout the brief journey home. As an apology for his snide comment earlier, Dom had filled the silence with forced compliments about the boys' performances. Robson stared moodily out of the window while Alastair flicked through a comic, sniggering occasionally. Once home, Dom whisked them off for a bath and Charlotte gathered together the necessary for hot chocolate. She fired off a text to Ruth, asking if they could meet up the next day. The desire to share her discovery was overwhelming. *A problem shared is a problem halved,* her mum used to say. *Still* said, even though she and Charlotte's dad lived in Florida and their telephone and FaceTime chats only happened twice a month. They were close, if not geographically, but Charlotte couldn't raise her fears about Dom's fidelity with her parents. Her mum, Rita, would get tearful and insist on flying over, whereas her dad, Pat, would disappear after a few gruff words claiming it was women's talk.

Hot chocolates drunk, teeth brushed and clean uniform located for school, Alastair and Robson disappeared to bed. Both were shattered, and Charlotte felt guiltily relieved to be off the hook for a bedtime story.

'Fancy a brandy?' Dom had changed into jogging bottoms and a tight T-shirt, which emphasised his athletic build. There was a gym near his office where he spent a lot of his lunchtimes. Or at least *claimed* to. Now Charlotte didn't know what to believe. She nodded, and he poured them each a generous measure. 'By the way, I have a later start in the morning, so if you could drop me off to get the car on the way to school, that'd be great.'

'Sure.' Charlotte took a sip, hoping the warming liquid would loosen her tongue and release everything she wanted to say. 'Dom, I need to—'

'Mummy!' A scream from upstairs jolted Charlotte out of her thoughts. Brandy slopped over the rim of the glass, and she hurriedly placed it on the table and sprinted upstairs.

Bursting into the boys' room, she saw Alastair cowering under his duvet. Robson stood on his bed on tiptoe, swiping at something on the wall.

'It's an enormous spider,' Alastair whispered, pointing at the corner where Robson was jumping up and down, wielding his favourite Harry Potter plastic wand. Both Alastair and Dom hated spiders. Normally Charlotte disposed of them — either gingerly picking them up or using a glass and a piece of paper — but lately Robson had got in on the act.

'It's tiny,' he retorted, prompting his brother to toss a pillow at his head.

'OK, one minute.' Charlotte dashed into the upstairs hallway, meeting Dom on the landing. 'Spider,' she mouthed, waggling her hands in suitably spidery fashion. He pulled a face and scurried into the master bedroom.

Opening the hallway cupboard that housed bed linen, spare towels and other sundries, Charlotte located a recent purchase: a bug-catching battery-operated device that sucked the little horrors into a tube for easy (and humane) disposal. Back in the boys' room — and relieved to see Incy Wincy hadn't vanished, otherwise Alastair would never sleep — she passed the sucker-upper to Robson with a wink. Grabbing him by the waist, she lifted him high enough to position it, push the button and ... *whoosh*, it shot up the tube.

Charlotte tucked the boys in again and perched on the

end of Alastair's bed. His thick auburn hair, so similar to Dom's, stuck up in spiky tufts. Robson's, damp at the ends, framed his cheeky, freckled face. Her chest swelled with pride at her two clever, funny and affectionate boys. Whatever happened, she would always put them first. Not a tiger mum, but a lioness protecting her cubs.

'Night night,' she said, reaching over to switch off the bedside lamp.

'Don't let the bugs bite,' said Robson, and she left the room to the sound of giggles.

CHAPTER 5

RUTH TURNED THE CARD OVER AGAIN, THEN PLACED IT BACK on the table.

'Well, what do you think? Pretty damning, eh?' Charlotte stirred two sugars into her double espresso. She rarely took sugar or drank strong coffee, but sleep had been as elusive as a pair of matching socks for the boys. By the time she'd knocked back her brandy, cleared up the kitchen and dragged herself upstairs, Dom was already in bed, reading the news on his iPad and grumbling about some politician or other.

Charlotte had washed her face, brushed her teeth, and contemplated fetching the card from her bag and tossing it in his face. But that wasn't the way to handle it. Quite how she *should* handle it plagued her through the night, between sporadic bursts of sleep incorporating vivid dreams with stampeding horses, screaming babies and a faceless woman shrouded in a silver cape.

'It doesn't look good,' Ruth agreed, 'but there might be a plausible explanation.'

'Like what?' Charlotte eyed her friend sceptically. While

Dom didn't actively dislike Ruth, and vice versa, they couldn't be described as close. Dom thought Ruth was flighty and didn't hide his disapproval — at least from Charlotte — at her propensity for younger men. He'd even hinted when the two of them went on nights out together about his fear that Charlotte might snag a toy boy herself. *Oh, the irony!* She didn't so much as flutter an eyelash at the men who flocked around Ruth, vying for her attention and plying her with drinks. OK, Charlotte was only human, and not averse to the odd compliment, but taking it any further? No, she would never cheat on Dom. But was he cheating on her?

'Well, maybe they worked together on a project or something, and she was just saying thank you.' Ruth shrugged, her expression sheepish. As explanations went, it was lamer than a one-legged donkey.

'Right. So what's with the "written in the stars" bit? Is this woman a part-time astronomer, or astrologer?' Charlotte was never sure which was which; not that she had any interest in identifying star formations or reading hokey horoscopes. 'And signing off with "big kisses" isn't the usual way of addressing a colleague.' Again, her rudimentary French had led her to Google Translate the expression. Technically, it meant 'lots of love', but still…

'You don't seem that upset, hon.' Ruth drained her coffee and gazed at Charlotte. 'Which either means you don't really believe Dom is guilty of anything, or—'

'Or what? That I'm not bothered if my husband is playing tonsil hockey with another woman?' Charlotte hadn't allowed herself to conjure up images of Dom and the French-speaking tart (her current title) getting beyond the basics. 'I'm still in shock, Ruth. Short of finding a pair of size ten skimpy knickers in his pocket, I can't imagine anything much more damning.' It was true, however, that Charlotte didn't feel a sense of boiling rage or an urge to weep uncontrollably. Until she got to the bottom of it, size ten or otherwise, she needed to remain cool, calm and collected.

'Look, you have two choices,' said Ruth. 'One, tear up the card and forget all about it. You've never had reason to doubt Dom before, have you?'

Ruth had once confessed that she found Dom a bit boring, which hadn't exactly been what Charlotte needed to hear two weeks before their wedding. Still, friends were supposed to be honest, and she'd put it down to too many margaritas and a teeny, *tiny* tinge of jealousy. They'd joked in the past about who would get married first. Ruth maintained she'd land a loaded octogenarian with an insatiable appetite for sex and a dodgy ticker, leaving the way clear for her to date men still wet behind the ears and maintain a luxurious lifestyle. Ten years on, Ruth remained resolutely single but comfortably off, thanks to her successful vintage clothes shop and a substantial inheritance from her grandmother.

'No, I haven't had reason to doubt him.' Charlotte had cast her mind back over the years, searching for any forgotten clues that might show Dom had been playing away. She could only think of a couple of occasions. Once, he'd come home reeking of perfume, but it turned out the girl at the department store fragrance counter had gone overboard spraying testers as he shopped for a gift for Charlotte's birthday.

The other time was when she'd heard him murmuring in French in the study, a few months ago. He'd blushed when Charlotte barged in, before showing her the language app on his phone. She hadn't been entirely sure, though, why he felt the need to learn French. They'd holidayed in Provence when the boys were little, getting by with 'Bonjour', 'Merci' and 'deux verres du vin rouge'; the latter upgraded to 'une bouteille' when the stress of two tired toddlers became too much. 'So, what's the other choice?' Not that Charlotte needed to ask.

'Confront him. Show him the card and ask him what it means. If he rubs his nose, he's guilty as sin.' Ruth believed in body language, convinced that every tugged earlobe, scratched head and sideways glance was a sign of something amiss.

Charlotte tugged her own earlobe, but only because the cheap pair of earrings she'd worn recently had left her with itchy patches. 'I will. I just have to find the right moment.' Preferably when the boys were out of the house, and she could catch Dom unawares while he unwound with a drink. She prayed that he wouldn't scratch his nose or, even worse, launch into a tearful confession before packing his bags and heading off to Miss Big Bloody Kisses.

Ruth left a short while later, after Charlotte had promised to let her know how things went. Her parting words were: 'If the bastard admits to anything, make sure you know where the loot's stashed.'

Charlotte had always left the financial planning and major bill-paying to Dom, but she knew he kept a bulging folder in the filing cabinet, filled with details of all their investments, pensions and insurance policies. The thought of divorce, dividing up their assets, even having to sell the house made her blood turn to ice. And the boys — how would it affect them? She pictured their innocent little faces, crumpled in confusion as everything they knew to be safe collapsed like a poorly constructed Lego house.

Driving home, Charlotte planned her strategy. Dom was due home around seven, and the boys had a sleepover at a friend's house. She'd make his favourite meal, spaghetti carbonara, and crack open something halfway decent. Once he was fully sated, with a good half-bottle inside him, she'd strike. Whatever the truth was, she had to know.

CHAPTER 6

'This? You've been getting your knickers in a knot about *this?*' Dom looked at the card, then at Charlotte, and burst out laughing.

Charlotte resisted the urge to stomp into the kitchen, retrieve the pan of leftover carbonara, and tip it over his head. Whatever reaction she'd been expecting, heaving guffaws hadn't been on the list. No nose rubbing or shifty looks, just an outburst of chortling usually reserved for the comedian Harry Hill. Charlotte couldn't stand the man — she found his stupid shirt collars and inane humour about as funny as an ingrown toenail — but Dom thought he was a comedy genius.

'Yes, I have, and I don't see why it's so amusing.' Images of tiny panties filled her head again, this time tangled in a silky heap after a sweaty session of—

'Darling, I can kind of see why you might be upset, but it's nothing, really.' Dom got to his feet and pulled Charlotte into his arms. 'She writes that stuff to everyone. Ask Jack; he'll tell you. She's a bit nutty, but harmless.'

Jack was a colleague of Dom's. Nice enough, with a wife

who wittered on endlessly about diets and the latest gym apparatus she'd bought for honing and toning purposes. After half an hour in her company, Charlotte felt compelled to inhale chocolate and jiggle her mummy tummy with gay abandon.

'I'm not going to ask Jack. I'm asking *you*. What future is she talking about, and what's written in the stars?'

Dom nuzzled her neck. Charlotte's slumbering libido gave a yawn, stretched a little, then gave a defiant two-finger salute. She stepped away, determined to see the conversation through to a credible ending.

'Amelie and I worked on something together. It came out better than we expected, hence the future reference. She's into stars and alignment and a lot of bollocks, to be honest. As I said, it's just her style.'

Charlotte looked at her husband. He looked back, guileless, with 'how could you think such terrible things?' written all over his face. He was either a serious Oscar contender, or—

'And the big kisses? Does she share those with everyone, too?'

Dom reached for her hands, and she accepted his grasp. She'd always loved his hands, big and strong in contrast to her dainty ones. He gave hers a squeeze, then cupped her face. 'Charlotte, trust me. There's nothing going on. I'm sorry you got the wrong end of the stick, but we're good.'

Approximately 95 per cent of Charlotte wanted to believe him. She leaned in for a kiss, and Dom reciprocated. For a few seconds she shoved her residual doubts aside and breathed in his familiar scent. No dodgy hint of another woman's perfume. Just the feeling of his lips brushing against hers, and the familiar cologne she bought him every Christmas. 'OK, I believe you. But if I find any more cards—'

Dom silenced her with another kiss. 'You won't. I promise. Now, I've got some work to do for tomorrow morning's meetings, so I'll let you chill with a bit of TV.'

Charlotte watched his departing back as he headed to the study. She rarely got to choose what to watch in the evenings. Dom dominated the remote control, and she generally binge-watched her favourite shows on catch-up during the day or when he was away on business.

With the dishwasher loaded, and a glass of wine in hand, Charlotte sprawled on the sofa. She was midway through a gritty crime drama, one episode into a frothy comedy with an irritating female lead, and dithering over a supernatural thriller with high ratings. Back and forth she switched, her attention span that of a bored amoeba. Exasperated, Charlotte switched off the TV and decided a bubble bath was in order. But first, she should update Ruth.

All OK. Just a silly message from an airhead colleague. Phew! C xxx

The reply popped up a few minutes later, as Charlotte sat on the end of the bed, peeling off her socks. She grimaced at her feet: chipped nail polish, and hard skin tough enough to grate Parmesan.

Right. That's good. As long as you're sure, hon. Later R xxx

Hunting out a foot file in the bathroom cabinet, Charlotte realised she needed a fresh towel. She wandered into the hallway, pausing as she heard the low mumble of Dom's voice behind the closed study door. Tiptoeing across the plush carpet, she pressed her ear against the door. She couldn't make out anything he was saying, but his side of the conversation was punctuated with chuckles. Maybe Harry Hill was on the line? Or maybe Amelie...

Charlotte sucked in a deep breath and moved away. Dom had told her his version of events, and she believed him. That annoying five per cent whispering in her ear could bugger off.

The bath was deep, hot and soothing. Charlotte scraped away at her callouses, vowing to remove the nail polish in the morning. She hoped the boys were having fun. She missed picking them up from school, hearing their excited chatter about the day's events, or carefully examining the latest handicraft. Her favourite two mugs in the world were hand-painted by Alastair and Robson. One featured a Jedi knight with a wobbly light sabre; the other an equally wonky heart with 'Love you, Mummy' written on the side. Their friend, Sam, was a sweet boy with an equally lovely mum, Jasmine. Charlotte imagined them all eating pizza or whatever together, before heading out into Jasmine's garden for a kickabout. It was Friday night, no school tomorrow, and Charlotte would pick them up some time in the morning.

Dom was closeted in his study. Charlotte was scraping dead skin off her feet. Shouldn't they be out on a date night, or something? It wasn't often they had the house to themselves. The boys were usually mooching around, needing help with homework or wanting either Dom or Charlotte to play some silly game with them.

Pulling the plug, Charlotte climbed out of the bath and wrapped herself in a fluffy cream towel. She ran a brush through her dark, mid-length hair and dabbed on some eye cream and moisturiser. Ruth often said Charlotte looked like a younger Elizabeth Hurley. As if! When she first met Dom, he likened her to Monica in *Friends*. Minus the neuroses. Charlotte would describe herself as reasonably attractive, or 'scrubs up pretty well' as an ex-boyfriend once commented.

Back in the bedroom, she located her tub of body butter and slathered it liberally all over. If Dom walked in, he might be overcome with lust at her glistening frame and bend her over backwards… Nah, if he grabbed her she'd more likely shoot out of his arms like a well-oiled rocket.

Donning her pyjamas, Charlotte slithered under the

duvet. Just then, Dom popped his head around the door. 'Ready for bed so soon? Sorry, still got a pile of crap to deal with. Sleep tight.' And then he was gone.

Charlotte tried to read, but the words swam before her eyes. Physically she had done little, but the emotional strain of challenging Dom about the card had taken its toll. She switched off the bedside lamp and took some deep, calming breaths. *In, out. In out. You do the hokey cokey and...* Mindfulness wasn't her thing, she figured. She'd tried yoga a few times, but could never switch off her brain sufficiently to get in the zone.

'Everything's fine. Everything's good,' she chanted in her head. Tendrils of sleep muddled her thoughts, and she drifted off. Until a sentence nudged its way in, and Charlotte's eyes sprang open again.

If I find any more cards—

You won't. I promise.

Did that mean there wouldn't *be* any more cards, or... Or that next time, Dom would make sure she didn't see them?

CHAPTER 7

THE NEXT MONTH DRIFTED BY IN A HAZE OF DOMESTIC DUTIES, the odd get-together with Ruth and a few other friends, and helping at the boys' school. Keenly aware of being a stay-at-home mum, Charlotte salved her conscience by volunteering to accompany class groups on outings or help with reading time and arts and crafts. Ruth berated her for feeling guilty — 'If I had kids and enough in the bank, I wouldn't be beating myself up for opting out of the rat race' — but that was easy for her to say. Ruth's business was her baby, and one which she'd nurtured and coddled from birth to its current, thriving status. Watching some other mums at school tapping frantically at their phones, their sharp suits and sharper heels in direct contrast to Charlotte's casual wear and Converse boots, did little for her confidence. Being a medical receptionist hadn't been an intellectual stretch, but she'd prided herself on her patience, and her willingness to chat and squeeze in last-minute appointments for the tearful and desperate.

Today they'd made the final preparations for Halloween at Little Upton Primary School. That evening, children, parents and friends would assemble for a spooktastic event in the school hall. Carved pumpkins would twinkle evilly on the periphery of the car park area. Tubs of apples were ready for bobbing, fake cobwebs decked the corners of the school hall, and plastic spiders dangled everywhere. Alastair was OK with fake ones, as long as Robson didn't drop one down the back of his T-shirt. Charlotte had been given the task of making Halloween masks and hosting Creepy Storytime. Earlier in the day she'd smothered balloons in gloopy papier mâché, gently peeling away the results and helping with the painting. Creepy Storytime would involve her sitting in a tent, backlit with a torch, and telling tales of ghosts, goblins and other terrifying creatures. The committee chair had roped her in at the last minute after another mum pulled out with a bad back.

Now, squatting on the damp ground, her face painted as a gruesome witch, Charlotte came to the end of her ghoulish story and wished she had a hip flask to hand. Her audience fidgeted, eager to get back to the sweets and fizz on offer. One little girl — Rosie, she thought — eyed Charlotte with disdain. 'You don't scare me!' she pronounced, adjusting the red devil horns clamped to her head.

Huh, you haven't seen me two days before my period. Charlotte smiled and signalled that the session was over. Off they scampered, leaving her to gather up her books, torch and a pointy tail which she suspected belonged to her nemesis.

'Oof!' She groaned getting to her feet. Charlotte had skipped a few gym sessions recently, putting her absence down to life getting in the way. If she didn't go immediately after the school run, the lure of coffee, cake and more pleasurable activities got in the way. People talked about 'muscle memory'; that the body remembered its fitness level as long as they maintained it. As far as Charlotte was concerned, her muscles suffered from a severe case of bloody amnesia.

'We're back!' Charlotte ushered Alastair and Robson through the front door. Both clutched goodie bags packed with enough sugar to have dentists rubbing their hands in glee. 'Right, you two, upstairs now. Goodie bags in the kitchen first — don't give me that look, Robson — and get your face paint off. But don't you dare pinch my cleanser. Soap and water, and as a treat you can shower in the en-suite.'

With squeals of delight, the boys disappeared at top speed. Charlotte collapsed on the sofa, psyching herself up to supervise the clean-up operation. Alastair and Robson loved the shower, with its giant rectangular head and smaller hand-held spray for rinsing. That bit was a particular favourite and usually resulted in the entire room being hosed down.

'Hey, how was the party?' Dom strolled into the lounge, shirt partly unbuttoned and a glass in his hand. His auburn hair needed a cut, although Charlotte quite liked the way it curled around his collar. Charlotte budged along to make room for him, but he stayed standing. 'Your face is green. And a bit black around the eyes.' Dom sipped his drink and gestured to his pristine white shirt.

'That's because I'm a witch. A tired, grumpy and very thirsty witch.' Charlotte pointed at his glass, then looked at her watch. It was after nine, the boys needed to get to bed, and all she wanted was a cup of tea.

'I'll deal with the terrible twosome. You fix yourself a drink and … your face.' Dom exited, leaving Charlotte unsure whether to laugh or cry. Getting to her feet, she glimpsed herself in the mirror above the fireplace. Lank, fake hair, topped by a droopy witch's hat. The complexion of a reluctant sea traveller on the verge of some serious vomiting. And dark-rimmed eyes that weren't entirely down to greasepaint.

Dunking a turmeric tea bag in a mug of boiled water, Charlotte yawned and tugged off the hat and wig. She went to pick up her phone, then paused. The one on the kitchen table looked identical to hers, but she hadn't yet emptied her handbag. It was Dom's. She turned it over, smiling at the grinning photo of the boys she'd had turned into a cover. To her shame, her phone cover boasted a smouldering picture of Liam Hemsworth. Bad mother. As she put it back, it rang. Charlotte hesitated, unsure what to do—

'Bloody work!' Dom dashed past her, grabbing the phone and glancing at the screen. 'Just when you think the idiots have got their act together, another crisis rears its head.' He scowled, shoved the phone in his pocket, and gave Charlotte a 'what to do?' look.

She lobbed her tea bag into the sink and faced him. 'Are the boys OK?'

'Yep. All clean and waiting patiently for a cuddle. I can read them a story if you like. You've probably had enough of that for one night.' Dom's phone pinged, signalling an incoming message. He ignored it and turned to go upstairs.

'Shouldn't you answer that? I mean, if there's a crisis at the office.' The niggling five percent of doubt reared its head again.

Dom shook his head. 'I've fired out an email calling a meeting tomorrow. If they'd just read the sodding info in the first place—' He rubbed the bridge of his nose, and Charlotte's doubt-o-meter registered double figures.

'OK. You go read to the monsters, and I'll scrub up and make us some supper.' She'd offered to make the boys scrambled eggs on toast when they got back, but they'd already stuffed their faces at the party. Charlotte wasn't hungry either, but for different reasons.

Standing in the bathroom, remarkably dry after the boys' ablutions, she wiped the steam from the mirror. Squeezing a blob of cleanser on to a damp muslin cloth, Charlotte wiped away the green and black make-up. She turned off the tap, listening to the faint sound of Dom reading to Alastair and Robson. They'd just got into the *Captain Underpants* books and — judging by the howls of laughter — were thoroughly enjoying the latest adventure.

Before returning to the kitchen, having decided a plate of cheese and crackers would have to suffice, Charlotte bobbed into the boys' room. 'Right, you two, time for lights out. You still have school in the morning, remember?'

Alastair groaned. Robson scrambled out of bed and rummaged through his book bag. 'Mummy, have you seen my spelling book? I need it for tomorrow, otherwise—' He halted, holding up the battered jotter, jubilation on his face.

Alastair looked at Dom, who placed *Captain Underpants* on the floor and grinned at Charlotte. 'Mum's the boss. Another chapter tomorrow night, if you don't sleep in and unleash the morning demons.'

Despite her unease about Dom, Charlotte giggled. They'd taken to referring to 'morning demons' on the days when everyone was running late, the toast got burned and the car wouldn't start.

'Do I need to brush my teeth?' Robson, normally obsessive about routine, crawled under his duvet.

Charlotte shot Dom a look, and he shrugged. 'Sorry. Thought they'd already done it. OK, in the bathroom now! Chop chop.'

The boys meekly followed Dom, Charlotte hanging back. She fluffed up their duvets, recalling how Alastair used to love her doing that while he was lying underneath. 'Give it a shake, Mummy! Again, please!' So many small rituals that gradually fell by the wayside as the years passed. How much longer before the boys refused to hold her hand? Turned their noses up at building Playmobil or Lego castles with her, or spending hours working on an elaborate jigsaw puzzle? Their teens were still a long way off, but Charlotte caught glimpses of the young men they would become. Alastair, a dreamer with a heart full of kindness. He might hate spiders, but he'd never kill one. Robson, precise and orderly. An accountant in the making, she thought wryly.

Kissing their scrubbed cheeks, Charlotte bade the boys goodnight. She joined Dom in the kitchen, opening the fridge in search of a chunk of Cheddar and some home-made pickle.

'Any chance of something more substantial?' Dom eyed the cheese and biscuits Charlotte plonked on a plate. 'I didn't have time for lunch.'

'It's late, I'm tired, and the best I can offer is this. Or reheated soup.' *Or make yourself a sodding sandwich.*

Dom retrieved his glass from the counter and fetched a second from the cupboard. Charlotte didn't really want alcohol, but something in his expression said she might need it. He poured the last of the wine, crouching down to ensure the measures were equal.

'What's up?' Charlotte cut the cheese into chunks. She bit into one, gulping frantically as it welded itself to the roof of her mouth. Dom handed her a glass of wine, and she downed most of it in one go.

'Stuff's been going on at work,' Dom said. 'I don't mean today's shitstorm; that's pretty standard when you work with a bunch of incompetents.'

Do those incompetents include Amelie? And why did he have to be so mean about them, anyway? Aside from Jack, Charlotte had only met a handful of Dom's team, who all seemed perfectly nice and normal. It pained her to think it, but Dom's ego had expanded recently. Since his last promotion he'd swaggered around, declaring that the next step up the ladder was just around the corner. Charlotte had celebrated with him — of course she had — but she didn't understand his need to keep shooting for a higher rung. They were comfortably off, with a pleasant house, the boys in a good state school and no big issues to deal with.

'I don't quite know how to say it, but… We might have to move.'

Moving was the furthest thing from Charlotte's mind. She felt paralysed, unable to process what her husband had just said. *Move?* He'd had his eye on a bigger property in the next village, with an extra bedroom, bigger garden and posher neighbours. But the additional cost would nuke their budget. Charlotte didn't need to move. She didn't *want* to move.

'Darling, they've offered me a transfer.'

Dom fiddled with a loose button on his shirt. Charlotte prayed it didn't fall off as sewing wasn't one of her strengths. Right now she didn't know what her strengths were, but dealing with out-of-the-blue proclamations wasn't one of them. She shivered, although she wasn't cold.

'To where?' Design For Life wasn't a big company, but its ethical stance and reasonably priced homeware meant an increasing presence in the UK and abroad. Small shops, often tucked away in remote industrial estates. Their stock was limited, but all sourced from artisan producers, with not a whiff of cheap labour. They planned to expand, though Dom had been tight-lipped about the ins and outs. Charlotte's chest tightened as she waited for him to continue.

'Overseas. But not that far: Switzerland. They're opening up more to international business, and it's a great country to live in. In fact, I've booked a trip for all of us to visit in two weeks.'

Charlotte's chest tightened another notch. *Two weeks?* Didn't he know that they could be thrown into jail (perhaps a mild exaggeration) for taking the boys out of school in term time? Was he insane? Did she even know this man, sitting there looking cooler than an iced cucumber?

'I don't get it. Why do we have to move? Isn't the head office here?' Charlotte tried to breathe normally, but her lungs wouldn't cooperate.

'They want me to head up a satellite office. Small, but hands-on, just to get things running. They reckon I'm the perfect man for the job. We're opening two stores, one in Lausanne and the other in Zurich. Early days, but it could be big. Charlotte, it's another step up the ladder. The company's already lining up schools to visit, and they'll pay the fees. Plus accommodation and relocation costs.'

Dom's eyes sparkled with excitement. Charlotte felt nauseous and dizzy.

'It's too good an opportunity to turn down,' he continued. 'You'll love it, I'm sure.'

Charlotte wasn't sure at all. Without a word, she left the room.

CHAPTER 8

'ISN'T IT STUNNING?' DOM POINTED OUT OF THE TRAIN window as it trundled past vineyards, now stark and devoid of fruit, and the boys oohed and aahed at the expanse of Lac Leman. It was mid-November, and the sun shone, although the outside temperature was only a few degrees above zero.

They would check into their hotel, freshen up, then embark on three school visits. The next day, a relocation woman had lined up a few rental properties for them to look at. Much would depend on the favoured school in terms of where they should live.

Charlotte loosened her scarf, the heat from the carriage making her sweat. She passed the boys extortionately priced sandwiches and bottles of water purchased on arrival at Geneva Airport. Switzerland was notoriously expensive, though Dom assured her that a downturn in international companies bringing in expats meant things had changed over the past decade.

'Prochain arrêt, Lausanne,' purred the train announcer. How could a simple announcement sound so much sexier in French?

'Mummy, will we have to wear a uniform at our new school?' Robson loved his embroidered polo shirt and grey shorts (trousers in the winter), whereas Alastair loathed them. If he could get away with casual, he'd be a much happier bunny.

'I think the first two schools don't have uniform, but the third does.' Charlotte had a pile of glossy brochures, each extolling the virtues of the relevant school.

'So can we skip the first two and just choose the third?' Robson gave Charlotte his best pleading face.

'We need to see them all,' said Dom sternly. 'You can't make snap decisions based on some photos and a blurb. It's important we agree on things like that.'

Charlotte stifled a snort of derision. There had been no consultation or discussion on the move to Switzerland; he'd presented it as a 'fait accompli'. OK, the boys were young and considered the whole thing an adventure, but her opinion had counted for nothing. For every reason she presented against the move, Dom had an arsenal of counter-attacks. The climate: sunny in the summer, crisp, clear and snowy in the winter. The safety aspect: less crime, fewer homeless people cluttering the streets. Charlotte had winced at that one. Those poor people huddled in doorways weren't criminals, just lost souls looking for help in a world that largely ignored them. She remembered Alastair crying once as they walked past a middle-aged man slouched in despondency, a handful of coins in his upturned cap. With little cash on her, they'd gone into a Costa coffee shop, bought a baguette and a flat white, and returned to the man. His expression had shifted from bewilderment to delight, his gruff thank you bringing an enormous smile to Alastair's face.

'The next stop is ours.' Dom pulled their bags off the overhead rack, the boys strapping on their backpacks. The plan was to jump into a taxi to the hotel which was only a fifteen-minute journey away.

They alighted from the train, buttoning up their coats against the chilly air. All around were signs in French, and the smell of coffee and pastries filled their nostrils.

Robson tugged at Charlotte's sleeve. 'Can I have a pain au chocolat?' Her mood lifted a notch at his perfect pronunciation. Ignoring Dom's moan that they needed to get a move on, she led the boys to the bakery stand.

'Deux pains au chocolats et…,' Charlotte hesitated, unsure of the word for the unctuous delight before her. She pointed, and the assistant nodded, placing the three items in a paper bag. Charlotte paid, then dished them out. She took a bite, a dollop of gooey cream landing on her chin.

Dom laughed before wiping it away with a paper napkin. 'Troops, it's time to get this show on the road!'

School one didn't hit the mark; the lady assigned to show them around seemed more concerned with keeping her long and swooping scarf in place than giving them information. Hordes of children, clad in everything from H&M to designer gear, swarmed around, clanging lockers and chattering excitedly. Alastair and Robson looked on in stunned silence, the contrast between this and their English school robbing them of speech. Dom barked out a few questions, but Charlotte was desperate to leave, hoping the next school would prove more successful.

It didn't. The head was a nice enough chap, who at least tried to engage the boys in conversation, but both remained shell-shocked. Like First World War survivors emerging from the trenches, they sat mute. Now, everything was pinned on school three.

'We run a tight ship here.' The headmistress, a tiny woman, sat behind her solid mahogany desk, where pens, papers and folders were lined up in an orderly fashion. The only anomaly was her dog, a scruffy hound of indeterminate breed, curled up in a basket. He regarded them all with an uninterested stare, passed wind, then settled down for a snooze.

'That sounds scary,' replied Charlotte, hoping the intended humour came across. An older pupil had taken Alastair and Robson off on a tour of the school grounds. First impressions were favourable when their taxi swept into the impressive entrance. The junior department, a picture-postcard wooden chalet, stood at the top of a winding pathway, while the senior school was a more familiar modern structure. There were tennis courts, an expanse of lawn, and an outdoor swimming pool. As it was break time, clusters of children in maroon and grey uniform milled around, teachers and support staff on hand to ensure all went smoothly.

The headmistress, Ms Chapuis, smiled. 'Not at all. What I mean is we adhere to standards, both educational and pastoral. With over fifty nationalities and differing backgrounds, we aim to provide top-level teaching, and a wider understanding of the world and our need to co-exist in harmony.'

Ms Chapuis explained the broad curriculum, with its focus on teaching both English and French from an early age, and its commitment to sport. 'All students have weekly ski lessons during the season, as well as a ski trip. We encourage participation in football — both boys and girls — and everything from tennis and hockey to badminton and cross-country running. We emphasise that it's not all about winning, but taking part.'

Charlotte didn't need to look at Dom to know his feelings on that one. His parents had two shelves of a cabinet devoted to trophies he'd gained over the years. Winning was everything in his eyes. Huffing and puffing at the rear equalled 'loser'.

'It all sounds wonderful.' Much to her horror, Charlotte's voice cracked. Dom reached over and squeezed her hand just a little too tightly.

Ms Chapuis sat back and steepled her hands, every finger bearing an ornate silver ring. 'Moving to a new country is always a challenge, Mrs Egerton. Many of the tears we see on day one are from parents, not children. All I can advise is to reflect upon your decision. Young children pick up on negativity all too readily and transitioning to a new country and school needs to be handled with care. Of course, we do all we can to make it as smooth as possible, but...' Her bright blue eyes regarded Charlotte with a mix of concern and compassion.

'You don't need to worry, Ms Chapuis,' said Dom. 'Charlotte's just a little overwhelmed, but we are one hundred per cent committed to this exciting new stage of our lives. Aren't we, darling?'

A tap at the door signalled the boys' return. They entered the room, both fizzing with enthusiasm.

'It's so cool here!' declared Robson. 'This is definitely my favourite.'

'I like it too,' added Alastair, 'even if we have to wear uniform.'

'Well, I think we've made our decision.' Dom got up and shook Ms Chapuis's hand. 'If you could arrange for your secretary to send over the relevant paperwork, we can get cracking.'

Moments later they left. The boys chattered nineteen to the dozen, each with at least one foot already firmly planted on Swiss soil.

Charlotte surveyed the surroundings and wished her heart agreed with her head. It was beautiful; the kind of environment thousands of people would want for their children. She needed to stop thinking of herself. They were a family and needed to pull together.

'All we need now is a place to stay, and it's all systems go.' Dom draped an arm around Charlotte's shoulders. She murmured agreement, and they set off for the waiting taxi.

CHAPTER 9

FINDING SUITABLE RENTAL ACCOMMODATION HAD BEEN MORE challenging than choosing a school. Charlotte balked at a communal laundry in two apartment blocks they viewed. Having an allotted day and time slot to tackle the mountains of manky clothing produced by the boys filled her with horror. Another place featured an open-plan bathroom, meaning anyone doing their business was in plain sight of whoever was in the bedroom. Two houses seemed more promising, but the asking price was out of their budget.

'What do you think of this one, sweetheart?' Their final viewing of the day was a three-bedroom house set on two levels, including a smallish private garden and patio. Leaving Dom to measure up for his monstrous four-burner BBQ (used four times in the summer), Charlotte followed the agent into the building.

'There is actually a fourth bedroom, although it is rather small,' the agent said in perfect, heavily accented English. 'It is normally used as a bureau. Sorry, I mean office.' Glancing into the room, tucked away to the right of the main door, Charlotte thought small was an understatement. If she had a cat to swing — not that animal abuse was her thing — the poor animal would ricochet off the walls.

'Mummy, where are our bedrooms?' Alastair tugged at Charlotte's hand, and her heartstrings tugged in sympathy at his use of the plural. The boys had been happy to share before, but she knew Alastair craved his own space. Unless the other rooms were considerably larger, the boys would share again. Not what she'd hoped for, particularly if — when — they had visitors.

'I bags this one!' Robson twirled around the space on the second floor, tucked into the eaves of the house. It was bigger than the cupboard-like office, thankfully. Enough for a bed, a desk and shelving for his books, toys and other detritus.

The remaining two bedrooms were considerably larger. One, clearly the master, had built-in wardrobes, an en-suite bathroom, and large windows overlooking the lake and mountains. The other could accommodate a double or two single beds, Charlotte quickly deciding on the latter. When visitors came — and Charlotte couldn't wait for Ruth to come — the boys could bunk up in one room and the other would suffice with a bit of tidying and primping.

'Is this one mine?' Alastair wandered over to the window which overlooked the garden. 'I don't mind sharing, but—'

Charlotte pulled him in for a hug. 'It could be, sweetie. Do you like it?'

Before Alastair could reply, Dom bounded upstairs, as enthusiastic as the puppy the boys desperately wanted, but were unlikely to have in the foreseeable future. Pets were a no-no in the properties they'd viewed. One owner, present during the viewing, had even eyed the boys with disdain and asked if they were 'well-behaved and quiet'. Charlotte's response that they loved playing electric guitars and singing 'Highway To Hell' at top volume hadn't gone down well.

'I've a good feeling about this one!' Dom announced,

prompting a glimpse of a smile from the agent. She shuffled a few papers around before backing out, presumably leaving them to decide. Charlotte wanted to back out, too. Not because the place was awful — it wasn't at all — but her heart kept pulling her towards everything and everyone she knew and loved at home. Home might be where the heart is, but right now Charlotte felt a dull pain in the chest at the thought of leaving all she held dear.

'What do you think?' Dom addressed the boys, no doubt worried Charlotte would find reasons to reject it. He'd given her a talking-to last night, along the familiar lines of not wallowing in negativity, finding the positives, blah, blah. Charlotte had nodded, with the rictus grin she'd perfected since Dom dropped the 'moving country' bombshell.

'It's, erm, nice,' said Alastair, tugging up the top of his sweatshirt and chewing on it. It was a habit he'd acquired recently and earned him a rebuke from Dom. Charlotte worried it was a sign of anxiety brought on by the upheaval ahead. She was trying to ignore it in the hope it would stop of its own accord.

'I love it! 'Specially the slopey roof and the funny window,' added Robson. 'Do you like it, Mummy?' His voice quavered with hope.

Charlotte raised the corners of her mouth as far as she could. 'Well, I need to check out the kitchen and living area, but it all seems fine,' she replied. 'Come on, let's see if the rest of the place matches up.'

The kitchen, with its seventies-style cherry wood cupboards and ancient floral tiles, was in stark contrast to Charlotte's sleek modern one, installed two years ago. Sludge-brown flooring and a dark wood-panelled ceiling gave it a claustrophobic feel, and the appliances were functional but dated.

'The owner will install a new dishwasher and double

oven,' the agent said, as Charlotte opened and closed doors, pleased at least to note the walk-in larder and sizeable fridge-freezer. 'He is also willing to discuss other minor changes, within reason.'

The living room was off the kitchen, with an open fireplace and a bright corner spot adequate for a dining table and half a dozen chairs. Not Charlotte's beloved dining set, which would never fit, and she didn't need Dom's tape measure to know their expensive suede corner suite was another no-go. Still, with some cheaper, smaller furniture and a few paintings and photographs dotted around, she could make it home. Or homely, at least. Somewhere the boys would be happy, and maybe she and Dom too. Marriage took work, and lately Charlotte had been too distracted by a silly business card and relocation fears to focus on her relationship. Dom worked hard, they had a comfortable life, and many women would give their back teeth to have the chances laid out in front of her.

'I think we should take it.' Charlotte moved next to Dom, whose face was a blend of disbelief and relief.

The agent scribbled on her notepad, and the boys high-fived each other. Dom kissed Charlotte, the boys groaned, and the agent beat a hasty retreat to her car.

* * *

'I LIKE CHEESE, BUT—' Alastair stirred the gloopy substance around, his face a perfect picture of discontent. To celebrate the whole school and house thing, they'd headed to a restaurant recommended by the agent: typically Swiss, with cheese fondue the speciality. A giant pot of the stuff simmered away, and each of them was armed with a skewer and a plate of bread and pickles. Liberally laced with white wine, the concoction lay heavy in Charlotte's stomach.

'Could I have a burger?' Robson carefully speared a wodge of bread and dipped it into the bubbling cauldron. 'They have burgers on the menu.' He gazed wistfully at the table next to them, where two boys of similar ages chomped on layers of bun, meat and miscellaneous fillings.

'This is what we're having.' Dom skewered a green pickle, known locally as a cornichon, and dunked it in the cheese mix. 'Delicious,' he added, although Charlotte thought that washing it down with half a glass of beer indicated the contrary.

Suppressing a yawn, she surveyed the room. Predominantly locals, gabbling away in French, with a smattering of tourists delving into fondue, raclette and other local delights. Charlotte sipped her glass of wine and wished she could crawl under the crisp hotel sheets and sleep for twenty-four hours.

Her wish came true an hour later. The boys were tucked up in their adjoining bedroom, Dom sitting at the desk and flicking through the paperwork for the house lease. They needed to sign for a minimum of eighteen months, although Dom was vague when pressed on how long his contract would be for. Charlotte told herself two or three years was doable. Then they could return to their lovely home, which was now on the rental market.

'School sorted, accommodation sorted. Now all we need to do is book a removal company and figure out what comes and what stays.' Dom put the papers in his briefcase and snapped it shut. Privately, Charlotte thought there was an awful lot more to do than that. She just didn't want to face up to all the practicalities of moving country just yet.

'I'm shattered, Dom. Any chance you could come to bed and we could get some sleep?' Charlotte hoped he wouldn't try to instigate anything else, not least because the boys were mere feet away. But a comforting cuddle would be nice—

'Sorry, something's come up. With work, I mean.' Dom picked up his phone, coat and hotel room keycard. 'I need to pop out for an hour. Got some issues to discuss with the team here.'

Charlotte squinted at the illuminated clock on the bedside cabinet. 'At ten o'clock at night? Can't it wait till the morning?' She knew the answer before the words left her mouth. They were on a mid-afternoon flight, and Dom liked to have a leisurely breakfast and minimal stress before travelling.

A hasty peck on Charlotte's cheek, and he left. She turned off the light and battered the pillow into submission. No sound from the boys, and only the distant rumble of passing cars disturbed the peace. She closed her eyes and pushed away the niggling worry over what — or who — demanded attention at such a late hour.

CHAPTER 10

'THIS IS BRILLIANT, MUMMY!' ALASTAIR GLIDED PAST Charlotte, closely followed by Robson: two blurs of emerald-green jackets, fluorescent helmets and swooshing skis. Blurred not because of speed, but because Charlotte's goggles had misted up.

'Charlotte, just do what I do. Stay focused and it'll all fall into place.' Dom sidled up next to her, skis perfectly aligned and goggles miraculously mist-free. Easy for *him* to say, she thought. Dom had started skiing at six, taken to France, Austria and Canada by his parents, Torquil and Jean. Or Torvill and Dean, as Charlotte privately called them, mainly because she always felt she was skating on thin ice around them. Dom had little to do with them these days, apart from the odd chat on the phone on birthdays and other special occasions. They sent the boys presents, always expensive and usually age-inappropriate.

The last time they'd seen Torquil and Jean had been at their golden wedding anniversary party in the summer. A lavish affair, with a giant marquee erected in the garden of their former vicarage home, and hired staff bustling around with flutes of champagne and postage-stamp-sized canapés. A 'no children' policy meant Alastair and Robson stayed at home with friends. Charlotte would rather have hung out with Ruth, wearing onesies and eating their body weight in cake and chocolate, but Dom had insisted they both go. He might not see eye to eye with his parents, but he had no intention of losing his substantial inheritance.

'Isn't this the perfect pre-Christmas break?' Dom removed Charlotte's goggles and wiped them with a tissue. 'Snow, sunshine and exercise. What more can you ask for?'

A comfy chair and a steaming mug of vin chaud, thought Charlotte, massaging a burgeoning bruise on her bottom. Dom's assertion that it would all fall into place only partially hit the mark. Charlotte had fallen over more times than she could count, and the stream of toddlers and infants sailing past her in perfect snow-plough formation compounded her humiliation.

'If you say so,' huffed Charlotte. Her feet ached in the hired ski boots, and she didn't know how much longer she could carry on. Dom had booked the five-day ski trip to Switzerland without telling her, presenting it as another fait accompli 'because it would be good for the boys'.

'They'll be skiing with the school,' he'd argued, as Charlotte eyed the boarding passes with a sinking heart. 'Maybe not this season, unfortunately, but a bit of experience now will stand them in good stead.'

Charlotte watched as the boys queued again for the button tow on the small practice slope. They'd mastered pulling it down and clasping it between their legs. Charlotte hadn't. Once, it rebounded and nearly took out her front teeth. On her fifth attempt, it snagged in her jacket pocket and dragged her several feet before she ended up in a heap, her pocket ripped to shreds.

'I was thinking of heading off for an hour,' said Dom,

passing back Charlotte's goggles. 'Maybe do a red or black run, just to get the old juices flowing again. Will you be all right with the boys?'

A small buvette serving drinks and snacks sat at the foot of the slope. No comfy chairs, just metal foldaway ones, but Charlotte reckoned she could install herself there and monitor things. Two Swiss ski school staff lingered close by, and the boys seemed totally at home.

'Sure. Just don't be too long.' Charlotte waggled her gloved hand at Dom, who called the boys over.

'Be good for your mum, and no daredevil antics,' he warned. 'I'll scope out some easy runs for you guys once you're ready. You too, Charlotte.'

Dom glided away towards the car park, Charlotte watching as he pulled out his phone and appeared to make a call. Work, no doubt, although why he needed to speak to someone when they were technically on holiday she never understood.

Taking off her skis — sheer bliss — Charlotte rammed them into the snow outside the buvette and slung the poles over their tips. Alastair and Robson joined her, demanding frites and Coke.

'With lots of ketchup, Mummy,' said Alastair.

'And salt,' added Robson.

Charlotte ordered three portions of frites, two Cokes and a chocolat chaud for herself. She declined the offer of a dash of rum, tempting though it was, and slumped into a chair. The boys darted back and forth, shoving in handfuls of chips (they'd always be chips in Charlotte's eyes) and lobbing snowballs at each other.

Charlotte dipped her chips in mayonnaise and looked up at the clear blue sky. A picture-postcard scene, where the snow-capped mountains glistened around her and the air was bitingly cold yet invigorating. A world away from home, where the weather usually dominated conversation, but not in a good way. Too wet, too dry, unseasonably chilly or unbearably hot. Switzerland adhered to the four seasons, or so Charlotte had been told. Climate change meant things were no longer as predictable, with the locals grumbling about less snow, spring flowers appearing then being destroyed by sub-zero temperatures, and summers rivalling the Mediterranean.

Tilting her head back, Charlotte relished the warmth of the sun. Her skin tingled, and she dug out the small tube of factor 30 cream from her breast pocket. Smearing a liberal amount over her face, she went to call the boys over for a top-up. But they'd re-joined the queue, chips forgotten and drinks half-drunk.

Drifting off, Charlotte felt the tension of recent weeks slip away. She badly wanted to take off those dratted ski boots, but had neither the energy nor the inclination. Instead, she focused on her breathing, and the joyful shrieks and squeals of the learner skiers honing their craft. Charlotte doubted she'd progress beyond the basics, but that was OK. She could tag along with Dom and the boys, content to join in with the après-ski eating and drinking.

Pulling out her sunglasses, Charlotte shuffled further down in the chair. She undid her scarf and folded it up as a makeshift headrest. Letting the noise wash over her, she closed her eyes and drifted away on a sea of thoughts. Maybe it would all work out fine. Perhaps her misgivings about Switzerland were nothing more than fear of the unknown. Plenty of people moved overseas and embraced an alternative lifestyle. Who knew, Charlotte might prove a natural on the slopes, sailing elegantly past Dom and the boys like a glamorous model in a perfume ad. Speaking French like a native as she browsed chic boutiques—

An anguished cry jolted Charlotte upright. *Alastair.* She

knew her boys' every sound, etched in her mind from birth. Leaping to her feet, she scanned the slope, a sea of bodies big and small making it impossible to see where he was. Then Charlotte spotted him. Alastair was tangled in the bright orange netting that ran along the side of the practice piste, flailing like a fish fighting for survival.

'Alastair!' Charlotte yelled, her eyes alighting on Robson slip-sliding towards his brother. As fast as the hideous boots would allow, she clumped her way upwards, digging her heels in in case she tumbled backward.

'Mummy!' Robson drew next to her, just feet away from where Alastair sobbed and fought to free himself. Before Charlotte could reach him, an older boy skied to his rescue. He discarded his skis, knelt down, and started working Alastair free from his trap. By then, several adults had gathered around, but they gave the teenager space to continue his mission.

'Is he OK?' Robson reached out his hand and clasped Charlotte's. His little body trembled, echoing Charlotte's own judders of panic. Was he? His sobs had subsided, and he didn't appear injured. No limbs jutting out at awkward angles, and no signs of blood.

'Sweetie, are you OK?' Charlotte dropped next to the junior Good Samaritan. He gave her a quick smile, before releasing Alastair from the last piece of netting.

One of the Swiss ski school staff gave Alastair a quick once-over, tickling him until he giggled. 'He is good,' the man said to Charlotte. 'No need to call an ambulance this time.' He produced a chocolate bar and passed it to Alastair, who accepted it gratefully. 'Your first time to ski?' Alastair nodded, and the man patted him on the head. 'Well done. If you do not crash into the barrier once, you are not a true skier.'

Alastair accepted Charlotte's relieved hug before splitting

the bar into four pieces. He shared it out with his brother, Charlotte, and the older boy who remained seated next to him.

'Thank you.' The boy, who looked maybe seventeen or eighteen, broke off a piece and popped it in his mouth. 'Alles gut.'

German, thought Charlotte, regarding Alastair's rescuer with gratitude and curiosity. He was a striking-looking young man, with balanced features and an air of calm that belied his years. She thought of hugging him too, then reconsidered. Instead, she sat quietly and ate her chocolate. The buzz of concern had abated, everyone returning to what they'd come to do.

'I'm so grateful for your help,' she said. 'I was so scared, but you dealt with it so well. Thank you. *Danke.*' Charlotte hoped it was the right word.

'It was nothing. I have had some bad ski experiences myself, but you pick yourself up, dust yourself off, and—'

Start all over again. Charlotte brushed away a random tear that threatened to slalom down her cheek. How did this stripling of a lad — now she was channelling her mother — know that song? Before Charlotte could ask, he grinned sheepishly and pulled out his phone. 'My father is a big fan of Nat King Cole, along with other oldies. He educates me in music, and I educate him in technology, like Instagram and Twitter.' He pressed something on his phone, and the song played out loud. Charlotte sang along, the boys puzzled but happy to listen.

'I thought Frank Sinatra sang it?' Charlotte didn't know much about the 'oldies', but she vaguely recalled her parents playing it aeons ago.

'Ah, he did, but this is the superior version.' The music stopped, and Alastair's helper got up and retrieved his skis.

'I'm sorry, I didn't even ask your name.' Charlotte saw

Dom in the distance, phone pressed to his ear and eyes scanning the area for his family. She waved, but doubted he noticed. Alastair got up too and did an awkward high-five with his helper.

'I'm Marcus. Very pleased to meet you, but I must go now. My father is waiting.' He slung his skis over his shoulder and marched towards the parking area. Charlotte spotted a red car pulling in, then Dom approached.

'What's been going on?' he asked, taking in Alastair's tear-streaked face and the strands of orange netting twined around his skis.

'Erm, Alastair had a minor mishap, but no harm done,' replied Charlotte.

'He smashed into the fence!' said Robson, milking the minor drama for all he was worth.

Dom crouched down and removed Alastair's helmet. 'Sure you're OK, buddy?' he asked, tousling Alastair's flattened hair.

'I'm fine, Daddy, honest. A nice man gave me chocolate and a big boy helped me get out of the stupid net stuff. Can we ski some more now?'

With a quick hug from both Charlotte and Dom, the boys kitted up and joined the queue again. People were leaving, and Charlotte wanted to head off soon too. Her toes were numb, and she yearned for a long, hot bath at the hotel, followed by a nice meal.

Dom turned on Charlotte, his eyes flashing with anger. 'I know it's only a baby slope, but he could have been seriously hurt.'

Charlotte bit back the response that maybe *he,* the experienced skier, should have stuck around instead of swanning off on his own. 'I was keeping an eye on them,' she snapped, deciding that Dom didn't need to know about her brief siesta. 'Anyway, I couldn't have done a thing to stop it, and Alastair's fine.'

Fifteen minutes later, they called it a day and lugged their gear back to the hire car. Dom fitted the adult skis to the roof rack, popping the boys' in the car boot. As Charlotte slid into the passenger seat, Dom's phone pinged. 'Give me a sec,' he said, wandering off to the other side of the parking area.

'Mummy, can we have Chinese for dinner?' said Robson, buckling up his seat belt. 'I saw a place right next door to the hotel.'

'Ooh, yes please!' Alastair chimed in. 'Spicy chicken noodles and spring rolls. Yum!'

Anything but death by cheese, thought Charlotte, as Dom returned and started the engine. 'Work again?' she asked.

'Yup. I might have to leave you guys to your own devices tomorrow for a few hours. Sorry.' Dom pulled an apologetic face, before backing the car out of the parking spot.

He didn't *sound* sorry, but Charlotte wasn't in the mood to pick a fight. A pleasant stroll along the lakeside, a spot of lunch, and a browse around the Marché de Noel would pass the time. The boys had already clocked the giant Ferris wheel, although the thought of getting on it made Charlotte's stomach do a pre-emptive heave.

'Right, let's hit those mountain roads,' said Dom. 'Last one asleep gets to wash my stinky socks in the morning!'

CHAPTER 11

'WHO'S THAT MAN, MUMMY?' ROBSON HALTED NEXT TO THE imposing statue, the figure raising a clenched fist to the sky. Bunches of flowers, old and new, lined the base. Tourists snapped photos and selfies next to it, waiting their turn to capture the moment.

'He's Freddie Mercury,' said Charlotte, patting her pockets till she found her phone. 'He was a very famous singer with a band called Queen. Right, stand on either side and... smile!'

'But why is there a statue of him?' asked Alastair. 'Is he dead?'

Charlotte nodded. She'd only been a little older than Alastair when Freddie died, but her dad had been a big fan and introduced her to Queen's music in her teens. 'There's a Queen museum near here, I think. If you'd like to go—'

The word 'museum' was enough to prompt some serious head-shaking. Robson twirled around and pointed at the McDonald's set back from the lake, affording possibly one of the most stunning views in the world for a fast-food outlet. 'Can we get something to eat? I'm starving.'

They'd ploughed their way through mountains of bread, croissants, boiled eggs and the ubiquitous cheese and ham platters at breakfast a few hours earlier. That wasn't even considering the banquet-sized portions of Chinese food demolished the night before. Considering they were both of slender build, the boys' appetites never ceased to amaze Charlotte.

'We're in Switzerland,' she said, steering them in the opposite direction. 'Let's find something typically Swiss we haven't tried before.'

Turning their noses up at tartiflette, more fondue and raclette, they opted for the very un-Swiss choice of paella. Perched on a wooden bench, they tucked in. Robson struggled to peel his prawns, Alastair nobly assisting and piling the discarded shells on a napkin.

'Can we go on the big wheel after this?' Robson licked his fingers, and Charlotte passed him a wet wipe.

'Do you think that's a good idea?' Charlotte had visions of them reaching the apex of the ride where she would hurl one of Spain's classic dishes over innocent passers-by. 'Maybe we should walk off the food first.'

They continued along the lake, Charlotte pointing out landmarks and the French border on the other side. She'd swotted up a little ahead of this trip, determined to prove to Dom — to herself — that embracing a new country and culture was doable. Experiencing the food smells, the chatter of the crowds and the locals going about their normal business filled her with a small bubble of hope.

'When do we go home again?' Alastair stopped at a stall selling churros, their sweetly fragrant aroma arguing with Charlotte's full stomach. She sighed, pulled out her purse, and bought a bagful.

'In two days. Plenty of time to get ready for Christmas.' That wasn't entirely true. Normally, Charlotte would have decorated the tree, wrapped all the presents and sent all the cards by now. Dom had nipped to Homebase the day before they left to pick up a tree, but it remained outside the house. She'd sent cards to close family and friends, but a bundle remained unwritten and unlikely to go anywhere this year. At least Charlotte had bought most of the presents for the boys, which she'd hidden at the back of her wardrobe. Nothing yet for Dom or Ruth, the only other person she shopped for at Christmas.

With the boys distracted by a stallholder performing magic tricks, Charlotte moved on a little further. A display of blown-glass ornaments hand-painted with festive scenes caught her eye. She picked one up: a tubular candleholder depicting the Christmas market, with indentations for tea lights. Charlotte paid and returned to Alastair and Robson.

'Mummy, he made a coin come out of my ear!' Robson grinned, and pointed at the silver two-franc coin in his hand.

'Can I get this?' asked Alastair. He touched a pencil case which promised to make the contents magically disappear.

'And can I get this?' Robson held aloft a mini-guillotine that looked capable of removing small fingers.

'Don't worry, it's perfectly safe,' said the stallholder, a swarthy man in his mid-twenties.

Charlotte knew both the boys, particularly Alastair, loved magic tricks. She dug out her purse again and paid, adding, 'Merci beaucoup' even though the vendor spoke perfect English. Minor triumphs.

He winked. 'De rien.'

'The wheel, Mummy!' Robson tugged at her sleeve, pointing at the massive structure carrying its occupants high into the chilly December air. 'We have to do it. Right, Alastair?'

Alastair shrugged, his pale cheeks trembling at the

prospect. He was always the more timid one, sticking to the gentler rides at fairgrounds and theme parks.

'It'll be fun,' urged Robson. 'You can hold my hand.'

A few minutes later they took their seats in the cubicle, exposed to the elements on all sides. As the wheel began its ascent, Charlotte made sure they all had their gloves and hats on. Robson squealed with delight as they reached the apex, passing the windows of an apartment block. An elderly lady appeared and waved, Robson and Charlotte returning the gesture. Alastair tucked his chin into his ski jacket and kept his eyes cast downward.

'Your cheeks are blue!' As the ride ended, Charlotte rubbed the boys' faces with her gloved hands. 'We need to get inside and have a hot drink.' Despite her reservations, Charlotte had loved the experience. Soaring into the crisp winter air, surveying the breathtaking views, fear dampened by the thrill of it all.

They found a small café serving chocolat chaud and pastries. As the remaining churros had cooled to an unappetising chewiness, they ordered individual slices of pizza with a pepperoni topping.

'We won't be needing dinner tonight!' said Charlotte, stirring the sachet of ready-made chocolate mix into the hot milk.

'Huh, that's ages away,' said Alastair, looking considerably happier than he had on the wheel.

'Will Daddy be eating with us?' asked Robson.

Charlotte checked her phone. No message from Dom, but he had said a few hours. She really didn't fancy trying to find somewhere to feed the boys on her own. The hotel menu was limited, and she wasn't confident of finding somewhere decent.

'Let's walk to Château de Chillon and burn off all that

food,' she suggested. 'It's over a thousand years old and one of the most visited castles in the world.'

Museums might not excite the boys, but they adored castles. They'd visited several in the UK, including Warwick, Windsor and Edinburgh.

'OK. Is it far?' Robson pinched a slice of pepperoni from his brother's pizza.

'Not really,' said Charlotte, who didn't know for sure. 'If you get too tired, we can always turn back. Come on, lazy-bones, let's get going!'

CHAPTER 12

'MERRY CHRISTMAS, DARLING.' DOM PRODUCED A BEAUTIFULLY wrapped gift from behind his back. Charlotte eyed him suspiciously. They always put presents for each other under the tree. The one they'd finally put up and decorated three days ago on their return from the Swiss holiday. As usual, none of the bloody lights worked, and Charlotte had spent a dusty and frustrating hour in the attic searching for her favourite red and gold decorations. She'd sent Dom out for replacements and bitten her tongue when he came back with lights that flashed like strobes and hideous green and silver baubles.

'What's this?' Charlotte asked, taking the gift. 'Shouldn't we wait for the boys?'

Alastair and Robson had been awake for ages, whispering urgently behind the bedroom door. They knew the rules, however. No sneaking downstairs until either Mummy or Daddy gave the signal that all was good. Meaning: Santa's presents were stuffed into their respective hessian sacks, Dom had half-chewed a carrot and left the remains of a mince pie on a plate, and Charlotte had knocked back a glass of sherry. That was also meant for Santa, but she figured it needn't go to waste. Alastair was definitely leaning towards the 'I don't buy this' camp, whereas Robson still clung to the belief that Mr Claus existed.

'I wanted you to have it now.' Dom gestured for Charlotte to open the gift. 'There's other stuff under the tree, but … this is my way of saying sorry.'

Sorry for what? Charlotte took a deep breath and picked at a corner of the wrapping paper. Was Dom about to confess to something awful, something about another woman? Surely not on Christmas Day, of all days.

'Open it,' Dom urged.

Heart pounding, Charlotte ripped off the paper to reveal a small padded envelope. She slipped her fingers inside and pulled out an embroidered fabric pouch. Glancing at Dom, who looked on the verge of exploding, she undid the popper. Within lay a fine layer of tissue paper, which she carefully unfolded.

'Oh! It's … it's … a ring.' The deep blue stone was unlike any she'd seen before. Around the stone were sparkling gems — diamonds? — all set in a silver band.

'It's tanzanite,' said Dom, taking her hand and slipping the ring on Charlotte's index finger. 'From Tanzania. Do you like it?'

Charlotte twisted the ring around. It didn't fit perfectly — a little too big — but it was stunning. 'I love it. Thank you. But why are you saying sorry?'

Dom echoed Charlotte's movements with his wedding ring. Except it fitted perfectly, even after ten years. 'Because I know you're still anxious about moving to Switzerland, and you weren't keen on going back again so close to Christmas. It's been a lot to take on board, and I feel bad that I haven't been more sympathetic.'

He raised Charlotte's hand to his mouth and kissed it. 'A

guy at work brought it back from a trip for his wife, but she turned her nose up at it. He offered it to me for a great price and I thought — hey, perfect for Charlotte!'

Right, second-hand goods. Charlotte's initial delight dropped a notch or two. Dom hadn't sought a gift to say sorry; he'd been handed one as if it had fallen off the back of a lorry.

'It's beautiful.' Charlotte swallowed a small lump of disappointment and forced herself to look at the positives. Dom felt sorry for his actions and his lack of sympathy, and the gift had nothing to do with guilt. Or at least, not the 'shagging another woman' kind of guilt.

'It was still pretty pricey,' he added, unaware his words were taking the sheen off the expertly cut and polished gem. 'Means I won't have to go overboard for your birthday!'

Before Charlotte could reply, she heard the unmistakable sound of the boys' bedroom door creaking open.

'Two minutes!' she shouted, heading for the kitchen and a coffee refill. Dom finished rigging up the digital camera and tripod he used to film the boys gleefully opening their presents, a ritual followed for the past few years. Charlotte hated it when he pointed the camera at her, as she was always in her dressing gown and had inevitably forgotten to brush her hair. She sipped her coffee and wished for the umpteenth time that her birthday didn't fall on the second of January. Too easily lost after the chaos of the festive period, and the perfect excuse for Dom to double up on the pressie front. Still, it was her fortieth, so—

'Santa's been!' Dom ushered the boys into the lounge just as Charlotte shuffled through, carrying her mug.

'My sack's bigger than yours,' said Robson, kneeling down to scrutinise the bulging bag.

'Size doesn't matter,' said Dom, winking at Charlotte. 'It's the quality that counts.'

'Mummy, can we open them now?' Alastair edged the corner of a large package out of his sack.

'Just a second.' Dom hurried over to the camera before giving the thumbs up. Charlotte took her usual place in the corner of the sofa, tucking her legs up and smiling at the boys' bubbling delight.

'Cool!' Alastair exclaimed, tearing open the wrapping paper to reveal a jumbo box of magic tricks.

'This is awesome!' declared Robson, unwrapping a Playmobil Mars Mission Rocket. He already had a castle and a pirate ship, the latter having caused great angst the previous Christmas when he tripped and snapped the mast in two. Dom hadn't been best pleased, and Robson's tears only abated when Charlotte ordered a replacement part online.

Within minutes reams of paper and piles of toys, games and clothes surrounded the boys. They pushed aside the clothes as they opened boxes and scattered pieces of plastic across the floor.

'Tree time next!' Ignoring the boys' grumbles, Charlotte and Dom stacked up the considerably smaller pile of presents from under the tree and placed them on the coffee table. Gift vouchers for everyone from Dom's parents, Star Wars Lego for the boys from Charlotte's folks, and fluffy pink slippers from Dom to Charlotte.

As Dom unwrapped the professionally packaged gift from Charlotte, she held her breath. It had been a last-minute purchase at Geneva Airport when she'd persuaded Dom to watch the planes take off and land with the boys while she browsed Duty Free. A Tag Heuer watch caught her eye, then made her credit card quiver with the six-figure price tag. Moving swiftly on, she picked up a Tissot model, a lot cheaper but still stylish. Or so she hoped.

'Thanks, darling.' Dom barely glanced at it before putting it to one side. 'Right, kitchen duties!'

Having watched her mum getting overly stressed every Christmas — parboiling sprouts, making stuffing, and chugging the brandy she used to anoint the pudding — Charlotte liked to keep things simple. A prepared small turkey crown, ready-to-cook veg and plenty of pigs in blankets, with ice cream and chocolate Yule log for dessert. The boys would pick at the food until they could play with their presents.

'Red or white?' asked Dom, holding a bottle in each hand.

'You choose,' replied Charlotte. 'Can you check on the turkey?'

Dom opened the oven and gave the crown a desultory poke with a fork. 'Looks OK to me. Shall I take it out and start carving?'

Charlotte nudged him aside and grabbed the oven gloves. 'It needs to rest first.' She located the kitchen foil and carefully swaddled the turkey as lovingly as she used to wrap the boys when they were babies. Admittedly, they hadn't been basted in butter or draped in bacon, but the action reminded her of their delicious baby smells. And of how they weren't babies any more.

An hour later, and both Dom and Charlotte's plates were clean. Alastair and Robson's looked like they'd merely shifted things around, aside from the pigs in blankets and a token Brussels sprout each.

'No pudding unless you eat more than that.' Dom frowned at the pair of them.

Charlotte passed the gravy, and they added a tiny splash to the mound of meat and stuffing. 'Two more mouthfuls, then you can have pudding,' she said, ignoring Dom's disgruntled sigh.

With the dishes cleared away and pots and pans left to soak, Charlotte and Dom settled in the lounge with the remaining wine. Alastair and Robson disappeared to their bedroom to 'prepare' a magic show for later, and Charlotte promised they would all watch the Christmas movie *Klaus* together later.

'You're too soft with them,' grumbled Dom, flicking on the TV. 'When I was their age, I had to eat everything, otherwise there was no dessert.'

Charlotte gave a mock-snore. If she had a pound for every story Dom told about Torquil and Jean's boot-camp approach to parenting, she could have bought that gorgeous buttery-leather handbag she'd eyed longingly at Geneva airport. Instead, she'd stroked it and focused on buying the watch that Dom didn't appreciate.

'So, for your birthday.' Dom changed the subject deftly, switching the TV off. 'How about just a few friends at a nice restaurant? We spent a fair bit on the Swiss trip, so maybe keep things low-key?'

Charlotte refrained from pointing out that Dom's fortieth birthday celebrations had included a week-long trip to an all-inclusive resort in the Dominican Republic, and a party for fifty people she'd organised as a surprise. 'Whatever. I'm not bothered.' Except she was, deep down.

Dom looked put out at her response. 'Sweetheart, there will be loads of opportunities to do amazing things when we get to Switzerland. It's a gorgeous country, with easy access to France and Italy. And we can do something special in the summer once we've settled in.'

At that point, Alastair and Robson swept into the room and began setting up their magic show. Charlotte sat down next to Dom and smiled as both boys gave an exaggerated bow.

'Ladies and gentlemen,' said Alastair. 'Prepare to be dazzled!'

CHAPTER 13

Packing day, and Charlotte desperately needed a coffee or something stronger. But the kettle was nowhere to be seen, despite her use of colour-coded stickers to mark what should and shouldn't be packed. Hugh and Des, the packing men (whom she'd already nicknamed Hump It and Dump It), were whistling loudly and tunelessly as they wrestled with reams of bubble wrap and assembled cardboard boxes at warp speed.

'Any chance of a brew, love?' Dump It, T-shirt straining to contain his ample girth, appeared in the kitchen. Before Charlotte could retort that boiling water required a vessel to boil it in, he whipped out her beloved red KitchenAid kettle from behind his back. 'That daft 'aporth nearly had this away,' he said, as Hump It huffed his way into the room. 'Blue to pack, red to keep aside. It's not bleedin' rocket science, Hugh.'

Luckily, the hapless Hugh hadn't got his mitts on the four mugs, caddy of tea bags and jar of instant sitting forlornly on an almost-empty shelf. And the boys had been beside themselves with joy when Dom whisked them off to McDonalds for a rare Sausage and Egg McMuffin treat, meaning the milk carton — usually upended over their cereal — still contained enough for their drinks.

Since they'd signed on the dotted line for both school and accommodation, the time had flown. In her twenties and early thirties, Charlotte had dismissed the notion that time speeded up the older you got. Now, barely into her forties, she firmly believed that the days and months had taken on a new and terrifying momentum.

As predicted, her birthday celebration took place at a local restaurant. Dom made a tipsy speech about trading her in for a younger model, greeted with a few muffled sniggers and a not-so-muffled 'moron' from Ruth. Charlotte's mood didn't improve when Dom presented her with his gift — a sparkly watch and earrings set which she knew came from a budget airline shopping catalogue. Charlotte was no snob, but somehow 'it's the thought that counts' didn't apply when he'd snapped it up alongside a bacon buttie and a mini bottle of Cabernet Sauvignon.

'Thinking of havin' another?' Des's gruff voice interrupted Charlotte's wistful reverie. She looked at her barely touched mug of coffee and shook her head. He laughed, a wheezing sound suggesting a serious nicotine habit. 'Not coffee, darlin', I meant another sprog. A fine pair you've got already, but time's a-ticking if you fancy a wee lass. Got four myself, two of each, and they're the best thing that's ever happened to me. Mind you, the missus says I need to tie a knot in it, or she's puttin' a lock on the bedroom door!'

Trying not to take offence at the implication that she was past her sell-by date, Charlotte gave a non-committal shrug. Leaving Hump It and Dump It to finish their tea and get on with packing the rest of the kitchen, she wandered outside. It was late March, and the temperature was pleasantly mild after a damp, cold winter. Small green shoots poked up through the earth, eager to blossom in the watery spring sunshine. Hanging baskets lined the boundary wall between their house and the neighbours'. Sadly, Charlotte wasn't so much green-fingered as a mortal enemy to all things floral and fragrant. She'd plant, water and add the recommended growth stuff, all to no avail. Like her shrivelling ovaries, the garden bore no fruit.

'What are you doing out here? Shouldn't you be keeping an eye on the removal men?' Dom appeared from the side pathway, Alastair and Robson trailing behind.

'We brought you a McMuffin, Mummy.' Alastair proffered a greasy bag. 'But it might be a bit cold.'

'Daddy let us have chocolate milkshakes too!' Sherlock Holmes wouldn't have struggled to work that one out, judging by the brown smears around their mouths and the dark stain on Alastair's top.

'I *have* been keeping an eye on them.' Charlotte took the paper bag and scowled at Dom. 'And, trust me, it hasn't been pleasant.' The sight of Des hunkered down, dismantling the TV stand, remained seared on her eyeballs. Not so much a bum crack, more a hairy crevice leading to unimaginable horrors. If his jeans had crept down another inch—

'Well, I'm here now.' Dom stood, hands on hips, cape flapping in the breeze. Not that he was *wearing* a cape, but his stance suggested the returning hero, fuelled by carbs, caffeine and confidence in his supreme parenting skills. Obviously, taking your kids to a fast-food joint totally trumped dealing with bottom-baring workmen questioning your childbearing abilities.

'In that case, I'm off.' Charlotte turned away, Alastair and Robson falling in behind her. Quite where she was off *to* remained to be seen, but bloody Superman could take charge for a bit.

'Darling, if you've struck up a rapport with the workmen, surely you should—'

Rapport? Yes, she and Hump It and Dump It were officially besties, destined to spend the rest of their lives trading tips on protecting fragile objects and not packing life essentials, thus avoiding nervous breakdowns.

'I'm going out.' Charlotte squirrelled in her pocket for her phone. Two missed calls from Ruth and one from her parents. They'd missed her fortieth celebration — 'We'd love to be there, but you know how life is?'— but were full of promises to visit them in Switzerland. Charlotte thought it was more likely that Santa Claus would be interviewed on Channel 4 News, revealing his true identity and his battle with obesity issues.

'Where?' Dom pulled out his phone. There they stood, mobile devices at the ready, squaring up for a cellular battle. 'Don't leave. I don't think...' He frowned, pressed a button, then turned from Superman to deflated dad. 'OK, I've some calls to make, but I can hold the fort. For a little while.'

Whoop-de-doo for you, thought Charlotte. She fired off a text to Ruth, knowing it was one of her rare days off, then stomped back into the kitchen, the boys still hot on her heels. Seconds later, a message appeared from Ruth. *No probs, honey. See you when you get here xx*

'Aren't you going to eat your McMuffin?' Alastair pointed at the bag which Charlotte placed on the counter.

'Maybe later, sweetie. I'm popping out to see Ruth, but I won't be long.'

Des appeared at that moment, wielding a gigantic roll of tape and a Stanley knife. 'If you don't fancy it, pet, I'm a wee bit peckish myself.' Charlotte gave him the thumbs up, expecting him to zap it in the microwave first. But no, he seized the congealing bun and devoured it in two bites.

Wiping his mouth on his sleeve, he grinned at Alastair and burped. 'Oops! Better out than in, eh.' Alastair giggled.

Dom came through the door. 'Seems like there's still an awful lot to pack,' he said. 'You will get it all done today, won't you?'

Des gave a mock salute and headed for the hallway, hollering at the top of his voice for Hugh to 'get his arse in gear'.

'Don't leave me with that Neanderthal,' hissed Dom. 'The amount the company's paying, you'd expect a better class of workmen.'

Charlotte doubted Hump It and Dump It would see much of the extortionate sum charged by Gulliver Removals. And despite their dubious eating habits and drooping jeans, they were a hardworking and decent pair.

Dom looked sternly at Charlotte. 'Two hours, max. Please. I've work to do.'

Charlotte rolled her eyes. 'I'll do my best. Can you double-check that the boys have put aside everything they need for the next few days? And book somewhere nearby for us to eat tonight. The cupboards are bare and I don't want to hang around in an empty house.'

They'd spend the night at the house — the beds were staying as they would rent it part-furnished — but tomorrow they moved into a hotel for one night. Then it was up and away to start a new life in a new country. Charlotte kissed the boys, waved at Dom, and wondered if Ruth might have something stronger than builder's tea...

CHAPTER 14

'IT'LL BE FINE, HON.' RUTH POURED A MEASURE OF TIA MARIA into each of their coffees before topping them with a squirt of canned cream. 'You're a survivor, keep on surviving, and all that malarkey.'

'But what if I don't make any friends?' wailed Charlotte. 'What if the boys don't make any friends? And what if Dom—'

'Runs off with another woman? I thought that was behind you, Charlotte. Anyway, if Miss Sparkly Card — Emily, or whatever her name is — is here, he isn't likely to be carrying on a long-distance affair.'

'Her name's Amelie,' replied Charlotte. 'And I've no idea where she's based. Oh God, I've just had a horrible thought!' She took a gulp of her drink, burning her tongue. 'Ouch. That's a French-sounding name, isn't it? What if she's Swiss, and she's part of the new team?'

Ruth shook her head in exasperation. 'That's an awful lot of "what ifs", sweetie. Look, I know you're not happy about moving. OK, you'd rather visit the gynae and have all your wisdom teeth out on the same day, but don't weigh yourself down with unnecessary worries. You'll make friends, no problem, and the boys will too. As for Dom— Well, if he does the dirty on you, I'll personally fly over and rip his testicles off.'

Charlotte laughed, her mood lighter now she'd unloaded some of her fears. Dwelling on things that might not happen was pointless and only added to her anxiety. If they were going to make this new life work, she needed to focus on the positives and stop being a negative Nellie.

'Speaking of testicles, are you seeing anyone at the moment?' Ruth kept quiet about her love life, probably because men flitted in and out of her life like testosterone-fuelled moths. Charlotte had only met a couple. Both seemed perfectly nice and besotted with Ruth. Perhaps that was the issue. Her friend marched to her own tune and didn't need — or want — the complications of a long-term relationship.

'Hmm, I might be juggling a few balls, so to speak.' Ruth winked and reached for the Tia Maria bottle.

Charlotte shook her head. She had to drive home (the thought of it being their last night there cut deeply) and hoped that Dom wouldn't be in a foul mood.

'Well, I'm having a top-up. Business is slow at the moment and knowing my bestie's leaving me is enough to drive anyone to drink.' Ruth's eyes filled with tears and Charlotte's followed suit. A full-on sobbing session ensued, the two entwined in a snot-filled and mascara-spilled embrace.

Charlotte pulled away first, looked at Ruth, and rummaged in her handbag. Producing a compact mirror, she angled it so they could see their reflected images.

'Good lord, we look like death warmed up,' hooted Ruth. 'Or a pair of Goths caught in a downpour.' Red-rimmed eyes framed with black smudges, foundation smeared and streaked down their cheeks.

'Should I take a selfie?' Charlotte pulled out her phone, but Ruth immediately slapped it away.

'If that ever got out on social media, I'd hunt you down and kill you. And given that I know your new address, it wouldn't be hard to do.'

Charlotte put her phone away and hugged Ruth again. She wanted to keep hugging her, to preserve the moment and stay exactly where she was. Freeze time — rewind it if she could — and make the sad stuff go away. But she had to leave, and return to Dom, to the boys, to whatever lay ahead. First, though, she had to repair her face. Slap on the war paint, then saddle up and gallop towards the future.

'Do you mind if I raid your make-up bag? If I go back looking like this, Dom will definitely run off with someone else. Even one of the removal men: Hump It and Dump It.'

'Who? Are they like the Chuckle Brothers? Charlotte, you're madder than a box of frogs, but I love you.'

Armed with Ruth's arsenal of under-eye concealer, hide-everything foundation and mascara that promised to give her lashes powerful enough to fan a small fire, Charlotte fixed the damage. The residual pinkness of her eyes she'd put down to an emotional parting. Heck, it *was* an emotional parting. She couldn't imagine meeting anyone else who understood her the way Ruth did.

'I don't know if I can do this.' Charlotte stood trembling on the doorstep. 'I feel like I'm on the edge of an abyss and no one will catch me when I fall.'

'But you won't fall.' Ruth held her by the shoulders and looked her straight in the eyes. 'You are smart, beautiful and more resilient than you know. I'm here, your parents are … well, they'd never let you down, and you can do this. Charlotte, *you can do this.*'

* * *

'How the hell did you deal with those morons?' Dom huffed around the virtually empty house, his angry voice ricocheting off the bare walls. 'Uncouth doesn't begin to describe them. And their constant demands for tea. Do I *look* like the office junior?'

No, you look like a petulant schoolboy who's been told to put away the stuff he left all over the stairs. Charlotte rubbed her temples, the start of a rare headache nudging at her vision. All she wanted to do was see Robson and Alastair, hug them till they begged for mercy, and eat dinner somewhere nice. 'Did you book a restaurant?' she asked.

The answer came in Dom's sheepish expression. 'I, erm, forgot. We could go to the pub, I suppose, or order takeaway.'

'Mummy! You're back!' Robson bowled into the room, wearing a strange combo of jogging pants and an ancient pyjama top. 'Everything's gone, and it's really weird, but I want a pizza. With lots of spicy bits and maybe pineapple too?'

'Pineapple on pizza is gross.' Alastair strode in, big brother laying down the rules. 'Pepperoni is fine, fruit is for weirdos.'

Dom reached for the drawer that normally contained takeaway menus, but Charlotte intervened. 'They've all gone in the recycling, and the cutlery and plates are packed.'

'We don't need cutlery and plates for pizza. Straight out of the box, only fingers required.' Dom gave Charlotte his finest 'I'm in the wrong, but you'll forgive me' look. Once upon a time it would have melted her defences as effectively as de-icer spray on a frosty windscreen. Now, however, she felt her backbone stiffen.

'We can go for pizza at the Italian ten minutes away,' she said. 'I don't want to eat here, and I need at least a half-carafe of Chianti to wash dinner down. The wine rack's empty, the corkscrew's packed, and I need to get out of here.'

Charlotte grabbed both the boys, giving them the hug that she knew would restore her equilibrium: temporarily, at least. Alastair relaxed into her embrace, but Robson wriggled furiously.'Do I have to change?' He looked at his mishmash of nightwear and sports gear. 'I don't know what else to wear.'

'Sweetheart, Luigi's couldn't care less if you turned up in your birthday suit, as long as the bill's paid,' said Charlotte.

Robson frowned and turned to his big brother. 'Do we have birthday suits? Are they like the black one Daddy wears to special things?'

Both Dom and Charlotte laughed. The sound broke through the tension in the room, and the boys joined in.

'It means going nudey,' said Alastair, proudly. 'Like, totally naked.'

'Eurgh!' Robson pulled a disgusted face. 'Who wants to eat looking at everyone's dangly bits?'

* * *

SETTLED in Luigi's with not a dangly bit in sight, they ordered two large pizzas to share. Alastair and Robson reached a compromise, with pineapple on one half and pepperoni on the other. Charlotte and Dom went for a marinara, and they waited for their drinks to arrive.

'Only two more sleeps and we'll be in Switzerland,' said Charlotte brightly, picking at the bowl of complimentary olives.

'Will the house be all ready when we arrive?' asked Robson, chewing an olive, then carefully placing the stone on his side plate.

Only if the magic unpacking fairies appear, thought Charlotte. She dreaded arriving, when she would face stacks of boxes, with no idea if everything would fit or not. Hump It and Dump It were due to arrive with the lorry shortly after they did. At least they'd ordered some new furniture in advance — beds, a sofa set and a compact dining table and chairs — for which the agent had organised delivery.

'No, darling,' she said. 'But we'll have fun finding places for all your things, and you can help Daddy build your new beds.'

'I'm afraid I'll be pretty much straight into work a few days after we arrive,' said Dom, nodding as the waitress poured the wine and gave the boys their soft drinks. 'The company's loaning us an extra car for the first few weeks, so you can get familiar with the area and drive the boys to school. Don't panic, I'll do the first few runs till you feel more comfortable.'

Charlotte nearly choked on an olive. Dom expected her to cope single-handedly just days after landing on foreign soil? She felt sick at the prospect, her mind racing at all the things she'd need to deal with.

'Pizza's here!' Robson clapped his hands in glee, then sneaked a piece of pineapple off his half.

'It'll be fine, Mummy,' said Alastair, and squeezed Charlotte's hand under the table. Her beautiful, sensitive boy, always quick to pick up on her mood. And he was right. Ruth was right. She *could* do this. How hard could it be?

CHAPTER 15

'I can't bloody do this!' Charlotte sat in the driver's seat. Her right hand fumbled for the gearstick, her brain failing to grasp what it needed to do.

'Charlotte, it's exactly the same as driving in England, just on the other side.' Dom waited as she started the engine, put the car into gear, and ... kangarooed forward.

'Don't make that bloody noise!' She slammed her fist against the steering wheel, Dom half-laughing, half-grunting at her efforts. 'It's hard enough to concentrate without you talking to me like I'm a halfwit.'

The previous twenty-four hours had been a whirlwind of activity. They'd arrived in Switzerland, laden with luggage, and staggered on to the train. Dom said the company wouldn't pay for a taxi, so public transport it was. At least they had first-class seats, although Charlotte saw nothing particularly first class about them. Fewer people, perhaps, but no snacks or drinks dispensed by a smiling trolley pusher.

The house had felt cold and unwelcoming. Their voices

echoed through the empty rooms, but they didn't stay empty for long. Hump It and Dump It soon arrived, unpacking and stacking cartons and crates with lightning speed.

'Nice gaff,' commented Des. 'Bit different to the old place, eh?'

Standing in the middle of the kitchen, an island of despair surrounded by boxes, Charlotte wanted to cry. But she couldn't break down in front of the removal men. And the boys were outside, discussing trampolines and goalposts which would have to be extremely compact to fit.

'Tea?' Charlotte rummaged in a box of groceries Dom had fetched from the village supermarket. She found the kettle, mugs and cutlery in a box marked 'kitchen essentials', and set about making a brew.

'Jeez, Louise. Look at that view, Hugh.' Des joined his mate at the large window in the lounge. 'Fair takes your breath away, dunnit.'

'Beats looking into my neighbour's garden and seein' her enormous knickers flapping in the breeze,' agreed Hugh.

Charlotte called the boys in from the garden. She needed to double-check the list of uniform needed for their new school. They had an appointment later to pick up blazers, polo shirts, tracksuits, book bags and all the other bits and pieces required to ensure they met the strict dress code of La Montagne. Thankfully, Charlotte had bought generic items such as shorts, trousers and socks considerably cheaper in the UK. Somewhere, in the depths of her carry-on bag, were name tags and a sewing kit. A fun-filled evening of labelling every sodding sock and PE T-shirt awaited.

But now she was driving Dom to his new office, so that he could pick up his work car. A considerably swankier model than the one she currently sat in. Automatic too, which meant no gears and only one leg to worry about.

'Charlotte, you're drifting over to the other side of the road.' Dom grabbed the steering wheel and tugged it hard. Charlotte gulped down the rude word teetering on her tongue. The boys were in the back seat, chattering and chuckling like Disney chipmunks. She envied their carefree attitude, their ability to take everything in their stride.

Had she always been a worrier? No. In her teens and twenties, not much had fazed Charlotte. She had breezed through school, even if her exam results didn't reflect much in the way of dedicated study. Boys came and went, as did her fashion style. One minute the wholesome girl next door, the next wannabe Debbie Harry — she loved all things' 80s — with overly bleached hair, black fingernails and skirts so short that her uncle Stan almost choked on a new potato when Charlotte bent over to open the oven.

When Charlotte met Dom, she felt comfortable in her skin, and his good looks, charm and ambition were the icing on the cake. All she'd ever wanted was to fall madly in love, get married, and have children. Hardly groundbreaking or glass ceiling-shattering, but then not everyone needed or wanted a high-powered career.

Charlotte had been content to be a stay-at-home mum in the early years, her focus on the boys and creating a stable and loving environment. But somewhere along the way, the worries grew, so subtly that she was barely aware of them gnawing away at her until she started waking during the night. A little voice whispering in her ear, berating her for being weak, for allowing others to walk all over her.

'We're here.' Dom gestured for Charlotte to take a left turn. She signalled, changed gear, and manoeuvred through the gates of a small industrial estate. 'It's just round the corner — take it easy, sweetheart — and voila!'

Switching off the engine, Charlotte looked at the unprepossessing façade. Grey concrete, glass doors, and Design For Life painted in the trademark green against a white background. A handful of cars sat in the forecourt, one of them presumably Dom's new mode of transport.

'Fancy a look around, boys?' Dom turned to Alastair and Robson, who shrugged in uninterested harmony.

'Do they have food, Daddy?' asked Robson. 'I'm starving.'

'Oh, I'm sure they'll have a biscuit or two,' replied Dom. 'Come on, troops. Let's go and meet everyone.'

The inside belied the austerity of the exterior. Turkish rugs in shades of turquoise and emerald green lay on high-end oak flooring. Charcoal and light grey sofas were accented with jewel-bright cushions. Low tables displayed Design For Life's latest catalogue and subdued lighting cast a warm glow over the reception area.

'Our first Swiss store opens next week,' said Dom proudly. 'Everything you see here will be available, as well as our new range of kitchenware and bathroom accessories.'

DFL had a long way to go before it knocked a certain Swedish company off its flat-pack perch, but Dom argued that they had different approaches to the market. Instead of volume, they focused on a faster turnaround of goods. More a 'buy while you can, then it's gone' philosophy. Generating a frenzied interest in quirky toilet brushes and spatulas shaped like guitars didn't grab Charlotte, but she happily accepted the freebies Dom brought home from time to time. A recent batch of fleecy throws, like discarded teddy-bear skins, now adorned the sofa set Dom had ordered with his employee discount. The company didn't do beds or dining tables as yet, so they'd sourced those from IKEA.

'This is Juliette,' said Dom, shaking hands with the attractive brunette behind the reception desk. 'Juliette, this is my wife, Charlotte, and our boys, Alastair and Robson.'

Juliette stood up and came round the desk. She was at least six feet tall, despite wearing stylish flat brogues. Charlotte pulled herself up to her full five feet five (in heels) and extended her hand.

'Lovely to meet you.' Juliette smiled at the boys, who mumbled hellos and eyed a jar of lollipops on the desk with barely disguised longing.

'And this is Antoine.' A gangly youth — although anyone under the age of twenty-five was a youth in Charlotte's eyes — bounded in. His shock of dyed red hair contrasted vividly with a milk-white complexion. Silver studs adorned each ear, and silver hoops protruded from his right nostril and bottom lip.

'Did that hurt?' asked Alastair, staring directly at Antoine's face. 'Doesn't the ring get tangled up when you blow your nose?'

Antoine laughed and patted Alastair on the head. 'Yes, eet was a little painful, but I am very careful eef I 'ave the rheume.'

'He means the cold,' explained Juliette, seeing Alastair's puzzled expression. 'Antoine speaks perfect English, but he likes to throw in the odd French word just to annoy people.'

Judging by her own accent, Juliette was also French (or Swiss), but with a hint of an American twang.

'Antoine is one of our buyers,' said Dom. 'He's got a brilliant eye for the unusual but practical. Things people don't realise they need till one finds its way into their trolley.'

'Ah, oui. The aprons with the built-in oven gloves were a triumph. As are our musical candles. They play a variety of songs, according to the occasion, and they burn for forty hours!'

If a festive candle played Jingle Bells for forty hours straight, Charlotte thought, she would either run screaming from the building, or chuck the bloody thing in the bin after ten minutes.

'Enchanté,' purred Antoine, reaching for Charlotte's hand and planting a kiss on it. 'You must be Charlotte. Your 'usband is a very lucky man.'

A frisson of pleasure ran down Charlotte's spine, not only because of the compliment, but the way Antoine pronounced her name, with the emphasis on the second syllable. It sounded sophisticated, *sexy*, even, although she'd bet her last Swiss franc that Antoine batted for the other team. Still, Charlotte took what she could get on the compliment front. It had been a long time since Dom had uttered more than a perfunctory 'you look nice', or more often, 'sorry, what was that?', when asked if he approved of her appearance.

'Boys, we have cookies.' Juliette produced a tin of biscuits and cartons of fruit juice. Alastair and Robson pounced on them in a way that suggested they hadn't eaten for a week.

'And here's the key for your car.' Juliette dangled a key fob in front of Dom. A BMW, according to the logo. Dom took it and signalled it was time to leave.

As they headed for the door, it opened and a petite blonde woman barrelled through. She didn't so much as glance at Charlotte and family, her focus on swerving past the desk and entering the room beyond. She reminded Charlotte of a fairy on top of a Christmas tree, if fairies wore silver-studded boots, fifties-style dresses and cropped leather jackets.

'Thank you for the biscuits,' chorused the boys, sucking noisily on their straws.

'See you tomorrow,' said Dom, steering Charlotte forward with his hand firmly placed in the middle of her back.

'Who was that?' she said, as Alastair and Robson squabbled in the doorway over the merits of chocolate versus caramel crisp.

'No one,' Dom replied.

And as if on cue, Antoine shouted, 'Lunch hour at bit on the long side, Amelie.'

CHAPTER 16

ALL THE WAY BACK, CHARLOTTE FOLLOWING DOM IN HIS SPIFFY new car, she concentrated as hard as she could on driving safely. The boys were with their dad, having insisted on swapping their car seats over so they could enjoy the plush leather interior and on-board computer. Leaving Charlotte free to let rip with every swear word she knew (and a few she normally abhorred), while struggling against the red mist of rage that threatened to steer her into a ditch.

'Bastard! Bollocking bloody two-faced lying cheating slimeball!'

Charlotte stopped at the traffic lights; Dom had got through before they turned to red. Glancing out of the window, she realised it was half-open, as was that of the car next to her. The occupant, a stern-faced man, gave her a disgusted look. Tempted to stick two fingers up at him, Charlotte turned on the radio instead. Pink blared out one of Charlotte's favourites, 'Fuckin' Perfect'. Grumpy man treated her to another look of disdain before speeding off.

Charlotte ground through the gears, finally locating first and jolting forward. Yes, it was *fuckin' perfect*, she seethed.

His protestations about Amelie being just a colleague — 'a bit nutty, but harmless' — replayed on a loop in her frazzled brain. They'd worked on something together, but what Dom had failed to mention was that *she* was *here!* In sodding Switzerland! Unless it was another Amelie? Hah, as if. Calming breaths were needed, and a change of radio channel. Charlotte stabbed at some buttons until a sultry female singer crooned about 'amour' and 'peine'. Cursing again, she killed the music and focused on undetectable ways of killing Dom...

* * *

'WHAT DID YOU THINK?' Dom uncorked a bottle of upmarket fizz, set aside to celebrate his first day at work in Lausanne. He didn't start till the morning, but Charlotte suspected he needed a drink to deal with the fallout from what she'd overheard. The faint sheen of sweat on his forehead and the fidgeting with his left earlobe were definite giveaways.

'About what?' Charlotte replied, salting a pot of water to cook the boys' favourite pasta. They'd hared upstairs on arrival, keen to challenge each other on the latest Play Station game. Charlotte dreaded the day they progressed from Spyro and Lego games to gore-filled battles featuring gruesome monsters and lethal weapons.

'My new office, of course.' Dom handed her a glass and began grating Parmesan for the boys' dinner. He might as well have 'guilty' tattooed on his forehead, since Dom doing anything kitchen-related — apart from opening wine and moaning about absent items in the fridge — was a rare sight. 'They're a friendly bunch, not that you met everyone.' He grated ferociously, wincing as a knuckle came to grief on the sharp blade.

'No, I didn't, did I?' Charlotte put down her glass and

snatched the plate of cheese away. 'You didn't introduce me to the late arrival. Now let me see, what was her name again?'

Dom flushed, grabbing a piece of kitchen towel to dab at his hand. 'Amelie, as you heard. And before you get the wrong end of the stick, there is nothing going on between us.'

Admittedly, Charlotte couldn't imagine anything going on between the rock chick fairy and down-to-earth Dom, but opposites attracted. And the fact he was so quick to deny any wrongdoing made her doubting antenna quiver alarmingly.

'She's here on a six-month contract.' Dom wiped the kitchen paper over his brow, leaving a red smear. 'Sweetheart, I knew that if I told you, you'd go off the deep end.'

Charlotte flinched. Had she become such a monster that her husband couldn't tell her the truth? No, she wasn't a monster. Just a woman who'd discovered a schmaltzy card in a suit pocket, and swallowed a story about stars and the future, and—

'You knew she was coming here, didn't you?' Charlotte stabbed at Dom's chest with her finger. For a moment she contemplated wiping the conciliatory half-smile off his face with the cheese grater. No, violence wasn't the answer. She needed to keep her cool and let Dom speak. Except this time, Charlotte wouldn't let him off the hook so easily.

'Erm, it was a possibility, but I honestly didn't know about it until a week ago.' Dom downed half a glass of fizz in one go, his free hand loosening the collar of his shirt.

'So you've known for a whole week, but you didn't think telling me was a good idea? Or were you hoping to keep it a secret? Silly old Charlotte, what she doesn't know won't hurt her. Well, Dom, I *am* hurt, and I need you to tell me the truth. Are you having an affair with that woman?'

The pot of pasta water chose that moment to boil over in a bubbling cauldron of fury. Charlotte felt an affinity with the pot, her rage echoing its furious hissing and spluttering. She grabbed the oven gloves — not attached to an apron — and shoved it to one side.

'No. I. Am. Not.' Dom moved towards her, but Charlotte stepped back. He tried again, and she reversed until her bottom pressed against the cutlery drawer. If the *Strictly* judges popped up, they might give them a few points for a cha-cha-cha.

Charlotte tried to wriggle away, but Dom grabbed her by the shoulders and thrust his face within inches of hers. 'You don't have to believe me, but nothing's happened between us. I told you the card meant nothing, and *she* means nothing.'

Squirming in his grasp, Charlotte made contact with Dom's crotch. *Oh my.* Either he'd stuffed the grater down his trousers, or become aroused by the situation. Charlotte didn't feel remotely turned on; the complete opposite, in fact. Maybe *he* was turned on by talk of Amelie, and thinking of all the things he liked to do with her—

'Mummy, is the food ready yet?' Robson appeared, still holding his PS4 controller. 'Why are you standing there like that?'

Charlotte executed a perfect pivot. Dom moved away and pulled on the joke apron she'd bought him for a birthday present, with *Mr Good-Lookin' Is Cookin'* embroidered on it.

'Mummy had something in her eye,' he improvised. 'I was just helping get it out.'

Robson shrugged and plonked himself down on a chair. 'You can't cook pasta if the water's not hot.'

Charlotte hastily replaced the pot on the hob and fetched a tub of home-made arrabbiata sauce from the fridge. 'If you sort out enough pasta for us all, it'll be ready in a jiffy,' she said, handing Robson the spaghetti measurer. She never used it, but Robson enjoyed sliding the strands into the correct-sized hole, ensuring no gap remained.

Dom dished up the food, playing the role of perfect sitcom dad to perfection. He listened intently to the boys chattering about their latest PlayStation game, what they liked about their new school, and who their new friends were. Charlotte tried to tune in, but her mind wandered back to the previous conversation. Specifically, had she got it all wrong — again — about Amelie, and what had brought on Dom's unexpected trouser salute?

'Mummy, can Nathaniel and Jodie come over for a play date next week?' Alastair expertly twirled strands of spaghetti around his fork, Robson going for the chop-it-up-and-shovel-it-in-with-a-spoon method.

'Who? Sorry, I mean of course they can,' replied Charlotte, staring at her own barely touched bowl. She still wasn't up to speed with their classmates, which she needed to rectify.

'Who's for ice cream?' Dom finished his pasta, giving Charlotte that twinkling smile she'd always adored, but which now only appeared on special occasions. High days, holidays, and when he fancied getting his leg over.

A few hours later, they were in bed. Dom sidled closer, and Charlotte bottom-shuffled towards the edge of the mattress. She hadn't raised the subject of Amelie again, but her biker-boot-clad, elfin figure might as well be snuggled up between them.

'Darling,' murmured Dom, his finger tracing a line down Charlotte's spine. Her treacherous body responded with a tingle of enthusiasm. It multiplied when Dom moved in for a neck nuzzle, his warm lips sending shock waves to the tips of Charlotte's toes.

'We're good, aren't we?' His soft voice tickled her ear as she turned around.

Charlotte hesitated before replying. 'Yes, we're good.' And, for the next half hour, they were very, very good.

CHAPTER 17

Two months into their move to Switzerland, Charlotte felt a little more settled. Yes, she missed the UK terribly, but Sadie, Pamela and a few other mums had helped her to feel welcome. They'd helped her to navigate the shops and advised her which plumber/electrician/handyman to call, and what to say. Charlotte still blushed when she remembered answering a cold caller in French and wondering why her response provoked hysteria.

'Erm, you said, "Je ne suis pas interessante", which means you're not *interesting*, instead of *interested*.' Pamela spoke excellent French, the result of spending several years in Paris as a student. Sadie muddled through, figuring that *bonjour, au revoir* and *ça va* would suffice. Charlotte had toyed with signing up for an intensive course, but toying was as far as she'd got.

She dropped off the boys, her driving confidence improved since the early days. Chatting briefly to Pamela, and arranging a catch-up later in the week, Charlotte headed back to the car. A familiar flashy red number was parked next to her, its driver leaning nonchalantly against the door as he vaped furiously. She hadn't seen Dickhead since the day of the incident, but Sadie had filled her in on his background.

'His name's Jürgen, he's German, and he's been married twice,' she revealed. 'His last wife buggered off back to Berlin, but they kept their son Marcus here because they didn't want to disrupt his education. He's seventeen and doing his International Baccalaureate.'

Coughing ostentatiously as a cloud of minty vapour wafted past her, Charlotte opened the car door. For good measure, she gave Dickhead her best look of disdain, one usually reserved for Dom when he left the toilet seat up.

'Is there something wrong?' Charlotte started as he touched her shoulder. 'You seem upset, or angry.'

He had a distinctive accent, and a deep, melodic voice. Glancing at his hand — and stepping away — Charlotte noted tanned skin set against a cufflink-adorned white shirt sleeve and a glimpse of an expensive gold watch.

'I'm fine,' she replied, in a tone suggesting the complete opposite. 'If you'll excuse me—'

To Charlotte's irritation, he blocked her way as she tried to climb in. 'Clearly you are not. Have I done something?'

'You could say that.' Charlotte squared up to him, aware of his height — well over six feet — and muscular build. She wished she had heels on but they were impractical on the school run, not least because of the hexagonal grass-filled tiles which formed the parking area. Only the brave or stupid risked breaking an ankle with inappropriate footwear.

'Enlighten me, please.' A smidgeon of a smile played across his face, which was as tanned as his hands and a contrast to his silver-streaked hair. Most people would consider him handsome, but Charlotte had no truck with his looks.

'You don't remember running me off the road weeks ago? I smashed my car into the wall,' — she gestured towards the school entrance — 'because you swung out too far. It cost a fortune to repair.' A little white lie, but his smirk had raised her hackles.

'Ah, a little bird told me someone blamed me for their run-in with the wall. Sadly, newcomers often misjudge the angle when making the turn from the left. I trust you are more practised now? I'm Jürgen, by the way. And you are?'

Ignoring the proffered handshake, Charlotte mumbled her name. The sheer arrogance of the man! Dumping the blame on her, when he had been in the wrong! 'I can assure you I'm a very able driver. With an unblemished record, until you got in the way.' Charlotte didn't feel the need to mention the time she'd rear-ended a car in England, or got herself jammed into a tight parking spot in a multi-storey car park.

'Jürgen.' Charlotte turned at the familiar voice of Pamela. She stood a foot away, her tone frostier than a snow-filled day in December.

'Pamela.' Jürgen gave a small bow. 'You look well. How is your husband?'

Charlotte sensed the tension between them. Perhaps Jürgen had also caused Pamela to prang her car? She couldn't recall Pamela telling her of any incident, although that didn't mean there hadn't been one.

'Are we doing coffee?' Pamela asked Charlotte, as Sadie tottered over in a pair of mid-heeled black shoes. She was being more brave than stupid, as she had an important work do with her husband coming up later in the month and was practising walking in unfamiliar footwear.

'Jeez, why didn't I opt for a full-length gown? At least I could wear trainers instead of these monstrosities!' Sadie almost came a cropper, saved from falling by the steadying arm of Jürgen. 'Thanks. Christ, I could murder an espresso and a pain au chocolat. Didn't get so much as a slice of toast or a sniff of caffeine this morning with the girls playing up.'

Gesturing to her car, Charlotte waited as Pamela and Sadie piled into the back seats. She nodded curtly at Jürgen. He smiled briefly, before climbing into his Ferrari or Lamborghini or whatever the heck it was. Seconds later he was gone, the noise of the engine ringing in Charlotte's ears.

Seated at a table in Le Petit Train with a round of coffees and pastries, the women waited for the caffeine to kick in. Sadie took off her shoes and massaged her feet, sighing with relief as she wiggled her toes. Pamela took out a compact mirror and checked her reflection, wiping away a tiny smudge of mascara.

'That Jürgen strikes me as an arrogant prat,' commented Charlotte, destroying the fern-like pattern in her cappuccino froth with ferocity. 'He bloody well blamed me for my car incident, when it was totally his fault.'

'Ah, he's not that bad,' replied Sadie. 'I think he's a bit shy, actually. And his son Marcus is a sweetie. Cute like his dad, too!'

If Charlotte looked up the definition of 'shy' in a children's dictionary, she was sure a picture of a strapping German with an attitude problem wouldn't be there. As for *cute...*

'Stay away from him. He's nothing but trouble.' Pamela finished fixing her make-up and ripped her cinnamon bun in two. Charlotte wondered if the bun represented Jürgen's throat, so venomous was the glint in Pamela's eyes. But what could the German road hog have done to warrant such a reaction?

'Pamela, methinks there's something you're not telling us. Did Jürgen's team beat you at the school quiz night? Or did his strudel trounce your cupcakes at the bake sale?' Sadie winked at Charlotte.

Charlotte noted the rising colour in Pamela's pale cheeks.

'Very funny,' Pamela replied. 'Just mark my words, steer clear of that man.'

Charlotte had every intention of steering clear, at least in the driving sense. Still, Pamela's comments left her wondering what had triggered such a strong dislike.

'Anyway,' Pamela continued, 'what's your dress like, Sadie? Got any photos?'

Sadie whipped out her phone, scrolled through, and thrust it in front of her friends. Both oohed and aahed over the slinky, one-shouldered silver number, complete with diamanté brooch.

'I told Rick I picked it up in the sales,' said Sadie. 'If he knew the actual price tag his head would explode. Still, I'm worth it, right?'

'Hello there!' None of them had noticed Alicia arrive, resplendent in head-to-toe cashmere, topped with a full-length burgundy leather coat. 'What are you all looking at?' Before Sadie could close the photo, Alicia peered at the screen. 'Lovely dress, darling. Is it Valentino?'

'As if,' murmured Sadie. 'No, it's from a small British designer. Not well known, but definitely on the up.'

Alicia sniffed, either from a cold or disdain at the dress's lack of big-name status. Without asking, she pulled up a chair and extended her perfectly formed legs. Judging by the trademark red soles, her shoes were Christian Louboutins. She snapped her fingers imperiously at the waitress, who — to Charlotte's delight — turned away.

'The service here is atrocious,' said Alicia. 'We should take our custom elsewhere: perhaps that new bistro in town. I hear their coffee beans are sublime. Apparently, they're extracted from civet poo. The prices are on the high side, mind you, but one gets what one pays for.'

Charlotte pulled a face. Drinking coffee produced from a

small animal's bottom? At home she was happy with a mug of Nescafé instant, or a mint tea if she felt virtuous.

Alicia finally placed her order, the waitress regarding her with all the enthusiasm of someone who'd trod in some poo, civet or otherwise.

'Right, I need to get more walking practice in.' Sadie wriggled her feet back into the painful shoes. Wincing as she stood up, she gestured to Charlotte and Pamela to join her. 'First to the car chooses where we go next. Shopping, yomping along the lakeside or back home for a snooze. Ready, steady, go!'

Fluttering hands at Alicia, they headed for the exit. Charlotte held back, Pamela next to her, as Sadie strode — tottered — ahead. Charlotte would drop them back at school to collect their own cars. She needed to sort out a few things at home. A sit-down with her book would be nice, but wasn't an option. Besides, she needed time to regroup. Meeting Dickhead face to face had rattled her, and something was definitely amiss between him and Pamela. However, judging by Pamela's still-stony expression, that was a subject she'd be wise to leave alone.

CHAPTER 18

'Peanut butter, flour, sugar, Cheddar, eggs, tuna, tomato paste, printer paper, tampons.' Charlotte stood at the supermarket checkout, mentally ticking off items on her handwritten list. 'Bugger! Forgot red onions.' Never mind, there were a couple rolling around in the bottom of the vegetable drawer at home. She could always cut off any squidgy bits.

Thankfully, Sadie had introduced her to other, larger shops not too far from home. Nowadays, Charlotte only ventured to the local one in moments of desperation. She still had bizarre dreams about sitting naked in a Marks and Spencer food hall, licking the chocolate off profiteroles and smearing her body with deli-style coleslaw. She hadn't shared these with Dom. Better he imagine her moans of pleasure in the small hours related to sexual fantasies, rather than a yearning for choux pastry and mayonnaise-drenched vegetables.

Digging in her purse for the shop's loyalty card — carte de fidélité — Charlotte recalled her moans of pleasure last night. Their sex life might not set the world on fire, but Dom still knew how to push the right buttons, and in the correct order. She straightened her face into a serious one, as the customer before her made payment and Charlotte's groceries advanced along the conveyor belt.

'Bonjour, Madame,' she said, the assistant echoing her words. She handed over the card for swiping, marvelling again at the subtle differences language could make. To Charlotte, fidelity meant being faithful in a relationship. And loyalty meant staying true to someone or something, but not in the same way. God, she had to stop over-analysing things, especially when doing a basic food shop.

'Cent vingt-cinq francs, s'il vous plaît.'

One hundred and twenty-five francs? OK, she'd snuck in two bottles of wine and a cheapo mascara, but Swiss prices still made Charlotte's head explode. She rammed her debit card into the machine, typed in the code, and said her 'Merci' and 'Bonne journée'. The pathetic quantity of stuff would barely fill the Bag For Life she'd folded into her handbag. Removing it, Charlotte started packing and — oh, for goodness' sake — half a dozen apples sought freedom and bounced towards the cigarette and magazines kiosk.

'Do you need some help?'

Charlotte looked up. Standing amid her apple uproar was Jürgen. He bent over, picked up two, and juggled them. Right, very impressive. She picked up a third and tossed it at him. Damn it, he carried on juggling. An elderly gentleman paused in his purchase of roll-up tobacco to give him a round of applause. A few other customers gathered, watching as Charlotte lobbed a fourth, then a fifth, then—

'My career in the circus did not last very long.' Jürgen gathered up the dropped apples and Charlotte held out her bag.

'Thank you.' He placed the slightly battered fruit in the

bag, then waited by her side as she retrieved the rest of her purchases.

'My pleasure.' Jürgen showed no sign of leaving. And no sign of having bought anything in the supermarket.

'Don't you have shopping to do?' Charlotte didn't want to dawdle with this man, wrecker of cars and — for whatever reason — arch-nemesis of Pamela. She planned on baking cookies and making cheese and ham sandwiches ready for Alastair's play date with his friends.

'All I needed was a supply of liquids for this.' Jürgen produced a vaping gizmo from the top pocket of his jacket. 'It is a poor substitute for cigarettes, but I have no wish to die just yet.'

'Right. Well, I have things to do, so... I guess I'll see you around.' Charlotte took in his effortless style. Designer suit: check. Designer shoes, polished to perfection: check. Not a greying hair out of place: check. Her irritation rose a notch, fuelled by a vaguely irrational but pulsating dislike of the man.

'Would you have coffee with me?'

Charlotte made a show of looking at her watch. Her cheap watch, in contrast to Jürgen's flashy number. Then she glanced at the supermarket café. 'I don't think—' It resembled a scene from hell. Customers were queuing for drinks, snacks and full-on meals, and jostling for tables already piled high with discarded trays and dismembered sugar sachets.

'Not here. There is a nice place just around the corner.' Jürgen nodded towards the exit. 'And they have delicious pastries and cakes, if you are not dieting like most women I know.'

Was he implying she was fat? Charlotte tugged her less-than-flattering Puffa jacket around her middle. 'No, I'm not. And I'm not hungry, so—'

With precision timing, Charlotte's stomach rumbled

louder than an approaching underground train. Jürgen grinned, touched her arm gently, and before she knew what was happening, they left the supermarket together.

'This is nice.' Charlotte sat opposite Jürgen, having both placed their order at the counter. Renversé, a Swiss-French variation on a latte, for her, and a double espresso for him. Conceding that skipping breakfast hadn't been the best of ideas, she'd opted for a croissant au jambon.

Jürgen had chosen a triple-layered chocolate confection, which he assured her tasted divine. 'Please, taste,' he said, offering her a second spoon. Charlotte hesitated — it seemed terribly intimate to share a stranger's dessert — but she took a small spoonful. It *was* divine.

'So, what brings you to Switzerland?' Jürgen downed his coffee and signalled to the waitress for another.

'My husband's work,' Charlotte replied. 'To be honest, I didn't want to come. But the boys are happy, and that's what counts.'

'Surely your happiness counts too?' Jürgen regarded her intently. The skin around his eyes was paler than the rest of his face. Charlotte assumed he was a summer sun worshipper or a ski bunny. Or both.

'Of course it does. I'm just struggling to find my feet, that's all.' *I don't have to justify my feelings to this man.* She finished her coffee and reached for her purse.

'Do you have to go already?' Jürgen smiled at the waitress as she set down his second cup. 'And this is on me. I'd like to get to know you better, Charlotte.'

Was he coming on to her? Maybe Mr Twice Married made a habit of prowling around supermarkets and homing in on women with dodgy packing skills. 'My son has friends coming over, so I need to get back and bake… things.' *Because baking a batch of cookies and slicing bread for sandwiches takes at least five hours.*

Jürgen stirred a sugar into his coffee and gestured for Charlotte to have more cake. 'You could always cheat and take some things home from here.'

'I could, but I enjoy baking for the boys. And the stuff here is a bit upmarket for an after-school get together.' Charlotte helped herself to a small sliver, washing it down with the glass of water that always accompanied the coffees.

'Perhaps you need to get out more,' said Jürgen, picking up his phone. 'Sorry,' he added, 'that did not come across very well.'

Charlotte glowered at him. Bloody cheek! Was he implying that she was some kind of hermit, only leaving the house for the school run and supermarket shopping? Mind you, she and Dom had gone nowhere together without the boys since moving to Switzerland. He was always too busy with work, or too exhausted in the evenings to do anything more than flick through Sky channels and top up his wine glass.

'Let's exchange phone numbers.' Jürgen passed his top-of-the-range iPhone to Charlotte. She took it, although every fibre of her being screamed 'No! This is not appropriate!'

'My son, Marcus, likes to babysit for extra pocket money,' Jürgen added. 'He is a good boy, and very patient with younger children. I believe your boys are younger, no?'

Charlotte nodded, relief coursing through her veins. Jürgen wasn't coming on to her; he simply wanted to find a revenue outlet for his teenage son. She keyed her number into his phone, and he fired off a quick confirmation text. So he now had her number, but where was the harm in that?

'Yes, Alastair is nine and Robson is seven. They're lovely — well, I would say that, wouldn't I? I'd hardly admit to them being little monsters!' She scrolled through photos on her phone, showing Jürgen a picture of the four of them taken at Christmas, wearing paper crowns and sporting cheesy grins.

'That's my husband, Dom, by the way,' she added, in case Jürgen thought they were posing with the postman.

'A lovely family,' he replied, beating a little tattoo on the table with his fingers. *Strong fingers,* thought Charlotte. Long, and topped with well-groomed nails.

'Do you have a photo of Marcus?' Jürgen nodded and produced an image of a smiling young man wearing a base-ball cap. Charlotte took his phone again and peered closer. That face was familiar. Of course, she'd probably seen him around at school, but—

'We've met!' She recounted the story of Alastair's skiing mishap, and how Marcus had come to his rescue.

'Yes, he mentioned something about it. He has a generous heart and always thinks of others.' Jürgen put his phone away, his expression one of quiet pride.

'So, do you have other children, or is Marcus an only child?' Charlotte already knew the answer, assuming her playground informant Sadie had reliable intel.

'Correct, Charlotte. He is my only child, and the reason I wake up every day. I have been married twice — I suspect you already know that — but I haven't given up on finding the one. The perfect match, as you say.' Jürgen stretched out his legs, taut thigh muscles straining against the expensive fabric of his trousers.

Help! Charlotte scanned the café in the faint hope of spotting someone she knew. She needed an excuse to extricate herself from this confusing, unnerving situation—

Oh, praise be to the god of all things gooey and calorific. Alicia waltzed in, designer handbag artfully placed on her arm. Mere mortals parted in her wake, although they might have been dithering over their sugar-laden choices.

'Alicia!' Charlotte's voice cut through the clamour of the café as keenly as a knife through the bread she hadn't yet bought. 'How are you?'

Jürgen stood up, frowning, his countenance that of a man with more to say. He gave Alicia a half-hearted wave, then tossed some notes on the table. 'Thank you for having coffee with me. I hope we've put the car incident behind us and we can be friends. Because I need friends, Charlotte.'

Charlotte swallowed, hard. When you made a judgement call on someone, it was difficult to unpick the stuff you'd knitted in your head. Jürgen was the bad guy: arrogant, entitled and going through wives like a Hollywood star with commitment issues. Or was he? Did she really want him as a friend? Mind you, Charlotte wasn't sure she wanted Alicia as a friend either.

'Oh, hello.' As Jürgen left Alicia approached, taking up the vacant seat. 'I see you know Jürgen. An interesting man, if a little intense for my liking.'

Alicia's order — a mint tea — arrived; presumably the coffee here didn't pass muster. She tore open the tea bag envelope, Charlotte marvelling at her perfectly manicured nails. She bit her own, chipped polish and ragged cuticles completing the unedifying look. Casually placing her hands out of sight, she smiled. Alicia smiled back, but Charlotte noted it didn't reach her eyes. In fact, her eyes, despite a liberal coating of mascara and lashings of smoky-grey eye shadow, looked pink and sore. Exactly how Charlotte's looked when she had a cold or … or she had been crying.

'Is everything OK?' she asked.

Alicia squished the tea bag into the tall glass mug, its colour spreading in kaleidoscope swirls.

'Yes. Of course. Why wouldn't it be?'

No idea. Buggered if I know why I bothered to ask. Alicia reminded Charlotte of the cool girls at her old school, the ones who stalked the hallways like young lionesses, ready to rip apart anyone who didn't meet their gold standard of casual ennui. Charlotte had kept out of their way, mostly, but many had suffered their withering put-downs and subtle bullying.

'Well, if you'll excuse me, I need to go.' Charlotte gathered up her things, leaving Jürgen's more than adequate payment on the table. 'See you soon.'

Alicia mumbled something Charlotte didn't quite catch. Probably 'bye', but it was hard to hear over the buzz of the café. She headed for the door, looking back once as she waited for an elderly lady pulling a laden bag on wheels to shuffle in. Alicia didn't look up, her focus on the mug of tea.

CHAPTER 19

'I don't like mayonnaise.' Nathaniel peeled open his sandwich and inspected the ham filling, his freckled nose crinkling with distaste.

'Here, have my cheese one.' Alastair swapped plates, eager to please his new friend.

Jodie, his other new friend, chomped on a slice of toast slathered in peanut butter. 'I'm vegan,' she had announced on the way up from school. 'My mummy says we shouldn't eat anything that has a face.'

Charlotte loved meat, but images of forlorn lambs, crestfallen chickens and sad cows filled her head as she wended her way past the vineyards. The vines were blossoming after the winter; fresh growth which would one day be transformed into Swiss wine.

'There's egg and cress too,' she said, pointing at the platter in the centre of the table.

'I can't eat eggs,' Jodie replied. 'Vegans don't eat eggs.'

Eggs don't have faces. Unless you paint silly ones on them at Easter. OK, Charlotte knew eggs hatched, so technically they did, but how could anyone live without eggs?

Popping another slice of bread in the toaster for her vegan guest, Charlotte checked her phone on the kitchen counter. A text from Dom, saying he'd be late home and wouldn't need dinner. Fine. No need to bother with the confit du canard and cassoulet she'd planned to prepare — well, dig out of the freezer and open the tin. Charlotte and the boys could have fish fingers, a tin of Heinz's finest — even if they cost three times the price here — and a side of oven chips. There'd be plenty of sandwiches left for Dom whenever he got home.

'What's a vegan?' asked Robson, reaching for the pickle jar. He spread a thick layer on his cheese sandwich, slurping his drink. Charlotte smiled and wiped away his milky moustache with a napkin. Robson flinched, embarrassed, and Jodie sniggered, unaware that she had a large blob of peanut butter on her chin.

'We talked about it in the car,' Charlotte said. 'Vegans don't eat meat, or fish, or eggs, or dairy products, or ... erm, I'm not sure what else.'

'That's silly. What do you eat when you go to McDonald's?'

Judging by the look on Jodie's face, a trip to the Golden Arches didn't feature on her social calendar.

With the children hunkered down for a cartoon-viewing session, Charlotte made a coffee and opened up her iPad. A number on her email inbox signalled a bunch of new emails. She clicked on the icon, sighing at the usual promo material, predominantly in German. Charlotte doubted she'd ever master French, never mind German. So many people in Switzerland were fluent in multiple languages. It was embarrassing, and a good reason to insist the boys work hard in their French lessons.

Hitting 'delete' on offers of discounted furniture and fitness gear, Charlotte grinned. An email from Ruth, buried beneath the special offers. They emailed from time to time, Ruth's missives packed with gossip, funny stories and assurances that life wasn't perfect in Blighty. Charlotte tried to reply similarly, keeping her gripes to a minimum. She opened the message, praying for no interruptions.

Hi, hon. How's things in the land of cheese and chocolate?

Hope Dom's behaving himself. I bought some new, super-sharp secateurs for the garden. Just saying.

Life goes on here, the usual lumps and bumps (and I ain't talking about my midsection). Or maybe I am. Sorry, rambling on. My mum's on a detox at the moment and she keeps sending me recipes of revolting green sludge that's supposed to cleanse your colon. Think I'd rather shove a hosepipe up my bum!

Work's super busy, which is good for the bank balance but not so good for my sanity. What's new with you? Have you made a new BF yet? Hope I haven't been relegated to the bottom of the friendship league...

Speaking of which, I need to get away for a bit (not that kind of 'bit', you filthy-minded mare!) Soooo, I was wondering if you fancied a bit of company in June. Can be flexible on dates, looking at staying maybe three/four days if you can put up with me for that long. Really need some girlie time, and a proper chat. All this texting and email malarkey is a poor substitute for getting together and chewing the fat. Oops, back to talking about blubber again!

Charlotte looked up as Alastair bowled into the room. 'We're still hungry,' he said, reaching for the biscuit tin. 'Do we have any biscuits Jodie can eat?'

A quick scan of ingredients revealed that Hobnobs and Digestives were a safe bet. Alastair piled them on a plate, and Charlotte made up a jug of diluted juice. Satisfied, Alastair disappeared into the living room, biting his lip with concentration as he carried the tray of snacks and drinks.

Charlotte returned to Ruth's email.

I can fly direct to Geneva and take the train to you if that's easier. Or you can book me a stretch limo with a hunky chauffeur and a fully stocked minibar. The choice is yours... Anyway, let me know how you're fixed and I'll get on to booking stuff asap.

Miss you loads. You leaving was a bit like getting my tonsils out (painful), and no amount of ice cream makes up for not having my bestie around. Although I'm currently inhaling a tub of salted caramel and soaking my tootsies in a basin of fragrant bath salts. I know, I'm so rock 'n' roll! Big hugs xxxxxxxx

Charlotte grabbed the paper calendar from the wall next to the fridge. Dom teased her about being old-fashioned, but she'd never got to grips with noting dates and appointments on her phone. Each page denoted a month, with columns for the four of them. Turning a page, she scanned the month of June. A few birthday reminders, a cheese and wine charity fundraiser at school and — ooh, a trip to Interlaken for both Alastair and Robson. Only a few nights away, but it coincided with Dom going on a business trip. Ruth adored the boys, but it would be lovely if Charlotte could have one night alone with her friend.

Jotting down the relevant dates, Charlotte fired off a reply.

Hi, gorgeous buddy. Squealing with excitement here! All OK and I promise you haven't been replaced. Haven't met anyone bonkers enough yet to step into your shoes. No need to bring sharp implements (won't be allowed in your hand luggage anyway).

Charlotte had already vented by text message about Amelie being around, and Dom's fervent denial of any wrongdoing. She hadn't mentioned the make-up sex, or the niggling question mark that remained over Dom's innocence. When Ruth arrived, they'd talk about anything and everything and hopefully put Charlotte's mind at rest. Ruth might not be Team Dom, but she always cut through the crap and found solutions to life's little problems.

Signing off, Charlotte realised Nathaniel and Jodie were

due to be picked up in five minutes. She hit send and went into the living room.

The four looked up, the TV screen paused on an episode of *South Park*. Alastair had the grace to look embarrassed, while Robson was intent on demolishing the last Hobnob.

'You know you're not allowed to watch that!' Charlotte seized the remote control and turned off the TV. She prayed that neither of the boys' friends would report their viewing choices to their parents, otherwise she would get a frosty reception at school.

'I wanted to watch a documentary about whales,' said Jodie haughtily.

'I wanted to watch *Monsters Inc*,' said Robson.

'So did I,' added Nathaniel.

Hustling the visitors into the hallway to collect jackets and bags, Charlotte heard a car pull up. Opening the door, she smiled at Nathaniel's mum, who was collecting both the children.

'Thanks so much for having them. I hope they behaved themselves!' She declined Charlotte's offer of a cuppa, explaining that she had to drop Nathaniel off for a guitar lesson and Jodie for a junior yoga class.

'Bye, bye.' Robson and Alastair waved at their friends. Jodie waved back with her right hand, the left intent on burrowing into her nostril. Charlotte shuddered as Jodie surveyed her finger, then popped the contents in her mouth.

'Right, you two. Time to clear up, then homework.' Charlotte closed the door.

Alastair sloped off to collect the empty plates and glasses but Robson stayed, a puzzled look on his face. 'Mummy?'

'Yes, sweetie?'

'Is snot vegan?'

CHAPTER 20

'You have a lovely home.' Juliette accepted a glass of pink fizz and a fish goujon, which she dipped into a bowl of tartare sauce. 'Such a stunning view, and space for your boys to play.'

Charlotte thanked her and also sent up a prayer of thanks for the wonderful weather. Despite her lack of enthusiasm for a party, she was glad she'd eventually agreed. And she was very relieved that the weather had upped its game. The previous two days had been unseasonably cold and wet, the mountains and lake obscured by low-lying mist. She'd checked out Meteo Suisse obsessively, relieved to see the evening of the party was forecast to be warm and dry.

'They seem to be enjoying themselves,' said Charlotte. Robson and Alastair were splashing around in the oversized paddling pool with Juliette's daughter, Sylvie, her husband, Olivier, watching with amusement.

'This quiche is simply to *die* for!' Antoine sidled up next to them, a slice of Charlotte's home-made asparagus quiche balanced on a paper plate.

Not for the first time, Charlotte pined for the scrummy

selection of pre-made party nibbles offered at M&S or Wait-rose. Scouring the supermarket shelves here, she'd found little to tempt her beyond spring rolls, jalapeno poppers and strange bread things topped with a gelatinous gloop. She'd baked a bunch of stuff and roped the boys into making chocolate brownies and butterfly cakes. Dom's contribution had been ordering cases of beer, wine and a selection of soft drinks for the designated drivers and children.

'Miranda, can you bounce a little less vigorously, please? Those little ones will be catapulted into outer space if you don't cool it!' Sadie stood next to the trampoline — another new purchase that had almost given Dom a nervous break-down during construction — as her daughter performed an expert backflip. Two tots, offspring of another of Dom's colleagues, scrambled to safety through the gap in the netting.

'Thank you again for inviting us.' Jürgen wandered over from the shade of the terrace where he'd been chatting to Sadie's husband, Rick. He clinked his beer bottle against Charlotte's glass of pink fizz. Marcus was organising some kind of skittles game for the children not occupied in the pool or on the trampoline.

'You're so welcome,' said Charlotte. It was the first time she'd seen Jürgen casually dressed, and his khaki shorts and white linen shirt suited him to a tee.

'Having fun?' Dom appeared, draping his arm around Charlotte's shoulders. Judging by his slight unsteadiness, he'd already knocked back several drinks, and he seemed on edge. Glancing around nervously, perhaps because there was no sign of Amelie? He'd told Charlotte he'd invited most of the office, but he hadn't mentioned her name. And Charlotte wasn't about to ask.

'It's a pleasure to be here,' said Jürgen. 'And to meet you, of course.'

'Likewise,' replied Dom. 'Now, there's a truckload of food that needs eating, and I suggest you fill your boots before the locusts descend.' He waved in the direction of the terrace where a borrowed trestle table groaned under the weight of canapés, assorted salads and cakes.

'The locusts?' Jürgen looked puzzled, turning to Charlotte for an explanation.

She laughed, and pointed at a dripping Alastair and Robson, wrapped in beach towels and heading for the food. 'He means the children. Once they get stuck in, we'll be scrambling for leftovers.'

Jürgen made his way to the table, stepping aside to let Juliette and her husband go first. They each picked up plastic plates and cutlery and began helping themselves.

'He seems all right,' said Dom, retrieving an unopened bottle of beer from his shorts pocket. 'No partner then, or has he waved the white flag after two failed marriages?'

Charlotte bit back an angry retort. She was sure she'd told Dom about Jürgen losing his first wife in an accident, but he'd no doubt forgotten. Or he hadn't been listening, which was more likely. But before she could speak, Antoine let out an eardrum-piercing whistle, and clapped like a demented seal.

'Fashionably late as always, sweetpea,' he announced, as a familiar figure rounded the corner of the house. Amelie, pretty as a picture in a vintage-looking pink halter-neck dress and silver espadrilles. Charlotte eyed the perfectly arranged ribbons wrapped around Amelie's perfectly shaped calves and wondered why she could never get the bloody things to stay in place.

'I ordered an Uber, but the idiot got lost and took me to another Chemin des Vignerons,' Amelie huffed. She and Antoine did the usual three-way kiss, then she picked her way across the grass towards Dom and Charlotte.

'I am so sorry to be late,' she said, holding out a heavily bangled hand to Charlotte. 'You must be Charlotte, although perhaps I am making the wrong assumption?'

'Yes, this is my wife,' said Dom, rather formally. He leaned forward as if to kiss Amelie on the cheek, but then shook her hand instead. She offloaded a canvas bag from her shoulder and passed it to Charlotte.

'Just a little something for the party, and for the hostess,' she said. 'The proprietaire — I mean, the owner — of the other house was a little surprised when I turned up bearing gifts. And as she was maybe seventy years old, I thought it unlikely to be you!' Amelie gave a tinkling laugh, and Dom joined in.

Charlotte attempted a smile, but her facial muscles struggled to respond. 'Thank you,' she said, pulling out a very expensive bottle of champagne and an exquisitely wrapped box of chocolates. 'Now, what can we get you to drink?'

'I'll deal with it, darling,' said Dom. 'You help yourself to some food, and I'll check if the sausage rolls are ready.'

Before Charlotte could reply, Dom and Amelie made their way to the drinks area where buckets of rapidly melting ice housed the beers. *I'll check if the sausage rolls are ready?* That was a first. Would Dom even know if they were ready? She checked her watch. They could probably do with a few more minutes.

'Can I help with anything?' Pamela appeared, with twins Rebecca and Elspeth in tow.

'I'm bored,' said Rebecca, blowing a stray strand of hair off her sweaty face.

'Don't be so rude!' admonished Pamela. 'Have something to eat or a dip in the pool. You remembered your swimming costumes, didn't you?' The pair shuffled off into the house, no doubt in search of their swimming stuff.

'No, everything's under control, thanks,' said Charlotte. 'It's a shame Martin couldn't make it.'

On arrival, Pamela had apologised for his absence. 'Summer flu, or man flu, to be more accurate. The slightest sniffle and he takes to his bed and expects to be waited on hand and foot. I left him with a flask of boiling water, a box of Lemsip and a fully charged iPad.'

Pamela scanned the twenty or so adults milling around the terrace and garden. Her gaze fell on Jürgen, tucking into a plateful of food and chatting to Rick. Her mouth tightened, as did her grip on the plastic champagne flute. 'So you invited *him*.' Pamela spat out the last word, as if its presence in her mouth was too foul to bear.

'Yes, I did. I think he's OK when you get to know him.'

Before Pamela could press Charlotte on *how* she'd got to know him, Charlotte remembered the sausage rolls. Having little faith in Dom, she excused herself and hurried to the kitchen.

'Oh, hello again!' Amelie was leaning against the worktop, nibbling a carrot stick. 'I was just saying to Dom that these look delicious.' She pointed at the sausage rolls, which were ever so slightly blackened round the edges. 'What a clever husband you have.' She smiled coquettishly at Dom, who stood a few feet away, a plate in one hand and a kitchen slice in the other. Charlotte noted her eyelashes fluttering at warp speed and felt an urge to snatch the kitchen slice from Dom and clobber Amelie with it.

'I'll take these outside,' he said. 'Have you eaten yet, Charlotte? Amelie, why don't you take one before they disappear?' She shook her head, once again smiling at Dom in a way that made Charlotte's hackles rise.

Dom headed off with the sausage rolls, leaving Charlotte alone with Amelie. Unsure what to say, Charlotte ran boiling water into the sinkful of dirty pots and oven trays and doused them liberally with washing-up liquid.

'Can I help?' Amelie stood next to her, Charlotte catching a whiff of her summery floral perfume. She realised she'd forgotten to squirt on her own perfume and prayed she didn't smell as sweaty as she felt.

'No, you're fine. Thank you. Erm, so you worked with Dom before? In England, I mean.'

Amelie gave her the look a cat gives a bird seconds before it goes in for the kill. 'Yes, we worked together. Very well.'

Charlotte focused on scouring the quiche dish, determined to remove every trace of stubborn pastry and distract herself from the thumping in her head. *Very well*. What the actual fuck did that mean?

'And you're happy to be here working alongside him again?' She knew she was straying into dangerous territory, but Charlotte needed to hear it from the horse's mouth. Even if the said horse was more menacing mustang than pert pony.

'I am. We are an excellent team. We work well together. We *all* work well together.' Amelie's bracelets jangled — as did Charlotte's nerves — as she snatched up a tea towel and wiped down the few items stacked in the drying rack before placing them on the worktop. 'Now, shall we return to the party?'

The party went on for several hours, with people drifting away as the sun set and the air cooled a little. Only a handful remained, including Sadie, Rick, Antoine and Amelie. Jürgen had left with Marcus at around eight, saying that he had an early start the next morning. Charlotte wished she'd had more time to talk to him, and didn't allow herself to question why she felt that way.

Finally, as the remaining guests bade their farewells, Amelie tapped Charlotte on the shoulder. There was no sign of Dom. Charlotte had noted the two of them keeping their distance on the whole. When they were together she sensed tension, as if they were engaged in a peculiar dance. Or was she reading too much into things? Too much, specifically, into what Amelie had said in the kitchen?

'Thank you for inviting me,' said Amelie.

'I didn't, Dom did.' Charlotte wished she could swallow the words when she realised how rude they sounded.

Amelie pursed her tiny mouth, her forehead wrinkling. 'Dom is a lovely man, and a handsome man, but a little too old for my taste. Just in case you were implying something, which I'm sure you weren't.'

A tooting horn signalled Amelie's Uber. She brushed her lips against Charlotte's cheek, and whispered, 'But never forget that men need tending, Charlotte.' Then she was gone.

CHAPTER 21

CHARLOTTE PACED AROUND THE ROOM, SEVERAL DISCARDED outfits strewn across the bed. She'd finally persuaded Dom they needed a night out, meaning a night out alone. Instead, they were going to a cocktail bar in Lausanne with a crowd of his work colleagues. Just what she didn't need so soon after the party.

'No, Amelie won't be there,' he'd said, before Charlotte even asked. 'She's away for a few days. Something to do with family, I think.'

Since the party, Charlotte had done her best to push all thoughts of Amelie away. Her parting words, however, still echoed in Charlotte's ears: 'Men need tending, Charlotte.'

What, like a bloody plant? Dom could keep himself fed and watered, and Charlotte had so far resisted tipping a bag of manure over his head. She probably shouldn't have quizzed Amelie on her history with Dom, but watching Miss Sparkly Pants flutter her impossibly long and probably fake eyelashes at him had pushed Charlotte's buttons.

Deciding on black skinny jeans and a silver-flecked top with bare shoulders, Charlotte twirled a few strands of hair around her curling tongs. Dusting some shimmery powder across her cheeks, she checked herself out in the full-length mirror.

'You look beautiful, Mummy,' said Alastair, as she made her way cautiously into the kitchen. Charlotte rarely wore heels these days, but the spiky scarlet sandals bought in last year's summer sales matched her lipstick perfectly.

'Like a princess,' added Robson. 'Fiona in *Shrek* when she wasn't an ogre.'

'Looks like the babysitter's arrived.' Dom peered out of the window at the sound of a car pulling up. Charlotte tottered over and glimpsed the familiar red car speeding away. Seconds later, the doorbell rang.

'Hi, Marcus.'

Jürgen's son was clutching a small bunch of flowers and a tray of clingfilm-wrapped biscuits. 'Hello, Mrs Egerton. Mr Egerton.' Despite Charlotte's protestations, he insisted on addressing them formally. 'These are for you.' He handed the flowers to Charlotte. 'They are from our garden. And my dad made these, which I hope the boys will enjoy.'

Jürgen made biscuits? Charlotte couldn't imagine Dom doing such a thing. He'd once cooked spaghetti for the boys when she'd been ill and burned it.

'Mummy says we can watch a movie on Netflix,' said Robson, grinning at Marcus. 'I want to watch *How To Train Your Dragon*, but Alastair says we have to watch *The Lion King*. Again.'

'And can we put on a magic show for you?' added Alastair.

Charlotte ran through the details of the boys' bedtime and routine and showed Marcus where everything was in the kitchen. 'Call if there are any problems,' she said, double-checking he had both their mobile numbers in his phone. Not that she foresaw any, and recalling Marcus's kindness and air of calm after the skiing incident, she felt the boys were in safe hands.

'All will be fine.' Marcus rummaged in his pocket and took out a one-franc coin. 'Now, we shall flip this to decide which movie to watch.'

Leaving the boys arguing over who got heads or tails, Charlotte and Dom slipped out to the waiting taxi.

'Seems a likeable lad,' said Dom. 'What does his dad do again?' He gave the bar address to the driver before slumping back in the seat.

'Erm, he made money in toilet rolls, I think,' said Charlotte. She'd never asked Jürgen directly how he earned a living. Sadie had mentioned the loo-roll connection one day during school drop-off, prompting Pamela to mutter something about him being 'full of shit'.

Dom snorted derisively. 'I guess there's always a demand for that. Must have been lucrative, judging by his wheels. Assuming that was his dad who dropped him off?'

Charlotte nodded, flipping open her tiny evening bag to ensure she had the essentials: phone, tissues, lipstick, credit card and keys. She had zero interest in cars beyond their ability to get you from one place to another. Jürgen owned a Ferrari — or was it a Porsche? Again, it didn't seem relevant. The handful of conversations they'd had touched on simpler topics, not the size of someone's bank balance or the value of their car.

The cocktail bar was jumping when they arrived. It was one of those places so dimly lit that Charlotte wished she had a miner's helmet to guide her through the gloom. God, she was getting old!

'Over here!' Antoine appeared, his formerly scarlet hair now a marbled mix of pink and yellow. It reminded Charlotte of a Battenberg cake, and the fact she hadn't eaten. She accepted Antoine's traditional three-way air kiss, and they followed him to a round table laden with weirdly coloured concoctions in jars.

'Glad you could make it.' Juliette stood up, and they went through the whole kissing rigmarole again. She wore heels this time, making Charlotte feel like a Lilliputian. 'You haven't met the others, no?'

Dom introduced Charlotte to the others seated or standing around the table. A flurry of hand-shaking ensued, with Charlotte trying to commit all the unfamiliar names to her memory.

'Hello again! Long time no see.' Dom's colleagues from the UK, Hank and André, joined the group, each clutching a pint.

'These guys are over here on a jolly — I mean, a training course. Isn't that right?' said Dom, slapping gum-chewing Hank on the back so hard that Charlotte feared he might choke.

'Are you enjoying Switzerland?' asked André. At least, she *thought* that was what he said. The clamour of the crowd coupled with his barely above-a-whisper voice made it impossible to be sure.

Charlotte smiled and replied in the affirmative as Dom passed her a glass of something clear and no doubt deadly.

'It eez a pity Amelie is not here,' said Antoine, clinking his glass against Dom's and Charlotte's. 'That girl eez the life and soul of the party.'

'Ah, yes,' mused Juliette. 'The last time we were here she started a conga around the room. She likes to be the centre of attention.'

Charlotte took a large gulp of her drink, its potency making her eyes water. Blinking furiously, she saw Dom's jaw tighten a fraction. Was that because of the mention of Amelie? Was he worried that his wife would grill him again on the subject, or did Amelie's absence mean more to him than he let on?

'We need to eat,' declared Hank, picking up a menu. 'I hope everyone's good with tapas, because that's what's on offer.' After several minutes of debating, Hank and André fought their way to the bar to place a large order for albondigas, garlic prawns, patatas bravas and empanadas.

The rest of the evening passed pleasantly enough. Charlotte chatted to Juliette and Dom ended up in a huddle with the menfolk, raucous laughter punctuating their chat. From time to time he caught Charlotte's eye. Was he making sure his wife was comfortable hanging out with his colleagues? Or wondering if he was in for the Spanish inquisition later?

At eleven, Charlotte signalled to Dom that it was time to leave. She'd told Marcus they would be home before midnight, and their pre-booked taxi was due shortly. He headed for the gents' loos, and she said her goodbyes to the group.

'We must do this more often,' said Juliette, giving Charlotte a hug. 'Next time I will ask my mother to look after Sylvie so that my husband can join us. He finds it hard to leave our little one, whereas I look for ways to mix with adults outside of work!'

Back home, Charlotte paid Marcus, who reported that the boys had been as good as gold. 'We watched both movies, although Robson fell asleep during the second one,' he said. 'And we ate all the cookies, but I used my phone to time them brushing their teeth!'

Marcus slipped out of the door just as the familiar red car appeared. Before Jürgen could vanish into the night, Charlotte tapped on his window.

'Are our boys now firm friends?' he asked, Charlotte catching a whiff of lemony cologne.

'Well, as they're tucked up in bed I can't ask them, but Marcus was already a hero in their eyes,' she replied.

Marcus blushed and thanked Charlotte again for asking him to babysit.

As he got into the passenger seat, Jürgen leaned further out of the window. 'Perhaps I can say thank you too by taking you for coffee again soon. Shall I text you?'

Charlotte glanced nervously back at the house. No sign of Dom. She nodded quickly, quelling the small knot of anxiety in her stomach. It was just a coffee, nothing more.

CHAPTER 22

'I THOUGHT WE SHOULD TRY SOMEWHERE DIFFERENT. WHAT DO
you think?'

Charlotte looked around the quaint café-cum-bakery,
customers queuing for fresh bread and chatting in French at
the tables dotted around. Somehow, people here never
seemed as loud as people back in the UK. And despite their
fondness for calorie-laden cakes and pastries, very few were
overweight.

'It's very charming,' Charlotte said. 'And not so easy to
find.'

The café was tucked away down a cobbled side street in
Vevey, minutes from the boys' school; she'd walked past the
narrow doorway three times before realising it was there.
Even more surprising was the small, sun-drenched rear
terrace where Jürgen had secured seats, a canvas parasol
providing some shade.

'So, how is life treating you?' Jürgen had already ordered
for them both. Renversé for her, an espresso for him, and a
selection of mini éclairs. Charlotte wasn't sure whether she

felt touched by the gesture, or annoyed that he hadn't waited to ask her.

'It's OK. Fine, I guess.' *Yes, let's go overboard with enthusiasm*, she thought. A sure-fire way of inviting questions she didn't want to answer. Charlotte had no desire to discuss the state of her marriage; certainly not with a man she barely knew and had misgivings about.

Jürgen didn't comment. He downed his coffee and pushed his sunglasses on top of his head. 'Please eat,' he said, 'before the icing melts.'

The éclairs were to die for. Charlotte had attempted to make some at home several years ago, but her choux pastry turned out like bathroom grouting. These were light as air, melt-in-the-mouth, utterly moreish, and—

'We know little about each other, would you agree?' Jürgen dabbed his lips with a paper napkin. He clearly hadn't shaved for a few days, and silvery stubble adorned his firm jawline. For one insane moment, Charlotte wanted to reach out and touch it. It was like the feeling when you stood at the top of a tall building and, just for a second, wondered what it would be like to fall.

'Well, we haven't exchanged CVs, or played twenty questions,' she retorted, her tone sharper than she'd intended.

Jürgen didn't flinch. He took out his vape, twirling it around like a mini baton. 'I will not use it here. The smell is a little strong, but the act of holding it is calming. Sometimes it is the simple things that give us peace when we are troubled.'

Charlotte smiled nervously. Lately, her troubled mind struggled to find any respite from the deluge of doubts and fears that prodded at her both waking and sleeping. Ruth had sent her a link to an online mindfulness course, but she hadn't made it past the introductory session.

'OK, why don't you start? I don't even know what you do for a living.'

Jürgen gave his vape another twirl. 'Well, I was fortunate to make some money in personal hygiene products many years ago.'

Charlotte's mouth twitched in amusement. 'You mean toilet rolls?'

'Indeed. Not very glamorous, but one of life's essentials. Nowadays I dabble in shares and do some consultancy work. It gives me the freedom to be around Marcus more and travel when I want to. Your husband, what does he do?'

Charlotte explained Dom's accountancy background and recent promotion within Design For Life. 'His current job is more of a managerial position, not that I know much about the business world. I worked as a medical receptionist for a while, which wasn't exactly exciting.'

'It sounds a very worthwhile job to me,' said Jürgen. 'Perhaps you can return to it one day when the boys are older?'

Charlotte shrugged. 'Maybe. Dom preferred me being at home.' She cringed inwardly, afraid Jürgen would think her a pathetic, downtrodden housewife with zero ambition. Which wasn't a million miles from the truth. She'd given up her job and relied entirely on her husband financially, not to mention moving abroad against her wishes.

They remained silent for several minutes. Charlotte racked her brains for something else to talk about. Before she could stop herself, she blurted out: 'Why don't you tell me about your marriages?' *Well, that was a sure-fire conversation killer.* Charlotte stuffed another éclair in her mouth, mainly to stop herself from putting her foot any further into taboo territory.

'If you would like to know, I am happy to talk.' Jürgen's direct gaze sent a shiver down Charlotte's spine. It was as if he could see into her soul, beyond the protective layers hiding her inner turmoil. It unnerved and excited her, this contrast between Jürgen and Dom. With Dom, she had to scream and shout for him to notice anything amiss.

'So, my first wife died almost twenty years ago, in an accident.' Jürgen didn't look away, but Charlotte lowered her eyes when she caught the flash of pain on his face.

'I'm so sorry. She must have been very young.'

'Twenty-five. We had only been married two years, and ... she was expecting our first child.'

His voice was calm and measured, whereas Charlotte wasn't sure she could trust herself to speak.

'We met as teenagers and Greta was the love of my life. I know it is a cliché, but it is true. We fitted together in every way, and she supported me in the early days of my business when others mocked me and predicted failure. My success and my money is all down to Greta, but it has been hard to enjoy it without her by my side.'

'How did... I mean, what happened?' Charlotte's curiosity overcame her desire to shut the conversation down. Jürgen wanted to talk, and for whatever reason, he wanted to talk to her.

'She was hiking in the mountains with some friends. Greta loved to keep fit, even more so when she discovered she was pregnant. I had a bad feeling that day, I think you say a premonition? I asked her not to go, but she laughed and said the exercise would be good for her and the baby. Two hours later, I received a phone call. Greta had slipped on a shingly path and fell over the edge. Her friends reached her, but... she suffered severe head injuries. She, and the baby, died in hospital.'

'I don't know what to say, except sorry again.' Charlotte reached out her hand and touched Jürgen's.

He clutched her fingers for a moment, then released them. 'There is no need to be sorry, Charlotte. Each year the pain grew a little less, but I had no interest in seeing other

women. I threw myself into my work, expanding my business, and investing in stocks and shares. I became wealthy,
but took no pleasure in my bank balance or those who
wanted to help me spend it.' Jürgen sighed. 'Until my second
wife came along.'

Charlotte ordered more coffees, and Jürgen described
how he had met Monica at a charity fundraising concert he'd
sponsored in Berlin. 'She was — she is — a musician. A
flautist, and a very talented one. She invited me for drinks
one evening, and for once, I accepted. It's hard to explain, but
she seemed different. Or should I say, *indifferent* to my social
standing.'

As they were now alone on the terrace, Charlotte urged
Jürgen to use the vape he was fiddling with again. He took a
long drag, exhaling a plume of peppermint which wasn't
unpleasant.

'Anyway, we dated and after some months, I asked her to
marry me. I wasn't in love with her, nor she with me, but I
realised I was lonely. And Monica was happy to accept, even
although her job took her away for weeks at a time. I thought
it was the best of two worlds; having a companion, but also
space to do our own thing.'

Charlotte thought she knew where this was going, but
kept quiet.

'We had Marcus, which was a surprise as Monica believed
she couldn't have children, and she found it difficult to adjust
to being a mother. I was over the moon, however, and
became a stay-at-home father as she continued to travel the
world.' Jürgen took another puff, the minty scent shrouding
Charlotte.

'Marcus was only five when I discovered Monica had
been playing with more than her flute. I went to one of her
concerts in Geneva and saw her at the bar afterwards with
the conductor. They weren't touching, but the electricity

between them was obvious. Sometimes it is not what people say or do, but what they *think* they conceal that is most telling.'

Charlotte gulped. Jürgen could be describing her situation with Dom. For months he'd denied any wrongdoing, and she'd believed him. But at their party, hadn't he and Amelie danced around each other? And as for Amelie's parting comment ... had that been a smoke screen?

'She married the conductor, Aaron, and they live in Berlin. Marcus stays with them every few months, but his home is here, with me.' Jürgen smiled and mimicked zipping his mouth. 'Enough about my sad history. Let's talk about cheerier things. The Montreux Jazz Festival, for example. Do you have tickets?'

Charlotte shook her head. She recalled the programme coming out in March, but hadn't got around to buying anything.

'Who's playing?' she asked, trying to remember the line-up.

'Sting, Elton John on his Farewell Yellow Brick Road tour and Tom Jones, to name a few. I got a couple of tickets for Elton, which will be a very special outdoor concert. Perhaps...' Jürgen's voice tailed off.

'Perhaps what?' Charlotte's phone beeped. A text from Dom. She glanced at it quickly. *Won't be home till late again. Soz. Up to my eyes in it. Xx*

'I just wondered if you would like to come with me. It's not really Marcus's scene. Maybe it's not your scene either, or... Sorry, it's a stupid idea. Please, forget I mentioned it.'

'That's very kind, but—' Charlotte imagined Dom's reaction if she said she planned to spend an evening with another man. Mind you, in recent weeks she'd felt increasingly invisible to him, their contact limited to rushed breakfasts with the boys and an hour or two in the evenings.

'I understand. Perhaps you could take both the tickets and go with your husband?'

Charlotte shook her head. 'I don't think Elton is really Dom's cup of tea. He's more of a Radiohead and Elbow man.' Whereas Charlotte, accompanied by Sadie, had gone to see *Rocketman* at the cinema, and spontaneously applauded at the end, much to the surprise of the more reserved locals.

'Think about it. Anyway, I'm sorry but I must go.' Jürgen took out his wallet and again refused Charlotte's offer to pay. 'It's been — what is the word — cathartic to talk to you so openly. Thank you for listening. You are an excellent listener.'

He touched Charlotte lightly on the arm, and left. She decided a quick trip to the loo was in order and made her way inside. Scanning the interior for a sign, she glanced at the window. Was that Pamela? She raised her hand to wave, but whoever it was scuttled out of view.

CHAPTER 23

Never had Charlotte been happier to see her friend. Standing in the arrivals area of Geneva Airport, she scanned the doors as passengers passed through. Some struggled with heavy bags, others skipped through with hand luggage, into the waiting arms of loved ones. When Ruth appeared, Charlotte ran towards her. They squealed in unison, startling an elderly gentleman who shot them a disgruntled look.

'I can't believe you're here!' Charlotte hugged Ruth tightly, inhaling her perfume and nearly dislodging the handbag slung over her shoulder. 'We're going to have the best time. Dom's out of town, the boys are away on a trip, and I have a fridge-full of food, booze and eye masks.' For years, she and Ruth had set aside evenings for pampering: giving each other pedicures, slapping on face masks and taking silly photos. They revisited their twenties, when life seemed simpler and the need for age-repairing treatments was redundant; but it was still fun.

'Hey, hon, so good to see you.' Ruth hugged Charlotte back before grabbing her wheelie bag. As usual, she looked immaculate. Or did she? She wore khaki jeggings teamed with a loose-fitting cream T-shirt and ankle boots, and her naturally curly brown hair was scraped up in a loose topknot. But her face was devoid of make-up. That was *so* not like Ruth. Admittedly, it had been an early flight, but—

'Are you OK?' Charlotte relieved Ruth of the wheelie bag and they made their way to the parking area. She found the ticket, paid at the machine, and they took the elevator to the right level.

'I'm fine.' Ruth climbed into the passenger seat, fumbled in her handbag, and produced a small bottle of water. 'Just a bit dehydrated.'

Charlotte manoeuvred the car through the barrier and on to the slip road. She passed a tin of extra-strong mints to Ruth, who took it and popped one in her mouth.

The journey took under an hour and Ruth was alarmingly quiet the entire time. Normally, she'd talk non-stop about everything from politics and annoying Z-list 'celebrities' to diet regimes and why getting a decent bra was akin to finding the Holy Grail. Now she leaned against the window and gave staccato 'yes' and 'no' answers to everything.

Unlocking the door to the house, Charlotte wondered if she'd upset Ruth. Maybe she hadn't kept in touch enough. They used WhatsApp to message, and FaceTime to chat, but life often got in the way. Their lives were poles apart, and they were both busy, for different reasons. No, there was something else going on. Charlotte knew it, just as she knew when the boys were unhappy or trying to keep a secret. Just as she knew when Dom had something to hide… But now was not the time to excavate that worry.

* * *

'I KNOW it's only lunchtime but what the heck, we found this amazing pink bubbly, so shall we celebrate?' Charlotte brandished a chilled bottle to accompany the assortment of pastries, mini sandwiches and charcuterie she'd arranged on a platter. 'I am so, so happy that my best buddy is here. I might not be fully integrated yet — and I doubt I ever will be — but I want to show you the sights. You can laugh at my crap French, eat amazing chocolate and even buy a cuckoo clock. I bloody hate them, personally, but each to their own!'

Charlotte's sense of something off with Ruth increased when her friend quietly asked for a glass of water and said she wasn't hungry. 'Maybe just a couple of dry crackers, if that's OK. Oh shit... Excuse me.' Before Charlotte could respond, Ruth launched herself out of the kitchen.

'It's on the left, just by the front door,' Charlotte called out, in no doubt what Ruth was looking for. And why she was looking for it.

Eventually Ruth reappeared, a sheen of sweat on her face, dabbing at a stain on her T-shirt. Charlotte didn't like to think what it was, but she needed to talk to her friend *right now*. No more prevaricating; no more bullshit.

'Are you pregnant?' The words hung in the air, hovering over the untouched plate of food and the unopened bottle of fizz.

'Yes, I am.' Ruth looked down, twisting the hem of her top between her fingers. 'And it's completely and utterly shit.'

Charlotte didn't know what to say. She'd been overjoyed with both her pregnancies, thrilled beyond belief at the knowledge that she carried a new life within her. Morning sickness was a mere blip on the rollercoaster ride to mother-hood. Stretch marks were carried as a badge of honour — although she wouldn't mind if they faded from view enough to allow her to wear bikinis again.

'Are you sure?' No sooner had she spoken than Charlotte wanted to claw back the idiocy of her question. Of course Ruth was sure.

'Erm, no, I just happen to be puking constantly, my tits are ballooning and I want to cry all the time. That's not a symptom, by the way — just my reaction when I look at the five different sticks I've peed on.'

'Oh.' Charlotte opened the fizz, anyway. She poured two glasses, took a hearty swig of hers, and placed the other in front of Ruth. 'Can I ask who the father is?'

Ruth looked up, her eyes awash with a mixture of tears and the feisty, kick-ass attitude that made her the best friend you wanted on your team. 'I don't know. Which makes me a complete slut, I suppose. I know you won't judge me, Charlotte, but you're living the perfect life, Dom's supposed indiscretions aside. Two gorgeous boys, money in the bank, sorted. I flit around from relationship to relationship, not thinking twice about where it's going. Except that now I've royally screwed up. Officially torn between two lovers, neither of whom has a clue what's happened. And they won't want to know.'

'How do you know that? Have you spoken to them?' Charlotte pulled her chair closer to Ruth and brushed a stray strand of her friend's hair off her face.

'And say what? Hey, guys, I've been sleeping with both of you, I'm up the duff, and there's a fifty per cent chance you're the daddy. Fancy going shopping for bootees?'

Despite the situation, Charlotte giggled. Ruth's ability to wisecrack no matter how dire things seemed was one of her trademarks — and one of the many reasons she loved her to bits. 'How far along are you?' There was no discernible bump, although Ruth's T-shirt could hide several months' worth of baby.

'Ten weeks, according to the doctor. Still early days, and time to deal with it.' She took a sip of the fizz and wrinkled her nose. 'God, not only am I chucking up like a demon, but booze tastes vile and the smell of coffee makes me dry-heave. Can I have those crackers, hon?'

Charlotte rummaged in the biscuit tin, producing an open packet of rye biscuits she only ever ate on diet days. Placing them on a plate, she helped herself to a sandwich; not that she felt hungry. 'What do you mean, time to deal with it?' Then an icy feeling in the pit of her stomach told Charlotte exactly what Ruth meant.

'Charlotte, I'm the wrong side of forty. I run a successful business and pretty much do what I want, when I want. Mr Right never came along, but I've been happy seeing men — OK, younger men — on my terms. I'm not stupid; I caught a tummy bug and I guess it screwed up the Pill's efficiency. Ironic, really, that a bout of vomiting leads to this.'

'You haven't answered my question.' Charlotte took Ruth's hands and squeezed them tightly. 'Please tell me you're not thinking of—'

Ruth shrugged. 'An abortion? Hon, it's pretty much all I've thought about in recent weeks. Me, a single mother?' She laughed, a harsh sound the opposite of her usual throaty chuckle. 'I don't think I'm cut out for *that* role, do you?'

CHAPTER 24

'HE DID *WHAT?*' SADIE PUT DOWN HER CUP, TEA SPILLING INTO the saucer.

'He made a pass at me.' Pamela picked up the complimentary biscuit and popped it in her mouth.

'Jürgen?' Sadie gaped at Pamela.

Charlotte said nothing. She'd heard what Pamela said the first time. As had Sadie, but disbelief had etched deep furrows in her brow.

'Yes, Jürgen. I know you've got a soft spot for him, Sadie, but the man is reprehensible.'

Charlotte still had reservations about the enigmatic German. OK, she'd met him once more for coffee, but his comment about needing friends had moved her. The fact she'd met him (not something she'd shared with either Dom or the two women sitting with her) prickled at her conscience. Yet, somehow, she couldn't square what Pamela was saying with the man she was getting to know a little better.

'Why are you telling us this now?' Sadie leant forward,

her brow relaxed but her fingernails drumming a tattoo on the table. 'We knew you weren't a card-carrying member of his fan club, but we never asked why—'

Charlotte nudged Sadie in the ribs. They *had* asked, several times. And Pamela had always clammed up, pink spots flaring on her cheeks.

'Does Martin know?' asked Sadie.

'Of course not.' Pamela's straying husband, welcomed back into the fold after his dalliance with the au pair, cut a forlorn figure these days. He lingered on the sidelines at school events, pulling the twins close as if realising how close he'd come to being a part-time dad. 'Because—' Pamela lowered her voice, forcing Charlotte and Sadie to lean closer. 'Martin would see it as my way of getting back at him for sleeping with that tart. Not that I've forgiven him, but I don't want to give him reason to think he's got the moral high ground.'

'But you said Jürgen made a pass at *you*. Surely Martin would be angry on your behalf?' Charlotte struggled to imagine meek and mild Martin building up a head of steam about anything. He reminded her of a turtle, minus its shell. His head was slightly too large for his skinny body, poking out of an ill-fitting, crumpled shirt — possibly because the au pair was no longer around to do the ironing. Still, he must have something going for him; perhaps an enormous—

'I'm not taking the risk. Anyway, my advice is to steer clear of him.' Pamela directed this remark at Charlotte, those pink spots turning a vivid scarlet.

Had Pamela spotted them together? Lurked behind a pillar, phone at the ready to take incriminating shots of … what? Charlotte seductively swirling a spoon through a latte, licking the froth as Jürgen deftly sliced up a millefeuille? No, they'd done nothing wrong. Two people chatting in a coffee shop, fully clothed and guilty of nothing more than a fledgling friendship.

'When did he make a pass at you?' Sadie brought out a hand mirror and checked her reflection. Tutting, she produced her lipstick and did a touch-up job.

'It was... I can't exactly remember. A few months ago. Yes! At school. During the seniors' disco. I'd volunteered to help serve drinks. Not alcohol, of course.'

'Jürgen came on to you at a school disco?' Charlotte tried but failed to keep a note of incredulity out of her voice.

'Not *at* the disco. Outside, when I realised I'd left my phone in the car. He followed me and ... he tried to kiss me.'

'Bloody hell.' Sadie smacked her lips together, puckering up at an old man sitting in the corner with a beer and an ancient dog drooling at his feet. He raised his glass in a toast. Sadie reciprocated with her mug of camomile tea.

Something was off; Charlotte could sense it. Pamela's version of events didn't ring true.

'I pushed him away, but he tried again.'

'That doesn't sound like Jürgen.' Sadie frowned, putting down her tea. 'Are you sure you didn't get the wrong end of the stick? Like, maybe he thought you were upset or something, and he was trying to comfort you—'

'I wasn't upset, and even if I had been, trying to stick your tongue down someone's throat is a funny way of comforting them.' Pamela's face contorted in fury, the redness spreading down her neck.

'OK, OK.' Sadie held her hands up in a calming gesture. 'Blimey, why didn't you tell us before?'

'It's embarrassing. And I didn't want you confronting him and causing a scene. I'm only telling you now because—' Again, Pamela's gaze fell directly on Charlotte.

Charlotte squirmed in her chair, praying Sadie wouldn't

pick up on the hostile vibes firing across the table. 'I'm so sorry, Pamela, that must have been horrible.' Charlotte wanted to leg it out of the café. Go home and do something mind-numbing yet soothing, like bake brownies or iron crumpled bedlinen. Anything to avoid thinking of Jürgen lunging towards Pamela. How *could* he?

'You're telling us now, because—' Sadie prompted. Charlotte made a show of looking for something in her handbag. Preferably an invisibility cloak or a device to zap her far away from the café.

'I wanted to warn you about him. Both of you, seeing as you think the sun shines out of his Armani-clad arse. But don't you dare say anything to him!'

Charlotte wondered how Pamela knew which designer label Jürgen wore. She didn't doubt it was expensive, but wouldn't know the difference herself. Dom had two or three fancy suits they'd picked up on a trip to Milan, but from a factory outlet.

'Don't worry, we won't.' Sadie patted Pamela's arm. Charlotte nodded in agreement, although her instinct was to confront Jürgen and find out exactly what had happened, straight from the horse's mouth. He'd probably deny any wrongdoing, which either meant he'd done nothing wrong, or he was a womanising liar.

'Sorry, Pamela. I've got to run,' said Sadie. 'I've got an emergency appointment to get my roots done. Luckily Veronique could fit me in at short notice, otherwise I'd be resorting to a bag over my head.' Blowing kisses in all directions — including the old man, who looked like he'd won the lottery — Sadie dashed out. Charlotte stood too, reluctant to stay with Pamela.

'Just be careful, that's all I'm saying.' Pamela shrugged on her coat, a heavy one despite the warmth of the day. 'You've got a fabulous husband and two lovely boys. The last thing you need is some creep who thinks he's God's gift destroying all of that.'

She headed out the door, leaving Charlotte unsure what, or who, to believe.

CHAPTER 25

FOR THE PAST TWO WEEKS, CHARLOTTE HAD TRIED TO CHAT TO Ruth every day. It wasn't always possible, as her friend continued to work crazy hours and Charlotte didn't want Dom or the boys overhearing their conversations in the evenings. At Ruth's request, she hadn't told Dom about the pregnancy.

The few days they'd spent together had been fun, but the spectre of Ruth's predicament had hung over them like a lowering cloud. They agreed not to talk about it all the time and focus instead on pleasant things, such as a trip to Gruyères to see the mediaeval castle and the bizarre museum and café dedicated to the late H. R. Giger, designer of the weird and terrifying creatures in the *Alien* movies. They'd also visited the cheese factory, but a whiff of the stuff made Ruth turn green and rush outside.

Sadie had given Charlotte two guest passes for the Montreux Palace gym and spa. As a member herself, she joined them for a lazy afternoon lounging by the pool and sweating in the sauna. She'd got on well with Ruth, the three of them roaring with laughter at the 'energetic soup' on the lunch menu.

'Does it sprint in here of its own accord?' said Sadie. 'That sounds far too healthy for me. I can heartily recommend the club sandwich with a side of fries — which I'll get next time I come and torture myself at a circuit class!'

On Ruth's final evening in Switzerland, both Alastair and Robson returned from their trip. They were exhausted, but bursting with tales of their camping exploits. Dom was due to return too, but had called earlier to say he'd be staying in Zurich an extra night.

'Still trouble in paradise?' Ruth had asked when Charlotte banged down the phone with unnecessary force. Charlotte had shared a little of her ongoing concern about Dom, but felt Ruth's dilemma was a far greater worry. And if she were honest, spending Ruth's last evening having a simple dinner with the boys and a few more hours to chat suited her better than having Dom around.

They'd both sobbed at the train station the next morning. Ruth was adamant she preferred to take public transport rather than risk vomiting in Charlotte's car. She still hadn't said for sure what she planned to do, and her decision — or lack of one — made Charlotte feel sick too.

'You really need to tell the two men,' she'd said, as they huddled together on the platform. 'Whatever you decide, they have a right to know.'

During their last chat, Ruth had finally revealed the identities of the two candidates: Will, a fitness instructor who specialised in home visits, and Simon, a dermatologist. 'And before you ask, I didn't get to know either of them through their professional lives,' she said. 'You know my allergy to exercise, and I haven't been bothered by eczema since my mid-twenties.'

She'd bumped into Will at a drinks party hosted by a

mutual friend. He'd tried to persuade her to sign up for a six-week personal training course — twenty per cent discount to celebrate his third year in business — and she'd feigned indignation. 'I told him it was bloody rude to imply that I needed to contort myself into horrible positions and get disgustingly sweaty. Which is what we ended up doing a few nights later, although the positions were rather lovely.'

Charlotte had mock-tutted, Ruth a picture of put-on innocence. 'And Simon? Is he an itch you couldn't help scratching?'

It turned out Simon's sister, Cara, was a regular customer at Ruth's boutique. He'd arrived there one day to collect her for lunch. Cara had asked Ruth to join them, with Ruth happily shutting up shop early. Cara had then dashed off after an hour to collect her poorly toddler from nursery. Lunch had stretched into late afternoon, and by seven pm Ruth and Simon were at his swanky bachelor pad admiring the view from his balcony and of each other.

'If you'd just stick to one bloody man at a time, life would be a lot simpler,' Charlotte had remonstrated. Not for the first time, but she didn't sit in judgement of her best friend. She knew that Ruth never lied to her partners and didn't pretend to want exclusive relationships. If a man so much as hinted that he expected to have her all to himself, she ended it immediately.

'Well, I've never been one for choosing the simple route,' replied Ruth. Except now she was caught between a rock and a hard place. She'd never be footloose and fancy free again if she went ahead with the pregnancy, but the alternative was too awful for Charlotte to contemplate.

'The thing is,' Ruth continued, then halted abruptly. She disappeared briefly from the screen, before popping up again. 'Sorry, just needed to grab some chocolate. Full-on 70 per cent dark stuff is one of the few things I can stomach. That, and sardines on toast, believe it or not!'

'What's the thing?' asked Charlotte. Ruth was looking downright sheepish, and not just because she was chewing fervently.

'Well, for the first time I can remember, I wondered if, just maybe, Simon might be more of a … a keeper. Don't give me that look, Charlotte!'

After much prodding, Ruth admitted to having stronger feelings for the dashing dermatologist than the squats and sit-ups expert. 'I'm not saying I'm in love with him, or anything like that. It's more like — I dunno — there's a connection I've never really felt before.'

Ruth said she'd cut ties with both men shortly after discovering she was pregnant. 'Will didn't seem that bothered, to be honest. I kind of suspect he has a string of lithe lovelies willing to step into my shoes. But Simon took it quite badly, even although I assured him it was me, not him.'

Rounding off the chat, Ruth dodged the 'you need to tell them' bullet again. But she promised Charlotte she'd decide soon.

CHAPTER 26

'I WAS THINKING OF GOING TO VISIT MY FOLKS FOR A FEW DAYS.'
Dom muted the TV, silencing the couple bickering over
whether they should build an extension to their home, or
move to a bigger place in the countryside. Charlotte threw
him a filthy look. It was one of her favourite UK shows,
although she rarely guessed correctly whether they'd 'love it
or list it.'

'Really? Is something up?' Charlotte wandered into the
kitchen where meat sauce for the boys' favourite lasagne
bubbled on the hob.

'Erm, Dad called earlier when I was at work,' said Dom.
He grabbed a beer from the fridge and popped the cap.
'Mum's been a bit off-colour recently — nothing serious,
mind — so I thought I should go over. Play the dutiful son
for once, seeing as they're not getting any younger.'

Charlotte sliced a chunk of butter and lobbed it into a
pan for the béchamel sauce. Nobody was getting any
younger, including themselves. She was still coming to terms
with turning forty over six months after the event. Torquil
and Jean were only in their early seventies and built of stern

stuff. Nothing short of a full-blown nuclear attack would fell those two, she thought.

'Do you want us to come too?' Charlotte metaphorically crossed her fingers in the hope Dom would say no. It wasn't as if his parents expressed any regular desire to see her or the boys. Occasional brief and stilted FaceTime chats comprised their contribution to grandparent participation. Not that they saw Charlotte's parents often either, but she hoped they'd visit at some point. And their online chats with Alastair and Robson happened most weeks and lasted up to an hour.

'There's no need, it's just for a few days. Anyway, the boys have summer camp coming up.'

With Dom adamant they couldn't book a summer holiday yet — 'too much going on work-wise' — Charlotte had enrolled Alastair and Robson in the school's expensive five-day camp. Running from mid-morning till late afternoon, it promised an action-packed programme of sports and craft-making activities, and included lunch and snacks. Sadie's kids were also taking part, as were Pamela's twins.

'What's wrong with your mum?' asked Charlotte, stirring the sauce frantically. Damn it, she'd need to sieve out the lumps.

'Oh, just a touch of the flu,' mumbled Dom. 'Nothing serious, but it's been ages since I saw them.'

He wandered off, clutching his beer and saying that he'd get on with booking his flights. Normally Charlotte dealt with family trips, but as he was travelling solo, she left him to it.

Robson appeared. 'Mummy, can I help with the lasagne?'

Hot on his heels came Alastair, with a 500-piece Harry Potter jigsaw and foldaway puzzle board in his clutches. 'Can I set this up on the dining table?' he asked.

Charlotte nodded, and Robson knelt on a stool next to

her. Lining up the lasagne sheets and sauces, she explained which order they went in.

From the hallway, she could hear Dom on the phone. He gave a low chuckle, but Charlotte couldn't make out what he was saying. Perhaps he was talking to his mum, though that seemed unlikely, as Jean Egerton was to humour what vegan burgers were to carnivores.

Dom reappeared, stuffing his phone in his shorts pocket. 'All booked. I leave tomorrow and I'll be back on Thursday. Will you miss me, guys?' He directed the question at the boys, although he winked at Charlotte.

'Why would we miss you, Daddy?' said Robson, sitting back to admire his culinary skills. The lasagne was a little lopsided, with white sauce oozing over the edges of the dish. 'You go away a lot, and sometimes you're not here at bedtime.'

Dom frowned and patted Robson on the head. 'Sorry, bud. I do my best, and you've always got Mum around. And your brother.'

Alastair looked up from his jigsaw. He'd picked out most of the border pieces and started lining them up neatly. 'I'll miss you, Daddy. Is dinner nearly ready?'

After dinner, which Dom pronounced a triumph, he insisted on helping Charlotte locate the various bits of kit the boys would need for summer camp. Charlotte tasked Alastair with scrubbing their filthy football boots outside, and Robson with tracking down their tennis rackets.

'How do they ever find anything in here?' Dom complained, pulling out a drawer packed with higgledy-piggledy socks, underwear and vests. 'It looks like an explosion in a clothing factory.'

Dom liked everything in his wardrobe and drawers arranged with regimental neatness — not that *he* was personally responsible for such order. Since they'd got married, it was Charlotte who paired the socks, ironed and hung up the shirts and folded T-shirts with military precision. She had followed in the footsteps of her mother, a woman who staunchly believed that a wife's duty was to cater for her husband's every need. Ruth had teased Charlotte about it often, calling her a Stepford Wife and asking if she had to charge her batteries each day.

'They're children, Dom, and it's not that bad,' Charlotte retorted, tossing a handful of school PE shorts on Alastair's bed. 'I spend enough time making sure your boxers are perfectly aligned without having to stress about the boys' stuff. It's clean, it's put away, and that's all that bloody matters.'

Leaving Charlotte to locate the last few items, Dom went off to pack his own carry-on bag. Passing their bedroom, Charlotte peeked in and saw several of his favourite shirts hanging on the wardrobe handle. She was about to offer to fold them — she usually did — but a general feeling of irritation washed over her, and she stomped downstairs.

'Glass of vino?' Dom joined her in the living room where she was curled up on the sofa with a hideously overpriced UK women's magazine bought from the village. Alastair had returned to the jigsaw, and Robson was outside practising his tennis moves with an ancient Swingball set.

'Sure.' Charlotte flicked to the beauty section, eyeing up the editor's picks of must-have serums and exfoliators. Some brands were impossible to find in Switzerland, and she'd had a nasty surprise early on when she ordered her favourite cleanser and moisturiser online. Her delight at receiving the package turned to disbelief when the postman demanded cash payment of taxes — almost half the cost of the products — on the doorstep.

Handing Charlotte a glass of chilled rosé, Dom plonked himself down next to her and squeezed her knee. 'I'll try to ping you once a day while I'm away, but I think Dad's got a few jobs lined up for me. Stuff in the garden, and you know Mum'll expect a few outings. If she's up for it, of course,' he added quickly.

'Fine. I'll be busy anyway, running the boys up and down to camp, and hopefully having some fun with the ladies.' Charlotte, Sadie and Pamela had already planned some shopping trips and a lunch outing across the lake to France.

'Good stuff. Enjoy.' Dom clinked his glass against Charlotte's and grinned. 'I'll pick you up something nice at the airport. What's your favourite perfume again?'

CHAPTER 27

THE FIRST DAY OF CAMP WENT WELL. ALASTAIR AND ROBSON greeted Charlotte with enormous sweaty hugs, bubbling over with enthusiasm. 'I won two matches in the tennis tournament!' declared Robson.

Alastair proudly displayed a papier mâché mask he'd made during craft hour. 'It's meant to be Egyptian,' he said. 'Miss Kirkwood said it was excellent.'

'That's fantastic,' said Charlotte, delving into her bag for juice boxes and Laughing Cow cheese sandwiches. 'How was lunch?'

'Meh.' Robson pulled a face. 'It was fish, and I don't like fish except for tinned tuna.'

'Hey, guys.' Sadie appeared, fanning herself with the local newspaper. 'Who fancies a barbecue back at ours?'

The children shrieked with delight. 'Have you got sausages?' asked Alastair. 'I love sausages.'

'Are you sure you want us to come over?' asked Charlotte. 'I don't want to put you to any trouble.'

Sadie shook her head. 'Rick's home and he loves nothing

more than donning his apron and wielding his tongs. And, yes, we have sausages: British ones!'

Out of the corner of her eye, Charlotte spotted Jürgen making his way up the path. Marcus, along with a bunch of older students, was acting as a volunteer helper at the camp. She gave Jürgen a brief wave, and he returned the gesture.

Just then, Pamela strode out of the chalet, a sobbing Elspeth clinging to her side. 'Bloody hell, it's not the end of the world,' she hissed at her daughter as Rebecca shuffled out behind them. 'I'm sure it was an accident.'

'What's up?' asked Charlotte, passing Elspeth a pack of tissues.

'Oh, they were doing some painting thing, and Rebecca tipped a cup of water over Elspeth's "masterpiece",' Pamela replied.

'She did it on purpose,' gulped Elspeth, blowing her nose vigorously. 'Cos mine was better than hers.'

'You'll join us for a barbecue too, won't you?' Sadie gave Elspeth a quick squeeze. 'I've made banoffee pie for afters.' She turned to Charlotte, and whispered, 'Should I invite Jürgen and Marcus too? The more the merrier, but...'

Charlotte wasn't sure how to answer. Based on Pamela's loathing of Jürgen, she didn't think it a good idea. Then again, they only had Pamela's version of events, and doubt still niggled in Charlotte's mind.

'Too late. They've gone,' said Sadie. Sure enough, Jürgen and Marcus were heading back down the path.

Rick greeted the group with a jug of Pimms and non-alcoholic fruit punch for the children. 'I promise it's not lethal strength,' he said, pouring the concoction into highball glasses.

'Missing Dom?' asked Sadie, fishing out a strawberry and popping it in her mouth.

'Hardly. He's only been gone one night,' replied Charlotte.

He'd rung to say he'd arrived safely, and that his dad was on excellent form, his mum less so. Relief swept over Charlotte when Dom said he couldn't stay on long. He'd talked briefly to the boys, then ended the call.

'I'm rubbish when Rick travels,' said Sadie. 'Even though we've an alarm system, I'm always convinced some random lunatic will break in and steal all our valuables.'

Crime rates weren't particularly high in the area, but there had been a recent spate of burglaries. A family at the school had revealed that thieves had broken in during the night and taken an expensive bracelet from the bedside cabinet as they were sleeping.

'I don't worry about stuff like that,' joked Charlotte. 'I keep an axe by the bed, and one look at me in my nightie and eye mask would be enough to scare anyone!'

Talk turned to summer holiday plans. Sadie and her family were embarking on a week-long sailing trip around the Greek islands. 'Miranda gets seasick on a pedalo, so I'm hoping the anti-nausea bracelet things work,' she said. 'It was Rick's idea. He's always fancied himself as an old sea dog, but he'll be in charge of mopping up the vomit!'

'We're taking the girls to Disneyland Paris, then for a week in Provence,' said Pamela. 'Can't say I'm a theme park fan, but it's only for two days. What about you, Charlotte?'

Charlotte shrugged. 'No plans at the moment. I've been checking out a few last-minute deals for Spain and Portugal, but pinning Dom down on dates is a nightmare.'

Their plates piled high with sausages, home-made coleslaw and cheese-stuffed mushrooms, the women took up residence on the comfy outdoor sofas in the corner of the terrace. Rick was entertaining the children with an impromptu badminton competition, faking spectacular falls to their delight.

Pamela put down her Pimms and dropped her voice a notch. 'A little bird told me that Alicia's having problems.'

'What kind of problems?' Sadie demanded. 'Is there an international shortage of civet-poo coffee? Is she having to slum it with supermarket own-brand?'

Charlotte snorted at Sadie's response, although a bit of her felt sorry for Alicia. She didn't appear to be friendly with many people at the school. Mind you, her imperious attitude probably didn't help.

'Rumour has it that her marriage is in trouble,' Pamela continued. 'A friend of a friend saw her with Derek in that swanky Michelin-starred restaurant up in Verbier. Apparently they were going at it hammer and tongs; so much so that a waiter asked them to quieten down or leave.'

'Lots of couples have arguments,' said Charlotte. Not that she could recall the last time she'd really argued with Dom. It was hard to argue with someone you barely saw. But having a full-blown war of words in a public place wasn't something she could imagine doing.

'That's not all.' Pamela glanced around, as if expecting Alicia to pirouette into view and clobber her with a Louboutin. 'I *also* heard that Derek's been spotted out and about … with a man!' She sat back with a satisfied sigh.

'And that proves what, exactly?' Sadie bit into a sausage and scooped up a mouthful of coleslaw. 'He's a successful businessman who must do a lot of wining and dining with other high-flyers.'

'Ha, but is it normal to hold hands with them?' Pamela's eyes glittered, her delight at delivering a killer punchline etched on her face.

Before either Charlotte or Sadie could react, Alastair and Robson bounded over. 'Mummy, Rick says we can go for a walk with him to see some donkeys. Can we, please?'

'There are two decrepit old dears in a field about five

minutes away,' said Sadie. 'They're a bit moth-eaten, but friendly enough if you tempt them with some apple slices.'

Charlotte checked her watch; still plenty of time before she needed to get the boys to bed.

'OK. Have you had pudding yet?'

The boys nodded as Rick approached with his girls in tow and a bag of chopped apples. 'Right, guys. All good with your mum? Excellent. We won't be long, Charlotte. Rebecca and Elspeth declined the offer to see Hee and Haw. I think they've taken refuge in the TV den.'

With Rick and the donkey posse on their way out, Pamela returned to her original topic. 'I always thought he was a bit, you know, effeminate. The way he walks, and I'm sure he checked out Martin's bottom once when we were at a school social.'

Charlotte had heard enough. Getting to her feet, she mumbled something about needing to burn off some calories. 'Wait for me!' she called to Rick, leaving Pamela and Sadie to carry on chatting — or bitching. If Alicia's marriage *was* in crisis, Charlotte didn't want to be part of analysing its demise.

CHAPTER 28

'WHAT DO YOU THINK OF THIS?' SADIE DID A TWIRL IN THE lightweight chambray dress she'd picked up from the bargain rail of the quirky French boutique. It was day two of summer camp, and she, Charlotte and Pamela had driven together to the small market town of Divonne-Les-Bains.

'Pretty,' replied Charlotte, flipping through a pile of pastel-coloured vest tops reduced to half price. 'Have you seen anything nice, Pamela?'

Pamela shook her head. She'd been in a funny mood during the journey, giving tetchy answers to questions and gazing at her phone as if waiting for an urgent call. 'My wardrobe's packed already, and half of it doesn't fit me any more.' She pinched her waist and pulled a face.

'You should join my Zumba class,' said Sadie, who was an enviable size eight at the most. 'I spent the first few sessions tripping over my own feet, but it's great fun and burns loads of calories.'

'Ha,' snorted Pamela. 'You're talking to the most uncoordinated woman on the planet. We bought the girls an old

Nintendo Wii system on eBay, because Martin thought it would be fun to challenge each other at stuff. They get all the shiny gold stars, and I get sweet Fanny Adams. I swear the bloody virtual yoga instructor smirked when I fell off the balance board doing a one-legged pose.'

Purchases made, the trio headed for a bistro highly rated on Trip Advisor, both for the quality of the food and the prices. 'I absolutely adore escargots,' drooled Sadie, as they perused the menu. It was good value, with two courses for fifteen Euros and three for nineteen.

'Yuck and double yuck,' retorted Pamela. 'How anyone can enjoy those nasty, slimy things is beyond me. When you see them slithering around, leaving those silvery trails, it's revolting.'

In response, Sadie stuck out her tongue.

Charlotte thought Pamela's remark was bordering on rude — not that she was a fan of snails herself. 'I'll have the mixed salad to start, followed by the ravioli tricolore,' she said. Pamela opted for the same, with Sadie choosing six escargots in garlic butter as a starter, with veal Milanese for her entrée.

An hour later, they piled back into Sadie's people carrier. Their children were all competing in a five-a-side football tournament at the camp and had insisted that mums (and dads) attend to cheer them on.

'I hope it doesn't go on forever,' moaned Pamela. 'Elspeth can't kick a ball to save her life, and Rebecca would be rubbish in goal. Why couldn't they run something else for the girls, like rounders?'

'Because the school believes in equality, both in the class-room and on the sports field,' replied Sadie, beeping her horn at a driver hogging the middle lane of the motorway. 'Any-way, I doubt it'll be more than an hour, and then we can get the wee blighters home.'

Dozens of parents sat around the pitch, some on picnic blankets spread out on the grass. A few had even brought picnics. Sadie unearthed an ancient tartan rug from the boot of her car and they spread it out in a quieter corner. Charlotte scanned the field, spotting Alastair and Robson huddled with their teammates. She waved furiously, but they were deep in conversation.

'Looks like Marcus is refereeing,' said Charlotte, indicating Jürgen's son with a whistle in his hand in the middle of the pitch. Two teams were playing, one from La Montagne and the other from another local private school. The La Montagne team wore their respective house colour T-shirts, with the opposition teams distinctive in their navy-blue and white striped tops.

'Can you see your girls?' asked Charlotte, nudging Sadie, who was passing around a tin of extra-strong mints.

'Probably hiding in the bathroom, knowing those two,' she replied. 'No, miracle of miracles, there they are!' Sure enough, Miranda and Louise appeared from behind a cluster of parents screaming encouragement at the players.

'Looks like that match is over,' said Pamela, as Marcus blew the final whistle. They didn't know the score, but judging by the whoops and cheers from some familiar faces, the home team had won.

'Alastair's up next,' said Sadie. 'It's a shame none of our darling husbands could make it, but Rick was adamant he couldn't escape some uber-important meeting. What about Martin, Pamela? What's his excuse?'

Pamela mumbled something about him being busy too. Charlotte quickly checked her phone, just in case she'd missed a message from Dom. Nothing. She'd texted him about the football tournament, expecting at least a word or two of encouragement for the boys. Sighing, she put her phone away and got to her feet as the match started.

'How are you ladies?'

Charlotte started at the familiar deep voice of Jürgen behind her. Turning, she shielded her eyes from the strong sun and smiled.

'All good. It's nice to see Marcus doing his bit. Is he an avid footie fan?'

'A devoted supporter of Man United,' he replied. 'I do not understand why, and I'm more of a rugby person myself. Not that Germany is renowned for rugby playing.'

Sadie patted the edge of the rug, signalling that Jürgen should sit down. Charlotte hesitated then budged up to make more room, but Pamela remained fixed in place, her back ramrod straight and eyes flashing daggers in Jürgen's direction.

'Thank you,' he said. 'I will stand, as my back is a little tender today. An old sports injury. I fear I may never get up again if I sit down!'

Charlotte watched as he made his way to the far side of the field. Sure enough, he seemed to walk awkwardly, in a way unlike his normal purposeful stride.

'Right, the match has started. Come on, lads and lasses!' Sadie stuck her fingers in her mouth and emitted a high-pitched whistle. Pamela winced and rubbed her ears.

'Alastair's pretty nifty with a ball,' said Sadie admiringly. Charlotte nodded, pride swelling inside her as her eldest dodged and weaved his way around the opposing team. He might lack the courage and confidence of his younger brother, but he always gave one hundred per cent.

At that moment, Charlotte's phone buzzed. She glanced at it: a text from Ruth. But before she could open it, Sadie let out a shriek and got to her feet. 'Oh, heck. Alastair's on the ground!'

Charlotte leapt up too, her heart thumping at the sight of

her son sprawled on the grass. Within seconds, a cluster of bodies blocked her view. She raced towards the scene, Sadie following in her wake.

'Let me through, please.' Charlotte pushed past Alastair's teammates and knelt down by his side. His face was ashen, and his left arm hung loosely by his side. The head of sports, Miss Liddy, crouched next to him, speaking quietly and urging the others to give him space.

'He took a bad tackle, Mrs Egerton,' she said. 'His legs got tangled, and he landed badly. I'm not a doctor, but I think his arm might be broken.'

Another staff member appeared with a makeshift sling. They gently manoeuvred Alastair upright and positioned it to support his arm.

'Does it hurt, sweetheart?' Charlotte stroked his other arm, her tears welling up and threatening to spill over.

Alastair shook his head, although he was trembling like a leaf.

'He's in shock,' said Miss Liddy. 'You need to get him to hospital for an X-ray.'

Charlotte looked up at Sadie. 'I'm not sure where it is.' She had a vague idea, but the thought of driving filled her with horror. A tight bubble of nausea rose in her throat, and she wobbled her way upright.

'I'll take you,' said Jürgen. Charlotte hadn't realised he was even there. 'It's only ten minutes away, and I can help with getting Alastair admitted and the formalities.'

'I'll take Robson home with us,' said Sadie. 'From experience, you could be waiting for hours.'

Jürgen and Miss Liddy helped Alastair to stand up. He pulled his T-shirt up and sucked on the collar, his face still grey-green.

'But what about Marcus? Don't you have to take him

home at the end of the tournament?' Charlotte felt useless, frustrated at her own timidity and annoyed that Dom wasn't around to help.

'He can cycle home,' Jürgen reassured her. 'It's not far and his bicycle is here.'

'It's no problem, Mrs Egerton.' With the match halted, Marcus had joined the group and now stood next to Alastair. 'I hope you're not planning on taking up any other dangerous sports,' he said to him, with a wink. 'Perhaps leave scuba diving for another day, eh?'

Alastair gave a wan smile, no doubt recalling the skiing episode.

Robson tugged at Charlotte's skirt, his face filled with concern. 'Mummy, is Alastair going to be OK?'

'He'll be fine, darling,' she replied. 'You carry on here, and Sadie will take you back to their house.'

'I'll drive him home when you give me the word,' said Sadie. 'Now off with you, and good luck.' She hugged Charlotte, and whispered, 'No hanky-panky with the hunky German while you're counting the hours in casualty.'

Charlotte blushed. Hoping Jürgen hadn't noticed, she followed him to his car. It suddenly dawned on her that it wasn't the swanky sports beast, but a more modest Audi. Clocking her expression, Jürgen grinned. 'Yes, I would have had a problem fitting both you and Alastair into my expensive toy.'

They got Alastair into the back seat as gently as possible. He hadn't said a word and continued to fiddle with his T-shirt. Once he was settled, Charlotte got into the passenger seat and buckled up.

'The Ferrari is in the garage for a small repair,' Jürgen explained as he started the engine. 'I had a minor disagreement with a wall the other day when I was reversing.'

Charlotte couldn't stop herself from giggling. 'I guess we both have a thing about walls,' she said, 'although you can't blame *me* for your mishap this time!'

CHAPTER 29

During the brief journey, Charlotte tried repeatedly to call Dom. Each time, his phone went to voicemail. She left a terse message, urging him to call back as soon as possible. Biting back her anger, she focused on keeping calm and chatting to Alastair. His colour had returned to near-normal, but he gave the occasional gasp as the pain kicked in.

'Here we are.' Jürgen pulled up at the entrance to the 'Urgence' department of the hospital. 'Let's get Alastair inside, then I'll park and help you get him checked in.'

Guiding Alastair to a plastic chair in the small lobby, Charlotte found her purse and dug out Alastair's private medical insurance card. She racked her brains for the words in French to describe what had happened, but got no further than il a tombé (he fell) and cassé (broken). Or was it caché? She always got those two muddled up.

Luckily, when Jürgen arrived, he spoke perfect French and the whole signing-in process took five minutes. A nurse directed them to the X-ray department and told them to wait. Shortly afterwards, another nurse came and administered a mild painkiller which Alastair swallowed gratefully.

'Will I be able to go back to summer camp, Mummy?' he asked, when Jürgen wandered off to get coffees from the vending machine.

'Sweetheart, I don't know,' Charlotte replied. Deep down she doubted it, and certainly not on the sports field. 'Let's just wait and see what the doctor tells us.'

Several more attempts to reach Dom failed. Sadie texted that they were safely home, Robson's team had won their match, and the children were glued to the TV. Charlotte scrolled through her phone looking for numbers for Dom's parents, but she couldn't find any. Then she remembered that she'd had a problem with her phone when they first arrived in Switzerland and lost all her contact details. And keying in Torquil and Jean's numbers hadn't been at the forefront of her mind.

'Here you go.' Jürgen passed Charlotte the plastic cup of coffee. 'I think I pressed the button for one with sugar by mistake. I'm sorry.'

'It's fine, honestly,' she replied, taking a tentative sip. 'Look, you don't have to hang around here. I can always get a taxi home when we're finished.' As she spoke, Charlotte realised she didn't want Jürgen to leave. His presence was comforting, but she felt guilty about him staying.

'I'm going nowhere,' he said firmly, fixing Charlotte with that direct gaze she'd become familiar with. 'My plans for a wild evening of watching TV with Marcus and whipping up an omelette can wait.'

Half an hour later, Alastair went off to have his arm X-rayed. Jürgen had popped outside to vape, and Charlotte paced up and down nervously.

It seemed an eternity until a doctor appeared, holding the X-rays and a lollipop for Alastair. He took it shyly and popped it in his mouth.

'You speak English?' the doctor asked. He looked in his

mid-forties, with thinning dark hair and a kindly face. Charlotte nodded gratefully.

'So, young man,' he continued, addressing Alastair, 'you have a rather nasty break here,' — he pointed to just above Alastair's elbow — 'which is a little more difficult to immobilise.'

Alastair gave Charlotte a puzzled look.

'It means it's harder to keep it still so that it heals,' she said, looking at the doctor for confirmation.

'Indeed,' he confirmed. 'We will first try to strap you up like an Egyptian mummy and see how that goes.'

Alastair's face crumpled when the doctor said there would be no sports of any kind for at least six weeks. 'Are you left-handed?' the doctor asked.

Alastair shook his head.

'In that case, you can use your right for writing or drawing, although playing computer games might be a little challenging!'

Jürgen reappeared as a junior nurse led Alastair off to be trussed up, and Charlotte filled him in on the diagnosis.

'Ah, that is not so good,' he said, his eyes filled with sympathy. 'But time will pass quickly, and he will soon be as right as rain. An English expression I always find strange, because what is right with rain?'

Charlotte smiled. 'Well, after three weeks of solid sunshine, we could do with some. No wonder poor Alastair broke his arm. The school pitch is rock hard!'

They waited together in companionable silence. A few staff members drifted by, and a young woman hobbled into another room, pain etched on her face. At least the doctor had assured Charlotte that swimming would be helpful as physiotherapy once the bone had healed.

'Did you reach your husband?' Jürgen touched Charlotte lightly on her hand, which she realised was holding her skirt in a death grip. She released the fabric and smoothed it down.

'No, it's going to voicemail. He must be somewhere with no signal.' *Or, a disturbing little voice whispered in her ear, he isn't where he said he would be.* She willed the voice to shut up, feeling the calm instilled by Jürgen's presence give way to a churning wave of anxiety.

An hour later, they left the hospital. Alastair was under strict instructions to keep the half-body cast dry, which meant shallow baths and damp flannels to wash around his upper half. 'Won't I get smelly, Mummy?' he asked, as they made their way home. 'If I can't wash under my arms, I mean.'

Jürgen signalled to turn into their road. 'Perhaps you can spray yourself with your dad's cologne. Or your family can all wear masks!'

Alastair giggled. 'That would be funny. Do we have masks, Mummy?'

Pulling up in the driveway, Jürgen insisted on escorting them into the house. He offered to make coffee for Charlotte, but she declined. Leaving Alastair installed in the lounge with Cartoon Network, she texted Sadie to say they'd returned. Once her friend had assured her they'd be on their way soon, she joined Jürgen in the kitchen.

'I'm so grateful, Jürgen. I'm not sure I'd have managed without you being there.' That wasn't *entirely* true; the process had been easy, even if she might have muddled up a few words. But having him there had been as comforting as a warm blanket on a chilly winter's evening.

'It was my pleasure. That's what friends are for.' And with that, he kissed Charlotte lightly on the cheek, called out a goodbye to Alastair, and left.

Charlotte was busy dolloping passata and mozzarella on a pizza base when the doorbell rang.

'How's the walking wounded?' asked Sadie, ushering in Robson, who immediately called out to his brother.

'He's OK,' said Charlotte. 'Come and see.'

Robson went into the lounge first and immediately exclaimed, 'That's so cool!' in response to Alastair's unorthodox attire.

Sadie followed Charlotte in. 'Oh, you poor lamb!' she announced, delving into her capacious handbag. 'I'm guessing no more footie for a while' — Alastair's face fell — 'but I happen to know you're an ace artist, so these are for you.' She produced a giant tin of Caran D'Ache colouring pencils and passed them over.

'Thank you,' said Alastair shyly, stroking the embossed lid with his good hand.

In the kitchen, Charlotte fixed iced coffees for Sadie and herself. Robson carefully measured out orange cordial in two glasses and topped it up with water, then took the drinks into the lounge.

'Is Dom dashing back to be with you?' asked Sadie, scooping ice into her drink.

Charlotte shrugged. She'd never confided her concerns about Dom and Amelie to her friend. Much as she liked Sadie, she'd only known her a few months, and with the whole Pamela/Jürgen situation she hadn't wanted to suggest anything was amiss with her own marriage.

'I haven't been able to get hold of him,' she said. 'I've left messages, but no call back so far.'

'What about ringing his folks? Didn't you say he was spending time with them? Sorry, dumb question. They'd be the next people you'd try, wouldn't they?'

Before she could explain about not having their numbers, Charlotte slapped her forehead. *Duh!* She might not have their mobile numbers, but she maintained an old-school phone book in which she kept contact details for friends and family. Dom had called her a dinosaur, but she found it satisfying to score out old addresses and note who did (or didn't) send Christmas cards. Torquil and Jean's landline number was definitely in there.

After Sadie left, Charlotte went in search of the phone book. She hadn't used it since Christmas and feared it might be languishing in one of the many boxes cluttering up the garage. Before embarking on the daunting task of looking there, she pulled out the drawer of the bureau in the hallway. Voilà! Charlotte wrestled the dog-eared book from under a pile of leaflets and catalogues.

Checking that the boys were OK first, she took the book into the kitchen and flicked to the letter E. Grabbing her phone, she keyed in Dom's parents' number, and waited.

CHAPTER 30

'HELLO? WHO'S CALLING?'

'Hello! Is that Jean?'

Of course it was. Charlotte would recognise that hoity-toity voice anywhere. She swore that Dom's mum had studied old recordings of the Queen's speech to perfect her received pronunciation. The woman came from Hull!

'Yes, who is this?'

Charlotte bit back a sarcastic response. Perhaps Jean's ailment had affected her hearing, and it wasn't as if they had cosy chats regularly. 'It's Charlotte,' she replied. 'How are you?'

There was a brief silence, broken only by the sound of a dog barking in the background. Clementine the corgi, no doubt. A squat little creature with a penchant for leaping into the laps of those who least welcomed it.

'Oh, hello, my dear. How lovely to hear from you.' If sincerity could be measured on a scale of one to ten, Jean's reply barely scraped a three. 'Is everything all right?'

'Yes. Well, no, actually.' Charlotte stammered over the

words. 'There's been an accident, nothing serious, but I just wanted—'

'Oh my goodness. Is it Dominic? Tell me what's happened!'

Jean called out to Torquil, and Charlotte overheard a muted response — muted both in the sense of him being far from the phone, and the whooshing sensation of blood rushing to Charlotte's ears. Why would Jean think it was to do with Dom? Unless…

'No, it's Alastair. He's broken his arm quite badly playing football, but he's OK. I don't understand why you thought it might be Dom. He's with you, isn't he?'

Charlotte shifted the phone to her other ear, aware of gripping it so tightly her fingers throbbed. She listened to a mumbled conversation between Dom's parents, picking up only the odd word. 'Alastair … accident … confused.'

'Are you there?' Charlotte realised her voice was shrill, verging on hysterical. She looked up to see Robson standing in the doorway, a questioning look on his face. Pointing at the biscuit barrel, she shooed him away with a handful of Bourbon creams.

'Yes, I'm here. And no, Dominic isn't. Was he supposed to be?' Jean's tone was wary, as if Charlotte had caught her cheating at her weekly mah-jong get-together with the twin-set-and-pearls group she called her friends. Except Jean wasn't the one being accused of cheating. If Dom wasn't with his parents, where exactly was he?

'Sorry, I thought… I mean, he said you'd been poorly, and that he was going to spend some time with you. I must have got it wrong. Sorry again.' Why the hell was she apologising? It was Dom who was in the wrong, not Charlotte. Or, for that matter, his parents.

Jean gave an irritatingly tinkly laugh which set Charlotte's teeth on edge. 'I'm perfectly well, dear. We haven't spoken to our boy since — Torquil, when did Dominic last call us?' There was another pause, then: 'Around two weeks ago, I believe. He's always so busy with work, but at least he calls regularly, unlike others I know of. Martha Hedgecock is lucky if she hears from her son twice a year. Quite shocking!'

Charlotte hadn't the faintest idea who Martha Hedgecock was and had zero interest in the frequency of her exchanges with her offspring. 'Well, I must have got things muddled up.' She bit her lip, determined not to give away the maelstrom of emotions surging through her body. In particular, her desire to rip Dom's head off and stuff it in the recycling bin.

'Indeed. It is rather strange, but I'm sure there's a simple explanation. Looking after two young boys in a foreign country must take its toll. Are you keeping well yourself?'

Great. Now Jean was hinting that Charlotte might have lost the plot, instead of concluding that her golden boy might be lying. 'I'm absolutely fine,' she snapped, knowing full well that she was a million miles from 'fine'. Devastated, nauseous and convinced her husband was a lying, cheating snake would be more accurate. Not that she could voice any of that to Mummy dearest.

'That's good. Well, Torquil has whipped up a delicious scallops and black pudding with beurre blanc for supper, so I'd best be off. Oh, and give darling Alastair a hug from us. And Robson, too. Bye for now!'

With that, Jean ended the call. Charlotte stared at the phone and resisted the urge to smash it repeatedly on the tiled worktop. Instead, she resumed making the pizza, shredding basil with ferocious intensity.

'Mummy, my armpit's really itchy,' wailed Alastair from the lounge.

Charlotte bunged the pizza in the oven, set the timer, and went to see the boys. 'Oh, you poor thing. It's because it's so hot, I guess,' she said, brushing a sticky strand of hair from his brow. The temperature had been in the high twenties for several days, and air conditioning wasn't a feature of the house.

'I'll get the fan, Mummy,' said Robson, leaping from the sofa and heading for the far corner of the room. He plugged it in and directed its cooling air towards his brother.

'Thanks, sweetie.' Charlotte patted him on the head and kissed the tip of his nose. Robson squeezed her around the waist and wandered off.

'I can't scratch it.' Alastair attempted to reach his armpit, but only a tiny gap remained between his underarm and the constrictive binding.

'I've an idea.' Charlotte dashed upstairs to Alastair's room and found his pencil case. She retrieved a plastic ruler and hurried back. 'Try this.'

Frowning, Alastair took the ruler and carefully poked it through the gap. He wiggled it up and down a few times before giving a sigh of relief. 'That's better. Oh, the oven's beeping, Mummy.'

With the boys duly fed, and ice cream and Gruyères meringues for dessert, Charlotte ushered them upstairs for a bath — or in Alastair's case, a hose down of his lower half with the shower spray and a perfunctory wipe-down of the visible bits of his top half. She read them a quick story, snuggled up together on Robson's bed, before tucking them both in and praying Alastair would get some sleep.

Back in the kitchen, Charlotte toyed with a cold slice of pizza. Her appetite was non-existent, shrivelled up like the three-day-old bag of salad she'd found lurking in the fridge. She poured herself a glass of white and set to cleaning out other past-their-best items as a distraction. An hour later she'd scrubbed the fridge interior, given the oven a once-over and mopped the floor.

What next? Charlotte glared at her phone. Nothing from

Dom. She could ring Ruth, but didn't want to burden her with this latest, kick-in-the-teeth instalment of her wavering marriage. Equally, she couldn't confide in her parents — not until she was sure of what was going on — and telling either Sadie or Pamela was a no-no. The only person she felt she could really talk to was Jürgen. He'd been in the same boat with his second marriage — Charlotte dragged her fingers angrily through her hair. Why was life so bloody complicated?

Checking on the boys, both thankfully fast asleep, she gathered together their bits and pieces for camp the next day. She'd already emailed Miss Liddy to let her know about Alastair, and she'd assured Charlotte that there would be plenty of activities he could take part in for the remaining days. Just not physical ones.

Charlotte turned on the TV and watched a few minutes of BBC News before hunting for some light relief. She flicked through the channels, settling on the live-action version of *Beauty and the Beast.* Belle was trilling away about a better, more exciting life when Charlotte's phone rang. She grabbed it. *Dom.* Deep breaths, in and out. It was showtime.

CHAPTER 31

'HOW'S IT ALL GOING?' DOM SOUNDED REVOLTINGLY UPBEAT for a man knee-deep in a swamp of secrets and lies. Not that he knew — yet — that she'd rumbled him.

'You took your bloody time replying to all my calls and messages,' retorted Charlotte. 'Even when I said something had happened to Alastair, you still didn't get in touch.'

Dom cleared his throat in that way he did when he'd been wrong-footed and was racking his brains for a suitable excuse. 'Sorry, sweetheart, I had some problems with my phone. I put it on to charge and it kept showing no battery. I think the cable must be faulty, so I borrowed Dad's.'

The sheer gall of the man! Charlotte pictured his nose extending Pinocchio-style as he blithely carried on the ridiculous charade.

'Anyway,' Dom continued, 'how's he doing? You didn't say much, just that he'd taken a tumble at football. It's not serious, is it?'

Tempted as she was to exaggerate Alastair's condition to amplify Dom's guilt, Charlotte couldn't. Not that guilt appeared to be an emotion her darling husband was familiar with. 'He's got a nasty break above the elbow of his left arm, and he's trussed up like an oven-ready chicken,' she said. 'I spent ages at the hospital with him, and he can't take part in any sports for at least six weeks.'

It had been on the tip of Charlotte's tongue to mention Jürgen's presence, but she decided against it. She doubted Dom would give a toss, seeing as he was up to something which she more than suspected involved a certain business colleague. And she'd bet her last Swiss franc it had nothing to do with Design For Life financial forecasts.

'That's too bad,' said Dom. 'Give him a cuddle from me, a gentle one, and tell him I'll be back soon. These things happen, although I've never broken a bone in my life, touch wood.'

Don't speak too soon, thought Charlotte, eyeing the unwashed pizza stone and picturing herself smashing Dom repeatedly in the face with it. She blinked away the brutal image. Charlotte wasn't a violent person, even if her mind was scrolling through myriad ways to make Dom suffer.

'And how are your parents?' she asked. 'You haven't said much about them.'

'Not bad, not bad,' replied Dom. 'Actually, Charlotte, Mum's waiting for me to help pack up a stack of old books to take to the charity shop tomorrow. She's feeling much better, thankfully, but now she's on a declutter mission, so I'd best be off. Love to you and the boys!'

And like mother, like son, Dom cut off the call, leaving Charlotte gasping like an escaped goldfish. She grabbed her wine glass and filled it, knocking half back in one gulp. How could he keep up the pretence so convincingly? All that bollocks about helping his mum! If she didn't know better, Charlotte would have swallowed the story, maybe even felt pleased that Dom was doing something useful.

Now she had two choices. She could call him back and

tell him she knew the truth — except she didn't, did she? — or she could wait till he got home. Charlotte pictured each scenario, weighing up her options as carefully as the flour and yeast she'd measured out for the pizza base. Knowing Dom (although Charlotte now thought of him as a shadowy stranger capable of dismantling their lives with calculating ease), he'd wriggle out of a phone conversation. He probably wouldn't even *answer* the phone. That meant forty-eight hours of letting her rage and hurt reach boiling point before ripping Dom apart face to face.

Tiptoeing into the boys' rooms for a last check before she dragged herself to bed, Charlotte listened to Robson's snuffly snores and smiled at Alastair's awkward position. She straightened up their duvets and kissed each of them on their warm cheeks. Her family, the perfect unit of four, to all appearances blessed. Then Charlotte headed to the bathroom, scooping up damp towels and neatly aligning the shower gel, shampoo and other mess.

Sitting up in bed, staring blankly at the pages of a book, Charlotte flipped between wanting to cry her eyes out, and stuffing all Dom's clothes in bin bags and lobbing them out of the window. Turning off the light, she thumped the pillow with venom, imagining it was her errant husband's smug face.

Charlotte curled up in her favourite foetal position, allowing the cooling silk pillowcase — meant to ease morning crease marks — to soothe her anger. As sleep proved a forlorn wish, the fabric grew damp...

CHAPTER 32

'HELLO, MY LOVELY. WHAT'S OCCURRING?' RUTH'S CHEERY voice was a welcome balm to Charlotte's jangling nerves.

It was the day before Dom's return, and her mood swung between icy calm and psychotic rage. The boys were at camp, Alastair content to follow indoor pursuits including origami, although how he'd manage that with one hand remained a mystery.

'I'm OK.' Charlotte attempted a smile at Ruth, although the corners of her mouth seemed set on a permanent downward trajectory. She'd covered her eye-bags with a liberal coating of concealer and hoped that on camera she looked better than she felt.

'I'm detecting a distinct lack of enthusiasm. What's up? Are you worried about Alastair?' Ruth was positively glowing. Possibly because of her pregnancy, a subject they hadn't broached for some time.

'No, not really. He's coping pretty well but the stupid cast thing keeps sliding around, so I might have to take him back to the hospital to see what they can do.'

Dropping the boys off that morning, Charlotte had

bumped into Jürgen and Marcus. When she explained her concern, Jürgen had offered to take them at the end of the day. He'd even called the hospital, spoken to the consultant, and been assured they had other options.

'So why the long face?' Ruth raised a mug of something, took a sip, and crinkled up her nose. 'By the way, if anyone tells you green tea is good for you, they can take a hike. It's bloody revolting, but coffee just makes me want to hurl.'

'Speaking of hurling, how are you? Have you, erm, you know, decided?' Charlotte hated that she wasn't with her best friend to lend a sympathetic ear and give advice. Being hundreds of miles apart was rubbish and speaking via the internet a poor substitute.

'Hon, believe me, I'm thinking of little else. I know I can't stay in limbo, but I still can't picture me as a single mum. Or a mum, full stop. Creaking up to the school gates in my fifties, surrounded by youngsters convinced I'm the wee bugger's granny.'

Charlotte giggled. 'Don't be daft, Ruth, you're only forty-two. Loads of women have babies later in life these days. Didn't that blonde actress who was married to Sylvester Stallone have a baby well into her fifties?'

'Brigitte Nielsen? Huh, that's fine if you've an army of nannies and staff to organise your life. I know how to run a business, but changing nappies, pureeing bananas and breast feeding is way out of my comfort zone.'

'It doesn't come easy to most mums. Trust me, I know from experience, particularly with Robson. He went from a placid little pumpkin to the squalling son of Satan within a week. Honestly, my eye-bags were down to my knees, and don't get me started on the state of my nipples.'

Charlotte shuddered at the memory. On the advice of her no-nonsense health visitor, she had thrown in the breast-feeding towel after six weeks. Dom struggled to watch her express milk with a pump, and Charlotte decided there was no shame in switching to formula. At least that way she could occasionally pass the buck — or the bottle — to her husband.

'You're really not selling this motherhood gig, are you?' Ruth gave a wry smile. 'Look, I know the clock's ticking — and I don't mean my biological one — but this is probably the toughest decision of my life.'

Charlotte nodded. Right then she wished she could reach through the screen and give her friend an industrial-strength hug.

'So, best friend wearing a palpable look of pain, are you going to fess up? Is it constipation, PMT, or something to do with darling Dom?'

Charlotte wriggled in her chair. She didn't want to burden Ruth with her fears, but the weight of Dom's likely treachery lay heavily on her shoulders. Taking a deep breath, she filled Ruth in on his cock and bull story about visiting his folks, and her suspicion about what he'd really been up to.

'Bloody hell, what an absolute bastard! And lying to you on the phone takes some serious balls of steel — which I'm happy to remove and remodel into a pair of earrings. When's the cheating turd back?'

'Tomorrow. I'm not sure what time, since I've barely spoken to him and he didn't bother telling me when he left. I just feel sick, Ruth. I mean, I don't have any proof that he's been with the tart, but what other explanation can there be?'

'Hon, I honestly don't know, but you've got the upper hand. Keep calm and for God's sake don't tear him to shreds if the boys are around.'

Charlotte swallowed a fresh wave of tears. Alastair and Robson's world would fall apart if they discovered what their father had done. And would there be any way back for her and Dom? Would he want to stay married to her, or would the truth set him free to shack up with Amelie? 'I'll do my best,' she replied, 'but right now I'm vacillating between sitting down to discuss the situation in a grown-up way, and smashing him in the face with a Le Creuset pan.'

Checking the clock, Charlotte realised she needed to get going. Her plan was to pick up a few groceries en route to the school, then go to the hospital again with the boys and Jürgen.

'Call me in the next couple of days,' said Ruth, blowing elaborate kisses at the camera. 'Or sooner, if you need me to find an excellent lawyer. A divorce one, not the criminal kind. Unless I see a story on the news about a man being bludgeoned to death by a cast-iron frying pan.'

* * *

'Is that better?' Charlotte looked at Alastair, now free of the sagging body cast and sporting a neoprene arm support secured to his torso.

'Much,' he said. 'I can scratch under my arm now!' To demonstrate, he did a passable impression of a monkey giving its armpit a good old going-over.

'Excellent,' said Jürgen. 'Now, what do you say to stopping off for ice creams before I take you back to your car?' He raised a questioning eyebrow at Charlotte as both Alastair and Robson squealed with excitement.

'Only if it's no trouble. You've already done so much for us, and—' Charlotte's voiced trailed off. She didn't want to dwell upon why spending more time with Jürgen felt so appealing.

'It is no trouble. There is a nice place right by the lake which I know does the best salted caramel and mint chocolate chip flavours. Or if you prefer, they do delicious Belgian waffles too.'

Fifteen minutes later, the four of them sat in a row on a bench close to the Charlie Chaplin statue in Vevey. They'd each opted for double scoops of ice cream, with sprinkles on top for the boys.

'It's so lovely here.' Charlotte swirled her tongue around the mound of vanilla she'd chosen, along with salted caramel. She pointed at the statue. 'I know he used to live here, but not much more than that. I bought a pile of tourist guides before we moved, but they're still packed in a box somewhere.'

Jürgen wiped a splodge of ice cream from the front of Robson's T-shirt. Robson thanked him and licked a few dribbles coursing down the side of the cone.

'Yes, Vevey was his adopted home for many years. He died in 1977 and is buried next to his wife, Oona, in a small graveyard near here. There is quite a new museum dedicated to his life and work, which is well worth a visit.'

Charlotte mentally added it to her list of places to go — assuming that they stayed in Switzerland. What would happen if her marriage collapsed? Dom was the one with the work permit. Would she and the boys have to go back to England and attempt to rebuild their lives? The shiver that ran down her spine had nothing to do with the chill of the ice cream.

'Mummy, can we go to the playground for a little while?' Robson crunched the end of the cone, and gave Charlotte his best beseeching smile.

'Sweetheart, Alastair can't exactly go on the swings or the climbing frame, can he?'

'It's OK, Mummy,' Alastair said. 'I can just watch Robson being rubbish at everything.' He poked his little brother in the ribs, and Robson stuck out his tongue at him.

'Fine. You scoot along for a few minutes, then we'll catch up. But be careful; I don't need any more trips to the hospital.' Charlotte looked at Jürgen, who nodded, and the boys took off for the playground.

'Forgive me for saying, but you seem sad, Charlotte. Your eyes, they do not have their usual sparkle. Is there something wrong?'

Charlotte turned away, sliding her sunglasses off her head to cover her traitorous eyes. 'I … well… I've got something on my mind, but I don't want to dump it on you.'

'Dump it?' Jürgen rubbed his chin contemplatively. 'Sometimes English expressions are not clear to me. You are saying you don't wish to tell me what is troubling you?'

'Yes. Well, no. It's not that, it's just … rather personal. And you don't need to hear my woes, not when you've been so kind.'

Jürgen shuffled along the bench, filling the gap where the boys had sat. He took both Charlotte's hands, the warmth from his easing the sense of panic broiling within her chest. 'Remember how you listened to me going on about my marriages? You did not yawn once or run for the door. You are a good person, Charlotte, with a kind heart, and if I can be of any help, it would be my honour.'

Still holding her hands, Jürgen waited. Charlotte's pulse quickened, and she felt a flutter of something in her stomach. A flutter that was wholly inappropriate for a married — for now — woman.

'It's nothing.' She snatched her hands away, hoping Jürgen couldn't see deeper into her soul and work out the feelings he had induced. 'We'd better fetch the boys.' Charlotte picked up her bag and stood up. Jürgen followed suit, and they made their way to the playground.

CHAPTER 33

CHARLOTTE PACED THE HOUSE LIKE A CAGED TIGER. DOM HAD texted his estimated time of arrival — around 4pm — and she'd arranged for Sadie to pick up the boys on the last day of camp. Much to their delight, Sadie had offered a sleepover too, with Rick in charge of erecting a tent for the children to spend the night in the garden.

'Are you sure it's not too much trouble?' Charlotte felt guilty for relying yet again on her friend. Depending on how things went with Dom — as in, would she be throwing him out? — she needed to pay Sadie and Rick back for all the times they'd helped her.

'Charlotte, the boys are adorable and Rick's never happier than when he's hammering in tent pegs and pretending he's a Boy Scout. He'll probably spark up a campfire and have them singing Ging Gang Goolie.'

The hands on the kitchen clock seemed to move painfully slowly. Charlotte checked her phone and her watch. Just under half an hour to go, assuming Dom was on schedule. She willed herself to breathe normally, feeling her pulse quicken at the confrontation ahead. A thought bounced around her head, one that had plagued her sleep, and to be honest her mind, for several days. *If Dom was having an affair, why don't I feel more upset?* Yes, she was angry and hurt, but was she heartbroken? When she prodded her feelings, she realised that the hairline crack in their relationship had widened into a gulf she didn't know how to fix. Or even if she wanted to fix it.

The sound of a car pulling up dragged Charlotte back to the present. She'd offered to pick Dom up at the station, but he'd insisted on taking a taxi. Maybe that was because he'd taken the train from the airport with Amelie and didn't want Charlotte to see them together. Assuming he'd *flown* anywhere. For all Charlotte knew, Dom might have been snuggled up in a cosy little boudoir a few miles away, oblivious to the world as the two of them writhed around on a king-size bed.

'Hey, I'm back!' Dom stood at the kitchen door, his bag slung over his shoulder. 'Where are the boys?'

'Still at camp, and Sadie's taking them to hers for a sleep-over.' Charlotte sat down, her fingers tracing the shallow score in the table where Alastair had pressed too hard with a compass.

'Aww, that's a pity. I thought we could all go out for dinner tonight to celebrate my return.' Dom dumped the bag on the floor and opened the fridge. 'Fancy a cold one?' He waggled two bottles of beer at Charlotte, who shook her head. 'Well, I need one — more than one — after all that time with the folks. Jeez, I love them and all, but they're hard work. How's Alastair's arm, by the way? I hope you haven't been letting him overdo things.'

The suppressed fury bubbling in Charlotte's stomach made a bid for freedom. He'd barely asked about the boys and was still continuing this ridiculous charade. Enough was enough.

'You know, something strange happened the other day.' Charlotte tried to keep her voice steady, but the words wobbled from her lips.

'Oh, what's that then?' Dom flipped the cap off the bottle and took a swig, his countenance as angelic as a choirboy.

'Well, I wanted to speak to you about Alastair's accident, but you didn't reply to my calls or messages. So I called your parents.'

Dom's countenance changed from choirboy to defendant in an instant. He didn't speak, but sat down opposite Charlotte and peeled the label off the bottle.

'You weren't there, Dom. Your mother thought I was barking mad, and I even questioned my own sanity. But there's no reasonable explanation I can come up with. You lied. And you're still fucking lying.'

Dom flinched, either because she'd caught him out or because he hated Charlotte using the F-word. Well, she had several more swear words up her sleeve unless he started talking.

'I… It's a bit embarrassing, but it's not what you think.'

'And how do you *know* what I think? Oh, let me see, most wives would probably think, "Hmm, my husband claims he's staying with his parents, but it turns out he's not. So what could he be up to? Ah, shagging another woman, that's what!"'

'Sweetheart, I—'

Charlotte shoved back her chair, the legs scraping across the floor. 'I want the truth, Dom. Right now. Or I'm heading upstairs to empty your wardrobe into bin bags and toss them out of the fucking window.'

Dom crumpled up the label, his eyes failing to meet Charlotte's.

'OK, OK, I get why you're upset, but I can explain. I didn't want to tell you the truth, because I thought you'd think I'd flipped, or something. The thing is … I went to a retreat.'

Charlotte gawped at him in disbelief. *A retreat?* Had Dom suddenly found religion, or a need to seek inner peace? For a second an image flashed into her mind of him wearing robes and tinkling a small bell. No, ridiculous. Dom was more likely to take up paragliding than—

'I needed to get away, Charlotte. Work's been crazy, and, well, we haven't exactly been happy, have we? I don't think you understand how much pressure I've been under, and all the nagging doesn't help.'

Nagging? Charlotte didn't nag. In fact, she prided herself on being infinitely patient, even when left to run the household and look after their boys virtually single-handed.

'Bullshit. If anything, *I'm* the one who needs a sodding retreat. Yes, you work hard, but so do I. Parenting two young boys isn't easy, Dom, and even less so when one half doesn't pull his weight.'

Dom looked wounded. 'I do my best, sweetheart. I'm sorry you feel that way, which is another reason I didn't want to tell you where I was going.' He reached for his bag, rummaged in the front pocket, and pulled out a piece of paper. 'Here. This is where I've been.'

Charlotte took the paper, an invoice as far as she could see, and scanned the details. At the top, an image of the Alps with a silhouette of a man standing on one leg in a yoga pose. Below the picture, the words: *Find Your Inner Calm. Destress, Detox & Delight At Alpine Oasis.*

She glanced at Dom, who'd recovered his equilibrium. In fact he was grinning, his inner calm duly restored. Charlotte hadn't seen her inner calm for days, and she doubted she'd find it soon.

'A yoga retreat? Seriously?' If he'd confessed to a secret

spot of Formula 1 racing or hot-air ballooning, Charlotte might have swallowed it, but yoga?

Motioning for her to sit down again, Dom took her hands in his. For a moment she remembered Jürgen doing the same. Then, she'd felt comforted, even though part of her said it was wrong. Now... Charlotte stared at Dom's familiar hands with their fine dusting of silky hair and the right thumbnail he chewed when anxious. Dom stroked Charlotte's palm, a gesture she once found a turn-on. Now, it irritated her, and she folded her hands in her lap.

'I still don't get all the cloak and dagger stuff. Surely telling me the truth would have been better than letting me think what I did. Were you scared I'd laugh, or something?' Indeed, Charlotte might have done, picturing Dom doing a Sun Salutation or wrapping his legs around his ears.

'I told you. I was embarrassed, and yes, I thought you'd find it funny. Anyway, I'm sorry I lied, but I'm not sorry I went. I feel better than I have in ages. Now, I'm going to grab a shower, then we can get a bite to eat at our local hostellerie.'

Charlotte gaped in disbelief at Dom's ability to act as if what he'd done was a mere blip on the radar. Not only had he lied, but he'd failed to react at the news of Alastair's accident.

'Why didn't you come home? When I messaged you about Alastair? Or were you too busy seeking spiritual enlightenment to spare him a second thought?'

This time, Dom looked genuinely remorseful. 'Sweetheart, you're absolutely right. I just assumed you'd have it all under control, as you always do. Forgive me.'

Dom pecked Charlotte's cheek, and she tried not to duck out of the way. Left alone, she looked at the invoice again. It was billed to Dominic Egerton for a single room, full board, with all yoga, meditation sessions and therapies included.

She boggled at the price: 2'500 Swiss francs, tax not included. Still, he earned the money, and could spend it however he wanted.

Trudging upstairs to freshen up, Charlotte wished she felt as rejuvenated as Dom did. Instead, she felt flat, wrong-footed and far from convinced by his story.

CHAPTER 34

ONLY ANOTHER TWO THOUSAND STEPS TO GO, AND CHARLOTTE would have aced her ten-thousand target for the day. She adjusted her earbuds and fiddled with her phone, looking for some rousing music to spur her on. 'Bad Romance' by Lady Gaga. That should do the trick.

Swigging from her water bottle, she carried on past the campsite: a hotchpotch of caravans, awnings, and tents set up for those attending the upcoming Montreux Jazz Festival. Charlotte recalled Jürgen saying that some 250,000 people swarmed to the event each year, filling up hotels in and around the area. Others either preferred or had to pitch up under canvas, which was fine as long as the current dry spell continued.

She took the path towards the lake, greeting a couple walking a panting terrier, its fur dripping after a dip in the water. Sidestepping quickly, in case it gave her an impromptu shower, Charlotte stopped at the entrance of the buvette. A blackboard listed the specials of the day — filets de perches avec frites; salade de chevre chaud, and steak de cheval. She couldn't bring herself to eat horsemeat, despite its popularity in Switzerland. Silly, really, when she'd happily tuck into a juicy entrecote du boeuf or a rack d'agneau.

The lake was as still as glass, the mountains a majestic backdrop. Charlotte paused the music, taking a moment to absorb the beauty surrounding her. Beads of sweat prickled her forehead, and she unearthed a tissue from her shorts pocket to wipe them away.

Dom had miraculously taken the day off to spend time with the boys, who'd had a whale of a time camping at Sadie's. If this had been motivated by guilt, Charlotte didn't want to know. Her mind remained a maelstrom of misgivings, but she needed to clear her head. Exercising, something she'd let slip since the move, helped a little.

As she scrolled through her phone for another upbeat tune, she noticed a car some twenty metres away: a familiar racing-green Jaguar convertible, its roof up despite the 28 degree heat. Charlotte moved closer, peering at the number plate. Yes, it was definitely Alicia's. Charlotte had a strange and rather pointless ability to remember number plates, though she struggled some days to recall what she'd eaten the night before.

Alicia sat in the driver's seat, looking down. For a moment Charlotte thought she was hunting for something she'd dropped, then realised she was banging her head on the steering wheel. *What on earth...?*

Hesitantly, Charlotte tapped on the window. No response. She tried again, harder this time, and Alicia looked up. Even through the tinted glass, it was obvious she'd been crying. A lot.

'Alicia, are you all right?' Charlotte grabbed the door handle, and it opened.

Alicia turned away, muttering something Charlotte didn't quite hear. Possibly 'go away' or 'mind your own business'. But Charlotte couldn't bear to see someone in deep distress.

Not even if that someone was an imperious pain in the arse with a superiority complex.

'Right, I'm coming in.' Charlotte went round to the passenger side and slid into the sumptuous cream-upholstered seat. A quick glance revealed a car as pristine as the day it glided out of the showroom. No discarded crisp packets, juice cartons or wads of pay-and-display parking tickets here. The only signs of disarray were several scrunched-up tissues scattered around Alicia's lap.

'Alicia, you don't have to talk to me, but I can't leave you like this. Please let me help.' Charlotte hoped her sweaty T-shirt wouldn't stain the leather. She leant forward, aware that her bare legs were also sticking to the seat. 'Erm, would you like some water?' She offered her half-drunk bottle, expecting Alicia to turn her perfect and possibly surgically enhanced nose up at sipping from a shared vessel.

To her surprise, Alicia took it and swallowed a mouthful. 'Thank you,' she said. 'I'm just having a bit of a moment. Please forgive my appearance.'

Alicia flipped down the sun visor and tutted at her reflection. It wasn't pretty: her eyes were swollen, mascara snail-trailed down her cheeks and a red line marked where she'd whacked her forehead on the steering wheel.

'Alicia, you're upset. Don't apologise for how you look. When I ugly-cry, my husband locks me in the basement and slides cream crackers under the door.'

Alicia rubbed at the mascara smudges with her finger. 'Really? Oh, you're joking.' A smidgen of a smile appeared. Charlotte realised she'd rarely seen Alicia smile; her default facial setting was haughtiness.

'So, would you like to tell me what's the matter?' she said.

'It's Derek. My husband.' Alicia twiddled with the solitaire diamond necklace framing her smooth throat. 'He's left me.'

Charlotte recalled seeing Derek at school. He'd struck her

as an odd match for Alicia: on the short side and paunchy, with a bad comb-over and a liking for loud shirts and clashing trousers. Still, they said opposites attract, and perhaps he had a delightful personality. 'I'm sorry,' she said. 'Has he … did he find another woman?'

Alicia pulled a gold compact from the glove compartment and set about repairing her make-up. 'No, darling,' she replied, dusting her face with powder. 'Another man.'

'Oh.' Charlotte didn't know what else to say. Pamela had been right. She waited for Alicia to explain further.

'It really shouldn't have shocked me. I knew — suspected — he was gay when I married him. But I told myself that we could make a go of things, and we have done for the past fifteen years.'

'But if you thought he was gay, and if he *knew* he was gay, why did you get married in the first place?' It made little sense to Charlotte. Surely their relationship had been a ticking time bomb from the start?

'Mainly for the money. Yes, I know that sounds callous and calculating, but when you were brought up with nothing, the promise of a better and financially sound life is very attractive.'

Alicia explained that Derek had made a fortune as a music producer, working with some of the biggest names in the business. However, he kept a very low profile, refusing interviews and any other media exposure.

'I grew up on a rundown council estate, with little interest in anything but dancing,' she continued. 'I got a scholarship to ballet school, which was my first step away from my origins. The next was changing my name, and after that … I met Derek.'

'Were you happy?' Charlotte asked.

'For a time,' replied Alicia. 'We had Jennifer, incredible holidays, a lifestyle I'd fantasised about as a child. But over the past few years, the façade crumbled. He'd spend more and more time away, supposedly on business, but I knew he was seeing other people. Other men. When he came home, we had little to talk about, whereas before, he was the one person I could confide in. The words just shrivelled up, and we began to regard each other with something like loathing. All the good bits crumbled away, exposing two people unable to communicate.'

'Isn't it a relief, in a way? I mean, it must be so hard for you and for Jennifer, but surely living a lie for so long must have been a terrible strain.'

Charlotte hoped she hadn't overstepped the mark. The interior of the car was now unbearably hot, and she longed to get out. Noticing her discomfort, Alicia put down the convertible's roof. A blessed breeze washed over them.

'Yes, I suppose so. It's the humiliation of it all. Not that I plan on telling people the whole sordid story — and I trust you won't share this with anyone.' Alicia fixed Charlotte with a steely stare, and she nodded furiously. Of course she wouldn't.

Charlotte glanced at her Fitbit. 'Erm, I really need to go. But if you need to talk again I'll gladly listen, although I'm sure you have good friends to confide in.'

Alicia laughed, a harsh, near-humourless sound. 'Very few, to be honest. Anyway, I'll be fine. Thank you.'

Charlotte moved to open the door, then paused. 'For what it's worth, maybe you and Derek will find a way forward, if only for the sake of Jennifer. As friends, at least.'

Alicia fluttered her hand in a gesture of farewell. 'Perhaps, although it's hard to imagine it right now. To be honest, we've reached the point of the disinterested meeting the couldn't-give-a-shit.'

'HOW WAS THE VEGETARIAN AND ORGANIC DIET?' ASKED Charlotte, whisking pancake batter for the boys, who were still in bed.

Dom had given Charlotte a glossy brochure from the retreat, detailing the various treatments and types of yoga on offer. Ashtanga, Pranayama, and a few others Charlotte could barely pronounce.

Dom looked up from his plateful of sausage, bacon and eggs. 'What's that?' He forked in a mouthful, his attention fixed on *The Times* app on his iPad.

'The food. How was it? I can't imagine that going meat-free for days helped your inner calm.'

'It was OK. Amazing, actually, how full you feel on a diet packed with wholegrains and fruit and veg. Mind you, we sneaked out one night for a drink. Alcohol-free was a little trickier!'

Charlotte stared at Dom. 'You just said *we*. Who was the other person?' The cat was now officially out of the bag. Let him dig his way out of this one.

'Oh, just another guy there on his own. We kind of teamed up, both being novices at this kind of thing. He suggested a cheeky pint, and I agreed. Willpower of an amoeba!'

For every question Charlotte lobbed at him, Dom batted back a plausible answer. Since his return she'd grilled him on the daily routine at the retreat, the names and backgrounds of the other participants, and how long it had taken to drive there. The promised bottle of perfume hadn't materialised (no flight, no duty free), but Dom had presented her with an edelweiss-patterned incense burner and sticks that smelled of eucalyptus oil.

Breakfast devoured, Dom packed his office bag and headed to work. He shouted a goodbye upstairs to the boys, receiving a sleepy 'Bye, Daddy' in return.

An hour later, Alastair and Robson were up, dressed and fed. With the temperature still in the high twenties, they took themselves outside to draw in the shade. Alastair was coping remarkably well with his restricted arm, but Charlotte couldn't wait for it to heal. Sadie had suggested a trip with the children to one of the local municipal pools, but Charlotte had declined. It seemed cruel for Alastair to watch the others splashing around in the water while he sat on the sidelines.

Relishing the peace, Charlotte curled up with a book in the lounge. The electric fan provided a little relief from the heat, and she'd put on her bikini with a lightweight cotton kaftan over the top. She'd deal with the laundry and ironing later when it was cooler. As she flipped through the book, trying to find her place, her phone rang. Dammit, she'd left it charging in the kitchen. Shoving her feet into her faithful flip flops, Charlotte hurried through and picked it up.

'Charlotte?' A familiar voice made her stomach flip.

'Hi, Jürgen. How are you?' They'd never talked on the phone before, only in person. His voice, amplified by the device, seemed deeper and more melodic.

'I'm very good. And you, are you OK?'

Charlotte hesitated. She'd been on the brink of confiding in Jürgen, but had held back for reasons she still didn't want to analyse. And she wasn't about to reveal Dom's elaborate cover story about chewing kale and standing on his head.

'I'm fine. Kind of glad the summer camp's over, to be honest. It's nice having the boys around, and I can keep an eye on Alastair's arm.'

'He will be fully mended before you know it.' Jürgen's words comforted Charlotte. Dom had barely paid lip service to his son's injury, instead relating the litany of sports injuries he'd incurred — minus breaks — during his youth.

'Well, thank you again for all you did. I mean at the hospital, and everything.'

'Charlotte, you have thanked me more times than my humble help warrants. It was my pleasure. I am always here if you need anything.'

A shiver of pleasure — and another emotion she pushed down — coursed through Charlotte's body. *I am always here*. The movie *Toy Story* sprung to mind: a perennial favourite of the boys, who adored their talking Woody and Buzz Lightyear toys. Charlotte loved the theme song, 'You've Got A Friend In Me' and they'd belt it out in the car on long journeys.

'Are you still there?' Oops. Charlotte had lost the thread of the conversation.

'Yes. Sorry, what was that you said?'

'About the tickets for Elton John. I don't want to push you, but I wondered if you'd reconsider coming with me? Or I am happy to give them to you, to go with your husband.'

Charlotte knew there was no way she'd accept tickets that had cost several hundred francs. She also knew Dom would have no interest in going, whereas Charlotte—

'When is it again?' Out of curiosity, she'd checked the Montreux Jazz Festival website and learned Elton was playing two outdoor concerts, but she couldn't remember the dates.

'This coming Saturday. It will be very busy, so we would need to go early to secure a good standing point.'

Before she could change her mind, Charlotte said, 'I'd love to come. With you, I mean, but I must pay you for the ticket.'

'It would be my treat,' insisted Jürgen. 'I can pick you up, if you like.'

'No, really, there's no need. We can meet somewhere near the stadium and walk to the concert together.' Charlotte didn't want Jürgen rocking up at the door in his Ferrari, and Dom making sarcastic comments. Quite how she would explain her actions to Dom remained to be seen, but then again she was an adult who could do what she liked. If Dom could sneak away for a three-day yoga retreat, she could go to a local concert.

'That is wonderful. Remember to bring a hat and sun cream, as the forecast is hot.'

'Yes, Dad,' laughed Charlotte. 'Shall I bring a picnic too?'

Assuring Charlotte that there would be plenty of food and drink stalls, Jürgen confirmed their meeting place and time, then ended the call.

Charlotte slumped back on the sofa. What had she done? The occasional coffee was one thing, but going to a concert with another man? She toyed with calling Jürgen back immediately and making some lame excuse about forgetting another engagement—

'Dammit, grow a pair, woman!' she exclaimed. She slammed her book down on the side table and went outside to check on the boys.

CHAPTER 36

THE DAY BEFORE THE CONCERT, CHARLOTTE WAS A BAG OF nerves. Not because Dom had objected, though. No, he'd raised an eyebrow when she announced her plans, with the other one twitching in harmony at the mention of Jürgen.

'You really want to see that old codger? Elton, I mean, not your German pal.' He'd laughed at his feeble joke, following it up with a crack about it being a miracle that the singer was 'still standing'.

'Yes, I do. I think he's brilliant, and this is his farewell tour.' Charlotte had gasped at the schedule posted online. Over three hundred shows around the world, ending in 2021. She figured Elton would need a long lie down at the end of it all.

Dom's biggest gripe was having to look after Alastair and Robson. 'You might have checked with me first, Charlotte. A few of us from the office were planning a beer and bowling night out.'

Tough, Charlotte muttered under her breath. Leaving Dom fiddling with his laptop, she'd sought sanctuary in the bedroom. Ruth had texted asking if she was free for a chat, and a chinwag with her friend would ease the butterflies fluttering around in her chest. It wasn't a *date,* for goodness' sake! Just two people going to a concert along with thousands of others. No big deal.

'How's it going, hon? Has Dom persuaded you to realign your chakras?'

Charlotte laughed. She'd already filled Ruth in via email about her husband's furtive foray into the world of sun salutations and coconut oil pulling, which sounded gross. Ruth, of course, had asked if Charlotte believed him. She'd said yes, although her conviction wobbled more than one of the boys' baby teeth. 'I'm quite happy with my chakras, whatever the hell they are. More to the point, how are you?'

'Well...' Ruth stretched the word out like a piece of elastic. 'I have some news.'

'Out with it, then!' Charlotte mentally crossed her fingers and toes that Ruth had decided. The *right* decision for her friend, even if Charlotte didn't agree with it.

'I bumped into Will — the fitness guy — the other day when I was picking up some shopping. We chatted a bit, and he invited me for a coffee. Or revolting herbal tea, in my case.'

'OK. And did you drop "I'm pregnant and you might be the daddy" into the conversation?'

Ruth shook her head vigorously. 'Didn't need to. He gave me chapter and verse on how his business was booming, and then bang, he dropped an absolute bombshell.'

'Yes? Come on, Ruth, don't leave me hanging!' Charlotte swiped a tissue over the laptop screen, which bore a fine coating of pollen.

'Turns out an ex of his, one of many I'd imagine, has popped back on the scene. Caroline, I think her name is. Will said they'd had a good thing going before, but he couldn't see it leading anywhere. Chiefly because she's absolutely desperate to have kids … and he can't.'

Charlotte heard Dom call out that he was heading to work. Alastair and Robson were holed up in their bedrooms, so she shouted a quick goodbye. 'Sorry. Carry on. What do you mean, he can't?'

'He had a pretty serious illness in his late teens, and afterwards the doctors said he'd never be able to father children. He didn't go into massive detail, and I wasn't up for a lengthy chat about sperm counts, but he was adamant. And not terribly bothered, to be honest. Will's the kind of guy who likes to march to his own tune without the added complication of raising a kid.'

'Hmm, that sounds familiar.' Charlotte gave Ruth a wry smile which her friend acknowledged with a waggle of her middle finger.

'Remind me why we're friends, bitch? No, don't bother. I'll always love you, despite your evil side. Anyway, you can see where this is going, right?'

Charlotte could. If Will wasn't a contender, the only possibility was Simon, the dermatologist. The man Ruth had hinted that she was rather more fond of.

'So is it time you had a little chat with Simon? Put him in the picture, and at least give him a chance to express an opinion?'

Ruth gave a pained look. 'I don't know, hon. If I tell him, will he put pressure on me to keep the baby? Or not want to have anything to do with it? Or—'

'Ruth, what's your gut feeling? Be honest, it's me you're talking to. Do you want to have an abortion, or take a leap into the unknown and become a mum?'

Charlotte watched as Ruth's eyes filled with tears. She said nothing, waiting for her friend to compose herself.

'I want to keep it.'

Charlotte exhaled loudly. Her sense of relief was enormous, even though she realised Ruth had a long, tough road ahead. 'And you'll speak to Simon? Promise me you will.'

'I will. In fact, I'll call him soon and ask if we can meet up. Oh God, Charlotte, I'm bloody petrified. About what he'll say, and the fact I'm going to do this with or without him.'

A commotion in the hallway indicated that the boys had emerged, probably seeking sustenance.

'Ten minutes, guys!' Charlotte hollered. She listened to the pair of them clattering downstairs and turned back to the screen. 'Remember when you told me I'd be OK moving to Switzerland? You said, and I quote: "You can do this." And I've managed so far, marital lumps and bumps notwithstanding. Ruth, you can do this, and I'll have your back along the way. Hell, I'll even come over to hold your hand during the birth, and you can call me all the names under the sun.'

Ruth dabbed at her cheeks, the tears now flowing freely. 'I bloody love you, Charlotte. Not that I want you to witness my screams of agony and all the gory stuff, but … I bloody love you.'

Assuring her friend that the feeling was mutual, Charlotte signed off. She sat quietly for a moment, Ruth's tear-streaked face etched on her eyeballs. She'd wanted to talk about Jürgen, but it wasn't the right time. What was there to say, anyway? They were going to a concert together, Dom didn't mind (or care), and it was completely innocent.

THAT NIGHT CHARLOTTE sat up in bed, trying and failing to read her book. The words swam before her eyes, little black dots that jiggled around without rhyme or reason. Dom sat next to her, cursing at *The Times*'s killer Sudoku. The boys were zonked, having spent most of the day chasing each other around the garden with water pistols. Robson had the unfair advantage of two hands — one to load, one to shoot — and Charlotte had reluctantly got in on the action. Reluctantly, but she'd had great fun. Whatever else was wrong with her life, playing with Alastair and Robson reminded her of the good stuff. She'd eventually waved the white flag, hair and clothes sodden, and set about cooking dinner.

'Bugger, this one's got me beat.' Dom closed his iPad and tossed it aside. 'Feeling a bit knackered, darling. All right if I switch off the light?'

Charlotte tossed the barely read book aside. 'Sure. I'm a bit tired myself, actually.'

Dom leaned across and pecked her on the lips. 'You've got a big day tomorrow. You, your German pal, and old Reggie boy. Hope you've brushed up on all the lyrics!'

Charlotte rolled over to the far side of the bed. She squeezed her eyes shut, the words to 'Sad Songs (Say So Much)' playing on a loop in her head.

CHAPTER 37

THE SHEER VOLUME OF PEOPLE DRIFTING TOWARDS THE stadium blew Charlotte away. Used to the relative sleepiness of her little Swiss village, it felt as if Glastonbury-goers had descended, minus the wellies and mud.

She'd found a parking spot ten minutes' walk away from where she was meeting Jürgen. Weaving her way through the crowds — a mixture of young and old, some sporting Elton-style over-the-top glasses — Charlotte hoped she'd spot him easily. She hoisted her canvas holdall up on her shoulder; the bag laden with chilled bottled water, sun cream and wet wipes. Once a mum, always a mum. She'd almost added little packs of raisins and chopped-up fruit, but remembered that Jürgen had said there'd be plenty of food at the concert.

'Charlotte, over here!' Jürgen stood a few feet away, waving furiously. She muttered excuse-mes, dodging a couple wielding beer cans and a group of middle-aged people dressed more for a hike than a concert.

'Lovely to see you.' Jürgen kissed her on each cheek, and she reciprocated. His cologne smelled fresh and citrusy, and his faint stubble brushed her skin. 'You look very fetching, if I may say so.'

Charlotte blushed. She'd spent longer than she cared to think deciding on a suitable outfit. She'd opted for a teal-blue T-shirt dress, cinched at the waist with a chunky antique-effect belt Alastair had picked out for her on a pre-Switzerland shopping trip. For comfort in the heat, she'd piled her hair up in a loose knot and brought a foldable straw hat with an extravagant pink bow.

'You don't look too shabby yourself,' she replied. Jürgen wore cream chinos, and an artfully crumpled — or possibly un-ironed — white linen shirt which emphasised his tan. He carried nothing; presumably the tickets and other essentials were tucked in a pocket.

They followed the crowd towards one of the entrances to the stadium, Charlotte already feeling sweaty despite a liberal application of deodorant.

'All is OK at home?' Jürgen placed his hand gently on the small of Charlotte's back, guiding her through the ticket checkpoint. A security guard quickly scanned the contents of her bag before giving them a nod to proceed.

'Yes, all good. The boys persuaded Dom to take them to a new burrito place in Vevey, then I guess they'll watch some TV, or whatever.' Apart from one jibe about missing out on the beer and bowling night, Dom had said little, only that he hoped Charlotte enjoyed herself. She fully intended to.

The atmosphere in the stadium was electric. A buzz of anticipation zinged through Charlotte's body as the sound and lighting crews made their last checks. People flocked to the front of the stage, but Jürgen pointed to an area on the left. 'It is quieter here, and we still have a magnificent view. Plus there is a beer tent within easy reach!'

Having no desire to get caught in the crush, Charlotte followed Jürgen to a grassy area which was relatively clear of bodies. Checking what she wanted to drink, Jürgen queued for a few minutes, returning with two beers in plastic cups. 'Not the finest you will ever taste, but it is cold and wet. Prost!' He raised his cup, and Charlotte tapped hers against his.

The show kicked off with 'Bennie and the Jets', Elton on fine form and loving the enthusiastic reaction from the fifteen thousand spectators. Charlotte whooped and cheered as each song ended and a new one began. From time to time she glanced at Jürgen. His expression was focused, his attitude less exuberant, but when he looked at her his features softened. As did the knot of residual anxiety in Charlotte's stomach which, along with relentless Elton John earworms, had kept her awake most of the night.

Charlotte fetched two more beers around the halfway mark; as they were both driving, they needed to keep within the limit. Jürgen bought two hot dogs slathered in ketchup and portions of piping-hot French fries.

'Delicious,' she declared, taking a hearty bite of hot dog. 'I can't remember the last time I had one of these. Probably on holiday somewhere with Dom and the boys.'

'Marcus would eat hot dogs every day if he had the chance,' replied Jürgen. 'It is remarkable he stays so slim considering his liking for fast food.'

'Ah, but he's very sporty, isn't he? And I guess he takes after you in terms of physique.' Charlotte gulped down a mouthful of beer, wishing she could also swallow her comment. Jürgen grinned and patted his stomach. 'A loose shirt hides a multitude of sins, Charlotte, but I do my best.'

There were times during the concert when Charlotte's emotions got the better of her. 'Candle in the Wind' brought a massive lump to her throat, as did 'Your Song'. At one point, Jürgen took her hand and raised it aloft, both of them swaying to the melody. When the song ended, he didn't let go.

'I think it's the finale,' whispered Charlotte as Elton sat down at the piano and the familiar opening bars of 'Goodbye Yellow Brick Road' echoed around the stadium. The audience sang along, a montage of images projected on the giant screen of his life in music, his charitable works, and at the end, his husband and two young boys.

Still grasping Jürgen's hand, Charlotte marvelled at Elton's incredible journey from troubled childhood to global megastar. What would her legacy be? Nothing as attention-grabbing or noteworthy. Just an ordinary woman who'd tried her best to be kind, adored her children, and...

Charlotte slipped her hand free and watched as people stamped, screamed and begged for more. They were caught up in a moment, a slice of history they'd relate to family and friends. 'We were there. It was incredible, like travelling through time. Unforgettable.'

Elton hadn't finished. He addressed the audience, exhausted but exhilarated by the love swirling around the stadium. 'I am sick to death of hatred, of racism and homophobia,' he said, breathless yet filled with passion. 'We should appreciate each other, we need to embrace everyone even if we do not agree with each other.'

Charlotte clapped as hard as she could. Jürgen clapped next to her, and the applause all around them made her ears ring. Then Elton took his last bow, and it was all over.

'Wasn't that incredible?' Charlotte kept close to Jürgen as they made their way to the nearest exit. She stumbled as a stocky youth barged past, his elbow connecting with her ribs. Jürgen wrapped a steadying arm around Charlotte's shoulder, the heat from his body welcome as the night air cooled.

'He is the ultimate showman,' agreed Jürgen. 'It is sad he is retiring, but I am glad we saw him before he did.'

'Hmm, unless he wallops through his money and makes a comeback. Didn't Cher retire years ago? Yet she keeps popping back up.'

'I think for some performers it is the draw of the live audience that they miss.' Jürgen pulled Charlotte closer as they edged through the crush at the gates. 'It is an addiction, I suppose, just like drugs and alcohol.'

'Well, Elton certainly had his fair share of those!' said Charlotte, recalling the scenes in *Rocketman* where he'd doused his cereal with vodka and snorted endless cocaine. It was a miracle he *was* still standing.

Jürgen insisted on walking Charlotte to her car, even though they'd parked in opposite directions. He'd removed his arm when the crowds abated, and Charlotte missed its solid comfort. He was just being a gentleman, nothing more.

'It was good to see you smiling tonight, Charlotte.' Jürgen faced her as she fumbled in the pocket of her bag for the car key. 'I hope things are OK at home, and that I can see you again soon.'

Charlotte found her key and purse and tried to hand over a wad of notes to pay for the ticket.

'Please, there is no need. The pleasure is all mine. Now, drive carefully and take care.' He kissed her goodbye and set off toward his own car.

Charlotte sat in the driver's seat for several minutes, reflecting on the evening. It was one of the most enjoyable she'd had for a while, but was that down to the concert, or the company?

CHAPTER 38

'Did you have a nice evening with Daddy?'

It was the morning after the concert, and Charlotte was home alone with the boys. While it was the weekend, Dom had taken himself off to an electrical store to buy cables and other paraphernalia.

'It was OK.' Alastair shrugged and Robson added another slice of bread to the toaster. His fourth, not that Charlotte was counting.

'You don't sound very enthusiastic. Didn't you like the burritos?' Charlotte sliced a banana over her cereal and added milk.

'They were nice, but really messy to eat. Robson spilled half of his down his front, and Daddy wasn't pleased.'

Nipping into the laundry room, Charlotte discovered Robson's T-shirt on top of the dirty washing basket. A lurid red stain adorned the front, and Charlotte sighed. Would it have killed Dom to chuck it in to soak? Not that he would know the importance of Vanish, unless you counted his ability to disappear at the drop of a hat.

'What did you do after dinner?' Charlotte hadn't had the

chance to ask Dom herself. By the time she got back from the concert, Dom was sitting at his laptop working on spreadsheets. He'd asked how it had been, but after talking for five minutes Charlotte realised his mind was elsewhere.

'We started watching a movie, then Robson wanted to play *Toy Story* Kerplunk, but Daddy said he had to make a phone call and it took *ages!*'

'Really? Who was he talking to?' A prickle of doubt laced with anger coursed through Charlotte.

Alastair rolled his eyes. 'Dunno. I think it was about work, but he went into the other room. We played the game, but it's better with more people.'

Charlotte touched his cheek and smiled. 'I'll play it with you later, promise. Now finish your breakfast and get dressed. Nathaniel and Jodie will be here soon, and I'm going to make something delicious *and* vegan.'

Neither of the boys looked particularly impressed at this, but Charlotte was determined to produce a lunch that satisfied all of them. She'd spent an hour on various websites and had hopefully come up with something tasty and nutritious.

'Your phone's ringing, Mummy.' With the radio playing in the background, Charlotte hadn't heard it. She dashed through to the lounge and picked it up. The caller ID showed an unknown number.

'Hello?' She waited, hearing heavy breathing down the line. About to hang up, Charlotte realised the caller was crying. 'Sorry, who is this?'

Finally, someone spoke. 'Hello, Charlotte. It's Alicia. I … sorry, I got your number from the school directory and I just … well, I needed someone to talk to.'

Charlotte had forgotten about giving her mobile number to one of the class reps when they were compiling a list of contacts. 'That's fine, Alicia, but — now really isn't a good time. The boys have friends coming over and I need to make chickpea burgers and quinoa salad.' Charlotte felt bad using food preparation as an excuse, but she had a pile of sun-dried tomatoes and herbs to chop.

'Oh, right.' Alicia's watery tone took on its more familiar haughty sound. 'Well, I'll leave you to it—'

'Listen, would you like to meet somewhere later on? Dom's out now but he should be back soon, so I could escape for an hour or so.'

'Yes, that would be good. Would you like to come to my place? Myriam, my housekeeper, is on holiday but I can fix some drinks. Do you have my address?'

Charlotte pretended to write it down. She knew exactly where Alicia lived; a waterside mansion once owned by a reclusive movie star and apparently costing in the region of 20 million Swiss francs. Sadie had been there a couple of times, and had spoken breathlessly of its infinity pool, private boat mooring and kitchen to rival a high-end restaurant.

'OK. I'll be there around four o'clock, and I'll text you if there's a problem.' Nathaniel and Jodie were due at noon, and Dom had promised to be back within the next hour.

Returning to her domestic duties, Charlotte wondered why Alicia wanted to talk to her. Yes, she had marriage troubles and few friends, but Charlotte wasn't sure how much help she could be. Still, she'd told Alicia she was happy to talk, and Charlotte considered herself a woman of her word.

Minutes after Nathaniel and Jodie arrived, Dom appeared, laden with electrical bits and pieces and a stack of DVDs. He eyed the platters of vegan delights with disdain, and fetched himself the makings of a ham and cheese toastie.

'Don't you want some, darling?' Charlotte enquired. 'I thought this would be right up your street after the retreat.' She watched Dom's face, looking for a sign that he'd been telling porkies all along. Though how he could have forged an invoice was something she couldn't figure out.

'It looks, erm, interesting, but I need something I can get my teeth into.' Dom plugged in the toastie maker and slathered the sandwich with English mustard.

'Do you know how pigs are killed?' said Jodie, painstakingly removing the sun-dried tomatoes and lining them up at the edge of the plate. 'They—'

'I don't think that's really a conversation for the lunch table,' interjected Charlotte, aware of Alastair, Robson and Nathaniel gawping in fascination. 'Now, who's for a second burger?'

Leaving the children to it — and hoping Jodie wouldn't give a blow-by-blow account of gruesome animal slaughter methods — Charlotte followed Dom into the small office.

'You're home for the day now, I assume?'

Dom bit into his toastie, a string of melted cheese dripping onto his chin. He chewed, swallowed, and gave a noncommittal shrug. 'Probably. How long are the minions hanging around for?'

'Till around three thirty. I'm going to visit a friend at four, so I need you here for Alastair and Robson. I promised I'd play a game with them; the one you didn't play because you were busy on the phone.'

Dom put his toastie down and wiped his mouth. 'I was talking to my mum, Charlotte. I thought I'd better explain the misunderstanding about where I was meant to be. Your tone is rather aggressive, don't you think? I hope you're not suggesting—'

Charlotte turned on her heel and marched out. *Misunderstanding?* More like outright lie. She toyed with ringing Jean to check if the alleged conversation had taken place, then dismissed it immediately. She'd only be digging a deeper hole for herself. Unless she told Jean how her darling Dominic had created an elaborate cover story, although a quick check of his dirty laundry had revealed a selection of gym kit.

Back in the kitchen, Charlotte stacked up the plates and loaded the dishwasher. To Robson's delight she suggested playing Kerplunk, and he dashed off to fetch the game.

'That was delicious, Mrs Egerton,' said Jodie sweetly. 'Perhaps you could incorporate more vegan meals into your diet, to see if you're ready to embrace it fully.'

Good God, how old was this child? Charlotte suspected her mother — a wiry woman with a penchant for ponchos and sweeping skirts — drilled Jodie daily on the merits of a plant-based existence. Not that there was anything wrong with being vegan or vegetarian or pescatarian or any other – arians that existed. Each to their own, and all that.

As the five of them settled down to play, the dishwasher groaned in the background like a mournful cow. Charlotte rolled the dice, took hold of a stick, and pulled.

CHAPTER 39

'COME IN, PLEASE. IF YOU COULD LEAVE YOUR SHOES AT THE door, there are indoor slippers to wear.'

Alicia pointed at a wall-hung collection of pink, cream and black slippers. Charlotte looked down at her sensible footwear, slip-on Skechers that were more comfortable than stylish. She hadn't trodden in any mud or cowpats en route to Alicia's, but she knew some people had a thing about shoes being worn indoors.

'Let's go out to the terrace,' said Alicia. Charlotte followed her through the enormous marble-floored hallway, complete with a chandelier that wouldn't have looked out of place on the set of *The Phantom of the Opera*. Fresh flowers adorned wrought-iron tables and imposing modern art covered most of the walls.

'You have a beautiful home,' said Charlotte, as they passed through a lounge roughly the size of the ground floor of her rented house. What struck her, however, was how minimalist and stark everything was, in contrast to the homeliness she favoured. Not a cushion was out of place, there were no family photographs and every surface gleamed.

The terrace was a sprawling affair, with the pool sparkling in the sun and a jacuzzi off to the side. Alicia gestured to a set of rattan chairs grouped around a glass table bearing a jug of something yellow garnished with fruit, and a platter of canapés.

'I made us mimosas, but not too heavy on the wine.' Alicia filled two glasses and handed one to Charlotte. 'I've been trying not to drink too much since Derek left, but sometimes you need something to take the edge off.'

Charlotte sat down, the charcoal-grey cushion almost swallowing her whole. She shuffled forward, anxious not to spill her drink.

'I do appreciate you making time to come and see me. I know I'm not the easiest person in the world to get along with, but I can see you have a kind heart.' Alicia toasted Charlotte before downing half her drink in one gulp.

'Oh, I'm no candidate for a sainthood,' replied Charlotte. 'Believe me, I have a dark side too.'

Alicia proffered the plate and Charlotte took a blini topped with smoked salmon, sour cream and chives. 'Doesn't everyone?' she said. 'It's just that some are more able to disguise it than others. I'm afraid my directness doesn't encourage friendship, but I've been content to live in my perfect little bubble. Until Derek decided to pop it, of course.'

'Has he been back? I mean, since he left.' Charlotte bit into the blini, balancing a napkin on her knees in case of spillage.

Alicia stretched out her long, tanned legs, wiggling a perfectly manicured foot. 'Oh, yes. He called to check I'd be out, then cleared out most of his personal stuff. Mind you, there's still a state-of-the-art recording studio in the basement, not to mention all the artwork and sculptures he's accumulated over the years.'

'Are you going to sell the house? It must be difficult staying here now that Derek's gone.' Charlotte was itching to see the rest of the place, but didn't feel she could ask for a guided tour. She recalled Sadie saying that it had at least ten bedrooms — all en suite — and a gym, guest quarters, and home cinema.

'Absolutely not! This is my home and I have no intention of going anywhere, at least for now. Derek has more than enough money to buy somewhere else for himself and lover boy. I believe they're currently shacked up somewhere near Geneva, not that I give a hoot.'

Charlotte pushed down the anxiety that always kicked in when she thought of splitting up with Dom. Without millions in the bank, they'd have no choice but to divide up their assets. *Don't go there,* she urged herself.

One mimosa down, Charlotte reluctantly declined a top-up. She still wasn't sure why Alicia had invited her. Perhaps she just needed a friendly ear, although she seemed very calm about the situation. So what had prompted the tears on the phone earlier?

'Erm, can I use your loo, please?' Charlotte's bladder was protesting at the drink she'd just finished, on top of several cups of coffee at home.

'Of course. It's this way.' Alicia led her back into the house and pointed to a glossy white door with a jewelled handle. 'I'll just check on Jennifer. She's supposed to be practising ballet, but I suspect she's glued to one of those awful reality shows.'

The opulence of the bathroom took Charlotte's breath away. Gold taps, flecked marble tiles and a toilet like nothing she'd ever seen before. It had a panel at the side with several buttons, and she wondered if it played music or rated the quality of your bowel movements. Tentatively sitting down and doing her business, Charlotte pushed one of the buttons and squealed as a jet of water caressed her nether regions. Crikey! She tried another, and warm air circulated around her bottom. Which, come to think of it, was also on the unusually warm side. A heated seat!

Back on the terrace, Charlotte helped herself to a breaded shrimp and wandered over to the edge of the pool. It looked so inviting that for a brief moment she wished she could dive in. Not fully clothed, of course, and she wasn't about to strip down to her mismatched undies.

Alicia joined Charlotte by the pool, her eyes red and her voice hoarse. 'Sorry,' she said. 'Jennifer was, as predicted, holed up in her room watching dreadful people screaming at each other. How shows like that pass for entertainment is beyond me.' She took a hankie — a cotton one, not paper — from her pocket and honked loudly into it. Charlotte couldn't have been more surprised if Alicia had performed an impromptu headstand.

'Are you upset with Jennifer?' she asked. Charlotte didn't know the girl, only that she was in her early teens and had a reputation for being wild. Whatever that meant these days. Perhaps her parents' unorthodox relationship had caused her to rebel, smoking behind the bike sheds and sharing illicit alcopops with friends.

'You could say that.' Alicia honked again, then stuffed the hankie back in her pocket. 'She's adamant she wants to live with her father and *that* man, which is absolutely not going to happen.'

'Oh dear,' said Charlotte ineffectually. She'd bet anything that the boys would want to stay with her if the worst ever happened. Not that they were mummy's boys, but they were measurably closer to Charlotte. Dom took them for the odd kickaround and trip to the swimming pool, but Charlotte mopped up the tears, administered the hugs and would give up her life for them.

'The thing is, there's no way Derek will want to have her living with them. A stroppy teenager mooching around his little love nest? I think not.'

'I'm sure if you talk to her she'll change her mind,' said Charlotte. 'If he's living in Geneva, Jennifer would have to change schools, wouldn't she?'

Alicia shrugged. 'Talking to my daughter is like trying to demolish a building with a feather duster. The girl is as stubborn as a mule, just like her father. The only thing that might sway her is if I cut off her monthly allowance.'

Now more composed, Alicia offered to make Charlotte a tea or coffee. Charlotte checked her watch. She needed to pick up a few bits on the way home, including Dom's suits from the dry cleaner. The thought dragged her back to the discovery of the card from Amelie —not that she had found anything incriminating since. 'Sorry, Alicia, I need to make a move. I wish I could be more help, but I'm always here if you need to talk again, or if I can do anything else.'

As Charlotte turned to leave, Alicia lightly touched her arm. 'I have something else to tell you, Charlotte. And you might want to sit down for it.'

Puzzled, Charlotte sat back down. A prickle of apprehension coursed through her as she took in Alicia's sombre expression.

'I may be speaking out of turn, but I'm a great believer in honesty.' She gave a brittle laugh. 'Perhaps not within my own marriage, but I hate to see other people being duped. Not everyone likes to hear the truth, but if I consider someone a friend... Well, let's just say if the boot was on the other foot, I'd want to know.'

The prickle turned to a fiery rush of foreboding. Whatever Alicia was alluding to, it wasn't good news. Charlotte grabbed the mimosa jug with shaking hands and poured a half-glass.

'Can you please just spit it out?'

Alicia reached over, patted Charlotte's knee, and drew a deep breath. 'I'm afraid I saw your husband with another woman. And, judging by their body language, they're more than just friends.'

CHAPTER 40

Canapés and alcohol churned in Charlotte's stomach, and she feared she might throw up. Instead, she got up and paced on the terrace, forcing herself to count down from fifty. By the time she got to fifteen she felt calmer, and ready to hear the rest.

'Are you sure it was Dom?' Although handsome, he might easily be mistaken for someone else, Charlotte reasoned. Then she wanted to slap herself firmly in the face. What was the likelihood of her husband having a doppelgänger living nearby? Not that Alicia had yet revealed where and when she'd seen him. *Them.*

'I'm sure, Charlotte. I wouldn't say anything otherwise. He didn't see me. I was picking up a friend who doesn't drive from a yoga retreat in Valais, and—'

'Wait a minute. Did you say yoga retreat?' Charlotte gawped in disbelief, hoping that somehow she'd misheard. Dom had shown her the invoice which clearly stated it was a solo booking, and— Charlotte thumped her forehead hard. She should get the words 'total sucker' tattooed on it, to remind her how naïve, how gullible she was. It had never

crossed her mind that someone else could have booked separately. In fact, that would be the logical thing to do when
attempting to fly under a wife's pathetically inadequate
radar.

'Yes,' Alicia continued. 'My friend — well, more of an
elderly acquaintance — goes twice a year, but she had to give
up her driving licence because of macular degeneration. I
dropped her off at the start and returned to pick her up at
the end. We were loading her bags into my car when I saw
them.'

For a moment Charlotte wished that Alicia had the eye
problem. At least then she might convince herself it was all a
mistake, but what were the chances of it not being Dom?

'As I said, he didn't see me, although he was only a matter
of feet away. Not surprising, really, as he was wrapped
around the woman like clinging ivy. The only way you'd
separate them would be with a bucket of water. Oh sorry,
that was brutal.'

Charlotte winced. Unbidden, an image came into her
mind of Amelie slithering around Dom like a sex-mad snake,
her little forked tongue probing his eager mouth.

'What did she look like? The woman, I mean.' As if she
could be referring to anyone else.

Alicia closed her eyes, trying to recall details of the trol-
lop's appearance. 'Petite, with blonde hair. I couldn't see her
face very well for obvious reasons, but her outfit struck me
as odd considering the high temperature.'

'What do you mean?' Charlotte pictured Amelie clad in a
fur coat — she was probably naked underneath — and
wearing vertiginous heels to bring her up to Dom's height.

'Well, she was wearing these strange silver-studded boots.
Not my cup of tea at all, especially teamed with a flouncy
summer dress.'

Charlotte left minutes later. She thanked Alicia both for

the drinks and for telling her that Dom was a duplicitous bastard. Taking a moment to compose herself in the car, she drummed her fingernails on the steering wheel. A million thoughts whirled through her head, most of them involving how to confront Dom with irrefutable proof of his infidelity. If only Alicia had taken a photo. He wouldn't have been able to wriggle out of *that*.

Before she started the engine, another thought struck Charlotte. Had Alicia genuinely told her as a friend, or was there an element of — what was that word again? — schadenfreude? Something about taking pleasure from someone else's misfortune. Whichever was the case, the outcome was the same.

On her way to the supermarket, a wave of nausea hit Charlotte. She pulled over and fumbled in her bag for a bottle of water. Gulping half of it down, she pulled out her pocket mirror and surveyed her face. Pale, wild-eyed, but otherwise normal. That German word, schadenfreude, played on repeat, and brought to mind the one person she really wanted to talk to before she talked to Dom. Charlotte grabbed her phone, scrolled through the numbers, and hit the call button.

'Hi, Jürgen, it's Charlotte. Yes, I'm OK — no, I'm not, actually. I wondered... I'm in Vevey and if you were free to meet at that little café... well, now. Sorry, I know it's short notice— You can? Thank you. I'll see you there in fifteen minutes.'

* * *

JÜRGEN STRODE through the café door precisely fifteen minutes later. Charlotte had touched up her make-up in the bathroom and hovered on the terrace until an elderly couple with a panting poodle departed. The harassed waitress was inside, dealing with a busy table of young mums and toddlers.

'Charlotte.' Jürgen greeted her with the customary Swiss kisses. 'I would ask how you are, but I think I already know the answer. I will fetch us something to drink. Perhaps a cold drink?'

He returned moments later with two iced teas and a selection of mini millefeuilles.

'That was quick,' said Charlotte, spying the waitress still scuttling around the room, mopping up spills and scribbling on her notepad.

'I am a very determined man, Charlotte,' Jürgen replied, rolling up his pristine shirtsleeves. 'When I want something, I generally get it.' A broad wink and smile tempered the underlying arrogance of the remark, making Charlotte's stomach flip-flop, and not in a feeling-sick way.

'Now, please tell me what's troubling you. I sensed before that you were unhappy, and seeing you unhappy makes me sad.' Jürgen's smile turned downwards, his eyes signalling concern.

'It's my husband, Dom,' Charlotte stuttered. 'Oh God, it's so humiliating, but I think he's having an affair with one of his colleagues.' Saying it out loud to someone other than Ruth felt strange, almost as if she were being disloyal to Dom. How ridiculous, when he was the one cheating on her!

'I'm so sorry, Charlotte.' Jürgen reached for her hand and she gladly accepted his comforting grasp. 'I know what it is like, as you know. I may not have been in love with Monica, but it still hurt, more so because of the effect on Marcus. Luckily, he is a resilient boy and quickly adapted to the change in circumstances.'

'I think that's what upsets me the most,' said Charlotte. 'If Dom *is* having an affair — if it's serious — it would be like a wrecking ball for our family. We'd probably have to leave

Switzerland and start all over again in the UK. It would be a bloody nightmare.'

As Charlotte's eyes swam with tears, Jürgen moved closer. The buzz of conversation around them faded as she gazed at his kindly, handsome face. 'You must not jump ahead, Charlotte, if that is the correct expression. Whatever the future holds, you will deal with it. You are stronger than you think, and I know you will find a way to make things good for you and your wonderful boys. Now, perhaps you should tell me why you believe your husband is seeing someone else.'

Without going into too much detail, Charlotte described finding the business card all those months ago, how Dom would disappear for late-night meetings and secretive phone calls, and Amelie's behaviour at their party. She ended with Alicia's assertion that she'd spotted Dom entangled with Amelie at the yoga retreat, but skipped the part about him claiming to be with his parents. That made Charlotte feel like a complete idiot, and she didn't want Jürgen to question her lack of intelligence.

'It sounds bad, Charlotte, but the only one who can give you answers is Dom. Considering what Alicia told you, I suggest you find a quiet moment to talk. Based on what you said, he may try to find an excuse, but please stand your ground.'

Try as she might, Charlotte couldn't imagine Dom squirming his way out of what Alicia had witnessed.

'Ooh, forgot to mention that Amelie *happened* to be at the retreat too — total coincidence — and then she accidentally tripped and fell and got all tangled up around my body! Ha ha! All totally innocent.'

' You do not have to answer this, but … do you love him?' Jürgen's gentle voice broke through Charlotte's thoughts. 'Whether he is guilty or innocent, do you still love him?'

Aware of the waitress hovering within earshot, Charlotte

shook her head. 'I don't ... I mean, I do... Sorry, could we maybe go for a walk?'

Leaving their drinks and cakes barely touched, Charlotte and Jürgen left the café and wandered through the cobbled streets of Vevey's old town. They headed to the lakeside, dodging cyclists and pram-pushers along the way. Finding a shady spot near where they'd had ice creams with the boys, they perched on a low wall. The lake glittered in the sunshine, and one of the stately paddle steamers sailed majestically by.

'I guess things haven't been great between us for a while,' said Charlotte, gazing out over the water. 'Since finding the card from Amelie — that's her name. Even though Dom came up with an excuse for it. To be honest, it probably started before that. The card just drove a deeper wedge between us, and moving here didn't help, especially when Dom failed to tell me *she'd* moved here too.'

'Have you spoken to anyone else? Perhaps your friend Sadie, or your parents?'

Charlotte shook her head. 'I've only told my best friend Ruth in the UK, but she's got a lot on her plate right now, so I don't want to burden her too much. And my parents live in Florida, and they'd just get upset and fret.'

Jürgen cleared his throat and gently turned Charlotte round to face him. 'It seems you put everyone else's needs first, Charlotte. You should be your top priority, and that includes deciding what makes you happy. If Dom is seeing another woman, he does not respect you. And you deserve so much more than that.'

Charlotte's lip wobbled at Jürgen's kindness. It seemed an eternity ago since she'd thought him an arrogant petrolhead. But now wasn't the time to dwell on that subject.

'What if I've neglected Dom? I'm so devoted to Alastair

and Robson that perhaps I've driven him into the arms of someone else—'

'Stop right there.' Jürgen pressed a finger to Charlotte's mouth and for the briefest of moments she imagined it was his lips. That thought absolutely wasn't helpful or appropriate in the circumstances. 'Every mother — well, almost — devotes herself to her children. It is the most important job in the world, and any husband or partner who resents that is a fool. Do not blame yourself, Charlotte. You have done nothing wrong.'

Charlotte quickly checked her phone. No messages or missed calls. Not that she had any intention of dashing back to Dom. Let him look after the boys for a bit longer.

'But I don't really *do* anything, Jürgen.' Charlotte fiddled with a loose thread on her jumper. 'I don't have a job, or any real hobbies apart from reading and walking. I feel like I've drifted through the past ten years without a purpose. And now I'm letting my husband walk all over me, like the pathetic doormat I am.'

A solitary tear trickled down Charlotte's cheek. She swiped it away, embarrassed at her words. And the fact that they were painfully true.

'Charlotte, listen to me.' Jürgen gently moved her hand away from the thread that was rapidly turning into a hole. 'You are much too hard on yourself. Moving to a new country and building a life there is not easy, particularly when so much is uncertain right now.'

Charlotte blinked back more tears. 'But I'm so scared of what might happen if we split up. I'm afraid I'll fall and never get up again.'

Charlotte stood, her bottom uncomfortably numb from the cold stone wall. She needed to go, grab some groceries and head for home. Taking a step forward, she almost collided with a rollerblading gentleman who must have been well into his eighties. He whizzed by with effortless grace and astonishing speed as Charlotte gawped in amazement.

'I tried that once, and fell over about twenty times,' she said, chuckling. 'The boys thought it was funnier than any cartoon.'

Jürgen rested his hands on her shoulders and fixed her with his mesmerising eyes. 'I'd teach you, Charlotte. And I promise, I'd never let you fall.'

CHAPTER 41

'YOU WERE GONE A LONG TIME,' GRUMBLED DOM, AS Charlotte put away the bits and pieces she'd picked up after leaving Jürgen. 'Did the ballet dancer give you a full-blown guided tour of her mansion?'

Ignoring his snarky remark, Charlotte filled the coffee canister with instant granules and put the kettle on. Seconds later Alastair and Robson bowled into the kitchen, complaining of starvation. With little enthusiasm for cooking, Charlotte unearthed a packet of crispy cheese and ham pancakes and a bag of chips and put the oven on to heat. 'Boys, this won't take long. Why don't you go play outside until it's ready? I'll give you a shout.'

They scampered off, Robson collecting a stray football from the basket of miscellaneous toys and play equipment in the utility room.

'Be careful with your arm,' Charlotte added. Alastair rolled his eyes but nodded in agreement.

Satisfied they were a safe distance away, Charlotte lined up the pancakes and chips on a baking tray. Dom hovered behind her, an open beer already in his hand.

'I thought we were having chilli tonight,' he said, taking a bottle of white wine from the fridge. 'Those things don't really float my boat, as you know.'

Accepting a glass of wine instead of making coffee, Charlotte faced the man she'd said 'I do' to ten years ago. She remembered the pre-wedding nerves, her mum fretting that her hat didn't match her outfit, her dad pacing up and down the lounge because the silver Bentley they'd ordered to take them to church was two minutes late. And Ruth, her best friend since childhood, telling Charlotte she was the most beautiful bride in the world, and Dom the luckiest man. Ruth, who'd asked Charlotte several times after they'd got engaged if she was one hundred per cent sure that Dom was the right man for her.

'Earth to Charlotte! Sweetheart, you're a million miles away.' Dom pinched her cheek playfully.

Charlotte swatted his hand away and took a swig of Dutch courage. 'I wish I *were* a million miles away, because occupying the same breathing space as a lying, adulterous bastard is seriously affecting my mental health.'

Dom attempted to arrange his features into a 'not that old chestnut again' expression, but his Adam's apple bobbed up and down as he swallowed hard. 'I've no idea what you're talking about, Charlotte. We've been over the whole Amelie thing, and I'm tired of being accused of something—'

'Someone saw you, Dom.' Charlotte cut him off, unable to listen to more lies tumbling out of his mouth. 'At the retreat, where you claimed to be alone meditating or whatever bollocks. And you were actually getting your leg over with that biker-booted bitch!'

Dom blanched at Charlotte's fury, but she could almost hear the cogs whirling in his head as he tried to come up with an explanation. 'It's not what you think,' he stammered, causing Charlotte to laugh out loud. 'If you just calm down, I'll tell you the truth.'

'Dom, I honestly believe you wouldn't know the truth if it slapped you round the face. So spit it out. You're having an affair with her, aren't you?'

Her husband slumped into a chair and studied his beer bottle. Charlotte checked where the boys were, relieved to see them at the bottom of the garden deep in conversation.

'Answer me, Dom. I've spent months with doubt gnawing at my insides after stupidly swallowing your pathetic excuses. Don't make me feel a bigger fool than I already do.'

'OK, OK, I've been an idiot, but I promise you I have not had sexual relations with that woman.' Dom gave her his finest doe-eyed look and Charlotte snorted in derision.

'What, you've turned into Bill bloody Clinton? Please spare me the bullshit, or you can pack a bag and get out right now.'

Before Dom could continue, the boys barrelled into the kitchen, screeching to a halt as they picked up on the frosty atmosphere. 'Is something wrong, Mummy?' asked Alastair. 'You look angry.'

'Mummy's fine,' Dom interjected. 'We were just having a little chat. Now, let's get your dinner on the table—' His voice tailed off as four sets of eyes took in the stone-cold, uncooked tray of food.

'Oops,' said Robson. 'Can we have some cheese and crackers while we wait?'

* * *

ONCE THE BOYS were in bed, Dom followed Charlotte outside to the small side terrace, which was well away from the boys' rooms. He carried the wine bottle and another beer, and Charlotte a bowl of mixed nuts. Neither of them had eaten much earlier, with Alastair and Robson scoffing six pancakes each and a mountain of chips.

'Whatever you do, don't start yelling.' Dom poured Charlotte a generous glass of white and scooped up a handful of nuts. 'We can talk like rational grown-ups, can't we?'

Could they? It had taken every ounce of self-restraint not to order Dom out of the house after getting the boys down for the night. As they sat around the table Charlotte had cringed at Dom's faux joviality, carrying on as if it were just another day. The perfect family, chatting about inconsequential stuff without a care in the world. She'd marvelled again at her husband's ability to put on a performance and decided that he was wasted in the world of business. Dom deserved an Oscar.

'So, Mr President,' Charlotte began. 'If you didn't have "sexual relations" — she formed air quotes with her fingers — 'what exactly *did* you have? A frisky fumble, a game or two of tonsil hockey, or a full-on grope?' She'd decided that sarcasm was a useful weapon, because it distracted her from the likelihood Dom and Amelie were way beyond first base.

'Charlotte, that's hardly an adult way of discussing this. I said I'd been an idiot, and I want to explain. Please, just listen and… Well, just listen.'

According to Dom, he'd mentioned the yoga retreat to Amelie, who was into such things as well as astrology, crystals, and fairy cards. Charlotte bit down another sarky comment at that one. What the actual fuck were fairy cards, and why would anyone be interested in them?

'She said she fancied a break too, and if I minded her booking at the same time. Separate rooms,' Dom added hastily. 'Stupidly, I agreed. Maybe I felt more comfortable knowing there was someone familiar there.'

'As opposed to your wife?' Charlotte arched an eyebrow. 'Oh, that's right. You were meant to be visiting your parents, not halfway up a mountain getting bendy with Miss Sparkly Pants.'

'You were busy with the boys at summer camp,' huffed Dom. 'And I needed the time away, as I already told you.'

'Yes, but *alone*, Dom, not with a woman you've repeatedly denied being involved with. Anyway, Alicia saw her all over you like a rash.' That, ridiculously, reminded Charlotte of Ruth's dermatologist beau. Right now she wanted to talk to her friend and hear Ruth's wise counsel, which would probably involve a string of expletives and a demand that she boot Dom's cheating arse out the door.

'Amelie's very flirtatious and touchy-feely,' countered Dom. 'I bet that shit-stirring cow witnessed Amelie giving me a friendly hug and twisted it out of proportion.'

Charlotte hesitated. She *had* wondered if Alicia drew some warped pleasure from telling her what she'd seen. Maybe she'd got it wrong or chosen to put a nasty spin on it. 'Have you kissed her?'

Dom looked distinctly uncomfortable. He squirmed in his chair, his gaze fixed on the grotty light fixture that barely illuminated the terrace and provided a home for dead insects. 'Once or twice,' he answered. 'I told you, I'm an idiot, but people make mistakes. I'm sorry, sweetheart, truly I am.'

Charlotte pictured the two of them snogging like hormonal teenagers and shuddered. 'You know, Dom, you're like the little boy who cried wolf. I've wondered so many times whether you were sneaking around behind my back, and now I find out that you have, and yet I'm supposed to believe that nothing much happened. In most wives' eyes, their husband kissing another woman is definitely crossing a line.'

'I know, I know. Look, it's out in the open now. I'm not proud of myself, but I'm only human.' Dom gave Charlotte a watery smile which she failed to return. Exhaustion washed over her, and she got to her feet.

'I'm going to bed now, and I'd prefer it if you slept on the sofa tonight. You can get bedding from the upstairs cupboard.'

'But what will the boys think if they find me there?' Dom's smile turned into a frown. 'There's no need to upset them, surely.'

'Oh, I'm sure you can come up with a convincing story,' said Charlotte, draining the last of her wine. 'You're very good at that.'

CHAPTER 42

'Maybe you should tail him next time he disappears on some dodgy errand. Just make sure you know how to take a bloody photo with your phone.'

Charlotte laughed, conceding that her expertise at taking photos left much to be desired. She tried to share snaps of the boys with Ruth regularly, but the shots often came out blurry, or with a finger over the lens. 'It's not my strong suit, nor is carrying on like 007. I don't *want* to follow him, Ruth. To be frank, I'm not sure I even care if he's screwing around behind my back. And that scares me.'

Charlotte had woken early after a night of checking the clock at hourly intervals. Her eyeballs felt as if goblins in hobnailed or possibly sparkly biker boots had danced across them, and three industrial-strength coffees had done little to dispel the fog permeating her grey cells.

'Sweetie, I'm gutted for you,' said Ruth. 'You deserve so much better than this, not least because he's dragged you to a country you didn't even want to go to, then done the dirty on you. Honestly, I'd tell him to pack his bags and go, at least till you've wrapped your head around it all.'

Charlotte nodded, the movement causing needles of pain to shoot through her head. She popped another paracetamol and downed it with a mouthful of water.

'Is he there now?' Ruth lowered her voice, eyes darting from side to side as if she expected Dom to leap into view.

'No. He took the boys shopping for some new shorts and T-shirts, and then a spot of lunch.'

Dom's night's sleep had clearly been as disturbed as Charlotte's. He'd stumbled around the kitchen complaining of backache, and his mood plummeted further when he discovered they were out of his favourite cereal.

'Going for a gold medal in the father stakes, eh?' quipped Ruth, familiar with Dom's less than sterling record as a hands-on dad.

'I guess so, although as a husband he'd be lucky to get the wooden spoon. God, Ruth, I don't know what to do. My mind leaps around like a demented frog, one minute convinced I don't want our marriage to end, the next thinking I don't even *like* Dom much anymore. When Jürgen said I needed to put myself first—'

'Whoa, back up there, girlfriend! Who exactly is Jürgen, and why has your face gone from glum to secret squirrel in a nanosecond?' Ruth waggled a finger at her in a naughty-naughty gesture.

'Oh, he's just a friend,' said Charlotte, hoping Ruth couldn't see the pink flush spreading from her chest. 'He's been really kind to me and the boys, and he's had experience of being cheated on in the past. I find it easy to talk to him, that's all.' Before Ruth could grill Charlotte further on Jürgen, Charlotte steered the conversation towards Simon and the big pregnancy reveal. 'You told him, right?'

Ruth nodded and grinned. 'It was honestly more terrifying than sitting my driving test, hon. All five attempts put together. I was shaking like a leaf, even though I'd prepared a speech.'

'And?' Charlotte's own heart thumped in anticipation of Simon's reaction.

'Well, he realised I was in a bit of a state, so he made a pot of tea — proper English stuff — and produced home-made apple cake. What's not to like about a man who can bake?'

Charlotte thought wistfully of the home-made biscuits Marcus had brought, then forced herself back to the more pressing matter of Ruth's revelation.

'Anyway, after two slices I felt better, but my planned speech had done a runner. I opened my big gob and just let it all out along the lines of, "I'm pregnant, you're definitely the father, and if you want nothing to do with me — us — I completely understand."'

'Wow.' Charlotte felt a wave of sympathy for poor Simon, who'd probably expected nothing more than a chance to pick up where he and Ruth had left off. 'How did he take it?' She imagined as a medical professional he was used to dealing with shocks, although lancing pus-filled boils and identifying rare skin conditions wasn't quite in the same league.

'Surprisingly well. OK, his face turned paler than a Japanese geisha's, but all things considered, his reaction was positive. A lot calmer than when I saw those bloody blue lines screaming "positive" on the test stick. Trust me, Charlotte, you would not have enjoyed my screams, which only multiplied the more sticks I peed on.'

'Please cut to the chase.' Charlotte didn't want Dom and the boys wandering in mid-chat. She checked the time at the top of the screen. Only half-past eleven, so that was unlikely unless her darling husband had had enough of the delights of H&M and bought Alastair and Robson a takeaway lunch.

'Once he'd processed it, which only took another cup of tea and a strong measure of whisky, he looked quite chuffed.

No, scratch that, he gave me an enormous hug and assured me he'd be there for me in whatever way I wanted. Shadowy partner, part-time dad, source of cash with no strings attached. He covered all the bases, including some I hadn't even considered. Mind truly blown, hon!'

Charlotte clapped with delight. 'Oh Ruth, I'm so, so happy for you. Now you won't have to go it alone. You must be over the moon!'

Ruth laughed. 'Don't go buying a wedding outfit just yet, hon. It's early days — well, not so much for my burgeoning bump — and I've no intention of diving head first into a serious relationship. Simon agreed we should start dating again, but baby steps for now. Oops, excuse the pun!'

'Speaking of bumps, didn't he notice you'd expanded around the middle?' Ruth was well into the second trimester, and should definitely be showing by now — unless she was one of those maddening women who only sprouted the tiniest of bumps in the final weeks. Charlotte had not been one of those.

'I'm not too enormous yet,' said Ruth, standing up and turning sideways. Sure enough, you'd be hard-pressed to notice anything. Charlotte's stomach often looked larger after a particularly carb-laden meal. 'Mind you, Simon's such a gent that he'd never comment on a woman's weight gain. Will, however, would have pointed out my paunch and prescribed a diet plan and some hideous abdominal exercises.'

Although Ruth made the comment in jest, Charlotte felt relieved that Will wasn't the father of the baby. She didn't know much about Simon, but the words 'decent' and 'kind' sprang to mind. Who knew what lay ahead for her best friend? Happiness, Charlotte hoped, and maybe love too.

After signing off with promises on each side to keep one another updated, Charlotte made herself a cheese and pickle sandwich. She'd taken one bite when she heard Dom's car pull up outside.

'A successful mission?' she asked, as Alastair and Robson bowled in with full carrier bags. Dom trailed in behind them, glued to his phone with an irate expression.

'Yes, Mummy. We got some cool shorts and tops *and* new swimming trunks. Look!' Robson delved into his bag and produced a lurid pair of Hawaiian-style board shorts with a flourish. Not to be outdone, Alastair scrabbled around with his good arm, and held up a pair featuring images of Bart Simpson.

'And we went to the funniest restaurant for lunch. Didn't we, Daddy?' Robson looked expectantly at Dom, who shoved his phone in his pocket and waited for Robson to continue.

'You had to choose things from a … a … what's the word again?'

'Buffet,' replied Dom. 'Listen, Charlotte, I need to head out for a bit. Antoine needs a hand assembling some furniture, and his partner is out of town. I won't be long.' He blew her a kiss which Charlotte ignored, focusing instead on Robson's excitement.

'See you.' Charlotte relieved the boys of their bags and they sat together at the kitchen table. 'OK, why was it funny?'

'Well, you picked what you wanted and piled it on your plate. I had hummus and a pasta salad thingy and lots of meatballs.'

'And I had couscous and chicken wings and big beans in a tomato sauce,' added Alastair.

'But when you got to the till, they *weighed* the food! Cos that's how they work out the price. Isn't that weird, Mummy?'

Charlotte smiled at their beaming faces. 'Just as well you didn't choose really heavy food, otherwise it would have cost a fortune.'

For the next ten minutes they chatted about their outing, which had also included a walk along the lakefront, now host to myriad food and merchandise stalls for the jazz festival. Under different circumstances Charlotte would have suggested a family outing to take in the atmosphere, but she didn't feel like hanging out with Dom more than was necessary. Any summer holiday plans had evaporated, although Alastair and Robson were content to see friends and play in the garden. And when Charlotte had mentioned getting tickets for a concert or two a while back, Dom had shown little enthusiasm. Sadie had a spare one for Rag 'n' Bone Man, but Charlotte hadn't committed to going.

Once the boys had disappeared to put away their swag, or more likely, scatter it all over the floor, Charlotte gazed sadly at the wall calendar. So little was planned, apart from Alastair's appointment in two weeks to check on his arm. Fingers crossed that he'd be liberated from his contraption, and they could venture to one or two of the lovely outdoor public swimming pools.

Taking a coffee outside, Charlotte slumped into a deckchair and soaked up the magnificent view. It was always breathtaking, even on those days when the sky darkened and dramatic bolts of lightning flashed across the lake and mountains. Alastair found the storms scary, but Charlotte and Robson loved them. They'd press their noses against the glass doors, squealing in delight every time the thunder crashed and the jagged forks touched down.

Inhaling the super-fresh air, laced with a hint of newly cut grass, Charlotte wished with all her heart for peace. Right now, her head felt like a small boat being tossed around on rough waters.

CHAPTER 43

Wandering along the lakeside in Montreux, Charlotte marvelled at how quiet it was — just a handful of joggers and cyclists, and a few dog walkers diligently picking up poop with the plastic bags provided by the local authority. It was such a contrast to the way it had been a couple of weeks earlier during the Jazz Festival, when people jostled for space, hunting for a spot to eat and drink amidst a sea of sweaty bodies.

Snapping another photo of Freddie's statue, and double-checking that it had come out OK, Charlotte continued towards the shopping centre. Alastair and Robson were at Nathaniel's for a play date, and Dom had left the house at seven for an early meeting.

Taking out a couple of folded shopping bags, Charlotte crossed the deserted market square and entered the building. The air conditioning cooled her skin and provided welcome relief from the midday heat.

As Charlotte popped a one-franc coin into the trolley release, she felt a tap on her shoulder. Twirling round, she saw it was Jürgen. He too clutched an armful of bags, and a broad grin stretched across his face.

'It is a small world, Charlotte,' he said. 'Although we have a habit of meeting up in supermarkets.'

Charlotte laughed, more pleased to see Jürgen than she cared to dwell upon. 'That's because my social life is pathetic. It's ridiculous how excited I get choosing the right ripe avocado or the perfect wedge of Brie.'

With a trolley each, they sauntered through the automatic barrier. Jürgen produced a handwritten list and a pair of glasses from his shirt pocket.

'I didn't know you wore glasses,' commented Charlotte. He looked good in them, the sleek, angular frame giving him an air of studious authority.

'Normally I wear contact lenses,' Jürgen replied, 'but they have been irritating my eyes recently, so I am having a break from them.'

They stood side by side in front of the fruit selection. Charlotte picked up a Charentais melon and a bag of mixed seedless grapes. Jürgen popped a pack of raspberries in his trolley. 'Tonight I will make home-made raspberry ripple ice cream for dessert.'

'Is there no end to your talents?' teased Charlotte. 'Next you'll be telling me you make your own meringues too!'

Jürgen chuckled, reaching for a bunch of bananas. 'Not when you can buy delicious Gruyère ones here, but I confess I make a mean pavlova.'

They strolled around, lobbing bits and pieces into their trolleys.

'I'm sorry I haven't been in touch since I last saw you,' said Jürgen. 'I wanted to give you time to process things, but it was difficult not knowing how you were.' He raised a questioning eyebrow.

'Dom admitted to something, but not to having... you

know.' Charlotte lowered her voice and glanced around. 'We've sort of reached an impasse, getting through the days without talking about it, but—'

'You do not believe him?' Jürgen placed a hand over Charlotte's and her grip tightened on the trolley handle.

'I don't know. And what worries me most is that I'm not sure how much I care.'

The shopping finished, they lugged their bags to a small café. Charlotte insisted on ordering, returning with two iced coffees and a giant chocolate-chip cookie. 'I thought we could share.' She broke it in half and handed Jürgen his portion.

He thanked her, took a bite, and laid the rest on a paper napkin. 'Charlotte, when trust dies, it is very hard to resuscitate. The pulse grows weak even if one person wants to make things work. My marriage to Monica was built on poor foundations, but it might have endured if she had not met someone else. Sometimes we tolerate things because we are afraid of the consequences of change. But fear of change is no reason to carry on when things are wrong.'

Charlotte gulped. It was as if Jürgen could see into her soul, nudging aside *what if* and *can't do that* with laser precision. He spoke so eloquently, cutting to the core of what had troubled her for months now. Did she and Dom have a future together? Charlotte tried to imagine a happily ever after, but the thought left a bad taste in her mouth.

'Talking to you … sharing things with you…' Charlotte snapped off a corner of the cookie and took a small bite. 'It's hard, but it's easy at the same time. Does that make sense? God, I'm babbling. Sorry.'

Jürgen sipped his iced coffee, leaving a smidgeon of froth on his upper lip. So used to wiping stray food and drink from the boys' faces, Charlotte leaned over and removed it with her napkin.

Jürgen took her hand and laced his fingers through hers. 'We have a connection, Charlotte. I don't mean to sound — how do you say — sleazy, but getting to know you has been a shining light in my life after many years of darkness.'

Coming from another man, Charlotte agreed that the words might sound sleazy — a come-on, hinting at a desire to take things further. But somehow, Jürgen was the real deal. He spoke from the heart, his face a beacon of honesty and empathy. Unlike Dom, who had got dodging and weaving around the truth down to a fine art. *But what about Pamela?* Not for the first time, Charlotte mentally hushed the niggling little voice.

'Give yourself time,' said Jürgen. 'Letting go of a marriage is never easy, even if the head says it is right to do so. Put yourself and the boys first. If the situation becomes intolerable, then you must act, but only in *your* best interests.'

Charlotte nodded and gently untwined her fingers from Jürgen's. If anyone spotted them, they'd jump to conclusions. The *wrong* conclusions, she reminded herself. Like in the movie *When Harry Met Sally*, and the discussion about whether men and women could be friends without the sex part getting in the way. Of course they could, although Dom had overstepped that boundary. By how much? Well, the jury was still out.

'It's been lovely to chat to you, but I need to get on.' Charlotte's plans for the rest of the day included giving the house a thorough clean, calling her folks for a catch-up, and enjoying a lazy hour or two in the garden. Hardly the height of excitement, but...

'Take care, Charlotte.' Jürgen stood up and glanced at the cluster of bags at her feet. 'Are you parked here?'

Damn it! Intent on stretching her legs, Charlotte had parked at the other end of town. Now she'd have to lug the shopping all the way back there in the stifling heat. She shook her head and explained her stupidity.

'Not a problem; I parked the Ferrari below. Please, let me drive you to your car.' Jürgen effortlessly gathered up his own bags and Charlotte's, his defined biceps visible beneath his pale-grey cotton shirt. Charlotte tried not to stare, aware of a group of women in their mid-thirties brazenly checking him out.

The journey to her car took under two minutes. Charlotte wished she'd parked several miles away as she relished the air whipping her hair around inside the open-top car. Passers-by stopped and stared as it roared along, the engine a growling monster. Casting a nervous glance at the speedometer, Charlotte saw they were well within the speed limit. God knows what it would sound like burning rubber on the autoroute…

'Thank you.' Swivelling out of the seat, Charlotte hoped she hadn't flashed her knickers at Jürgen, who was holding the door open for her. She tugged down her skirt and accepted her pile of shopping bags. 'My car's just here.'

'If you ever need me for anything, just call,' said Jürgen. 'Any time, day or night.' He brushed his lips against her cheek, then stepped back.

'I will,' said Charlotte, a wave of sadness washing over her. She loaded up the boot, got into the car and listened to the sound of Jürgen's departure. As the roar faded, she leant on the headrest and closed her eyes for several minutes.

CHAPTER 44

JULY TURNED TO AUGUST, THEN SEPTEMBER. THEY'D FINALLY managed five days at a converted farmhouse in Umbria, Dom adamant that he couldn't afford more time away from work. Alastair and Robson loved it, especially the kidney-shaped pool and the friendly Italian waitress, Graziella, who served their favourite gnocchi with pesto every lunchtime.

In the evenings, they sat outside on the tiny private patio and played card and board games. Dom did his best to put on a show of unity, but Charlotte struggled to do the same. He often wandered off to make a phone call, but she no longer questioned who he was calling, particularly as she'd texted Jürgen several times. Nothing more than chatty, innocuous messages, which Charlotte told herself were no different to her exchanges with Ruth. But deep down, she knew their bond ran deeper than friendship.

With the boys back at school, time weighed heavily on Charlotte's hands. She saw Sadie and Pamela for the odd coffee and catch-up, and tried to fit in a walk at least three times a week. She deliberately kept her distance from Alicia, uncomfortable with the knowledge that she had about Dom.

It appeared she had persuaded her daughter Jennifer to stay, as Charlotte saw her frequently, hanging out in the school grounds with her band of mini-skirted friends.

In October, Sadie suggested their families went to the Montreux Palace together on Christmas Day. Charlotte laughed in surprise. 'That's two months away! I haven't even got my head around what to do for Halloween, never mind Christmas.'

'Trust me, if you don't book now, you'll be lucky to get a table.' Sadie flicked through her phone and brought up a series of photos of herself, Rick, Miranda and Louise seated round a beautifully decorated table, all sporting Santa hats. 'We went last year for the first time and loved it. A bloody enormous buffet serving everything you can imagine, and — get this — an entire room devoted to cheese, desserts and an enormous chocolate fountain.'

Charlotte mentioned it to Dom, who blanched at the price but told her to go ahead, if that was what she wanted. Alastair and Robson's eyes lit up with glee at the mention of the dessert room, and the idea that they could eat as much as they wanted. For Charlotte, spending the day with another family would dilute the ever-present tension between herself and Dom. Not to mention giving her a break from cooking and cleaning up afterwards.

At Dom's insistence, they went on another couple of nights out with his work colleagues. He didn't mention Amelie, and Charlotte's relief when she didn't show up was palpable. Perhaps she'd left the company, or moved some-where else? What struck Charlotte as strange was that no one else mentioned her either. And Charlotte couldn't help feeling that Antoine and Juliette acted a little awkwardly around her, compared to their warmth and friendliness before.

In the run-up to Christmas, Dom announced that he had

to spend a few days in Zurich. 'Look,' he said pointedly, opening his laptop and gesturing to an agenda of meetings and presentations.

'Will *she* be there?' The words came out before Charlotte could stop them.

'You have to get over this, Charlotte.' Dom slammed the laptop lid down and faced her. 'It's like a bloody elephant in the room, and I don't know how much more of your attitude I can take.'

'*My* attitude?' Charlotte glowered back at him. 'I'm not the one who confessed to kissing someone else.'

'I said I was sorry.' Dom puffed his cheeks out in exasperation. 'And no, she won't be there. You have my word.'

'And your word means such a lot, doesn't it?' Charlotte hissed in response. Unbidden, an image of Amelie blown up to elephant size and pirouetting round the room in a tutu filled her mind. She giggled, and Dom looked at her as if she'd flipped her lid.

With Dom out of the way, Charlotte relaxed a little. She didn't know how to fix her marriage — or if she even wanted to — but the boys deserved a wonderful Christmas.

With the tree already up, and brunch for eight booked at the Palace, all that remained was to pick up a few presents for the boys. Charlotte had ordered stuff online, but she always enjoyed browsing through a toy department for quirky bits and pieces. What could she do with Alastair and Robson, though? They were on holiday now till early January, and Charlotte balked at asking Sadie to have them again. Perhaps... She found Jürgen's number and rang him.

'Hello, Charlotte. How lovely to hear from you.' His warm voice wrapped around Charlotte like a comforting blanket. 'I hope you're well.'

'I'm good,' Charlotte replied. 'And you?'

'Fighting a head cold, but nothing serious.' Jürgen coughed and apologised.

'I wondered if Marcus might be free this afternoon to babysit the boys. Just for a few hours, while I do some Christmas shopping in Lausanne.'

'Give me a second.' Charlotte heard the phone being put down and muffled voices in the background. A moment later, Jürgen returned. 'Marcus would be delighted to babysit. I can bring him over, say around two o'clock?'

'Perfect,' replied Charlotte. 'I'll give them lunch and maybe Marcus can help them build a snowman.' There'd been a decent snowfall overnight. Not enough to put Charlotte off driving — the Swiss were super-efficient at clearing the roads, with the ploughs out around 5 am.

'He will love that,' said Jürgen, giving a throaty chuckle. 'We will see you soon.'

* * *

WHEN JÜRGEN ASKED if he could accompany Charlotte on her shopping trip, she didn't hesitate to say yes. Leaving the boys and Marcus pelting each other with snowballs, they set off in Jürgen's car. He'd insisted on driving, and Charlotte relished being in the powerful machine once more, although this time with the heating cranked up to the max.

Wandering around the toy section of Globus, Charlotte picked up some packs of Playmobil figurines and browsed through a stack of jigsaw puzzles.

'I adored jigsaws when I was younger,' said Jürgen. 'There is something very soothing about spreading out all the pieces and making them into a complete picture.'

Charlotte added one featuring characters from one of the boys' favourite Disney films. 'I did a thousand-piece one when

I was pregnant with Alastair. Some old Dutch artist's painting; I can't remember the name now. It took me ages, and I ended up having it framed because I couldn't bear to take it apart.'

'Yes, it's sad when you finish it only to pack it all away again.' Jürgen tucked a colourful 500-piece puzzle featuring a bustling Swiss village market under his arm. 'I will revisit my youth one evening, when Marcus is bored with keeping his old father company.'

After picking up some wrapping paper and gift tags, they ended the outing with coffee and cake in a nearby café. With outdoor heaters providing warmth, they huddled round a circular table, watching shoppers dart past laden with bags.

'You seem happier,' said Jürgen, stirring sugar into his espresso. 'Are things better between you and your husband?'

Charlotte met his steady gaze, filled with concern and tenderness. When had Dom last looked at her in that way? His recent expressions had shown guilt, frustration and defensiveness more than any fondness or desire.

'No, not really.' Charlotte tipped the small pot of coffee cream into her cup and stirred vigorously. 'I feel like I'm adrift at sea and the only person who can save me is myself. Which is a bloody terrifying thought, to be honest.'

Before she could take a sip of her drink, Jürgen shuffled his chair closer, and reached towards Charlotte. A buzzing in Charlotte's brain replaced the buzz of the street as he inched closer, his lips seemingly aiming for hers. Their mouths connected, the heat of the exchange spreading from her head to her toes. The world faded to black, all thoughts of Dom banished by the kiss. *Oh my God, we're kissing!*

Charlotte pulled away, a hot wave of shame replacing the excitement of kissing another man. Not just any man, but Jürgen. Her friend, someone she relied on, the man Pamela insisted had forced himself upon her—

'How dare you!' Charlotte hissed across the table. 'How

could you take advantage of me when I'm vulnerable? Then again, it isn't the first time, is it?' She ignored the sneering voice saying that she'd agreed, not willing to process that she'd crossed a line. A line which made her no better than Dom.

'I'm so sorry, Charlotte, I didn't mean... I was trying to... your hair.' White-faced, Jürgen pointed to the right side of Charlotte's head. Puzzled, she ran her fingers through her hair and a fragment of silver tinsel fell into her lap. She gazed at it, recalling that she had brushed past the beautifully deco-rated tree beside the Globus doorway as they left.

'I noticed it before, but it looked pretty sparkling in your hair,' said Jürgen. 'Then I thought you might not appreciate it being there. I was just...'

Charlotte twiddled the tinsel around her middle finger. Jürgen hadn't instigated the kiss; she had. Although he hadn't exactly objected.

'Charlotte, what did you mean when you said that it wasn't the first time?' Jürgen gazed at her, hurt all over his face.

'Pamela said you'd hit on her at a school event months ago,' stuttered Charlotte.

Jürgen looked as stunned as if Charlotte had slapped him hard on the cheek. 'I would never hit a woman. I don't understand what you are talking about.'

'No, not *hit*, not physically. She claimed you'd tried to kiss her against her will.'

Charlotte watched realisation dawn on Jürgen's face. He gave a sad smile that tugged at Charlotte's insides. 'I do not like to speak ill of anyone, Charlotte, but I'm afraid the oppo-site is true. Pamela tried to kiss me — I gave her no encour-agement — and I moved away immediately. That is the truth.'

Charlotte wished she could rewind the last few minutes. Not only had she kissed Jürgen, she'd accused him of forcing himself upon Pamela. Something she'd always known couldn't be true. If stupidity were an Olympic sport, she'd be a shoo-in for a gold medal.

'I'm sorry.' Charlotte stared at Jürgen, willing him to meet her eyes. He didn't, his attention focused on fumbling in his pocket.

'I think I'd better take you home.' He produced his car key, and they left the café, the silence between them almost unbearable.

CHAPTER 45

THE FESTIVE SEASON PASSED WITHOUT INCIDENT. ALASTAIR and Robson relished returning to school in January, excited to begin their weekly ski lessons. After a week off work Dom headed back to the office, with several trips to Zurich and the UK lined up. Charlotte had detected a shift in his mood and behaviour over the holidays. He was more affectionate towards her, even attempting to instigate sex on several occasions. She turned away every time, her mind and body unwilling to co-operate.

No matter how hard Charlotte tried, Jürgen occupied her thoughts more than was healthy. She still saw him regularly at school, but neither of them mentioned meeting up again. Her cheeks still flamed with embarrassment whenever she remembered the kiss, and her unfounded accusation regarding Pamela.

'Should I say something to her?' Charlotte asked Ruth, having related the whole sorry story during one of their chats.

'Hon, I wouldn't bother. Sounds to me as if she wanted to get back at her cheating husband and thought locking lips with your hunky German would do the trick. When he didn't play ball, she relieved her hurt feelings by spreading nasty rumours about him.'

'He's not *my* hunky German,' Charlotte said indignantly. 'I told you: we're friends, and the kiss was just a misunderstanding.'

Ruth snorted derisively before standing up and stretching with a groan. 'Yep, your lips accidentally collided. Happens all the time. Oops, didn't mean to snog you.'

Charlotte laughed at Ruth's gigantic bump, now dominating the screen. With the baby due any day now, she'd ballooned over recent weeks and complained of constant backache and heartburn. 'It wasn't a snog, anyway. I'm a married woman, in case you've forgotten.'

Ruth slumped back into her chair and pursed her lips. 'Hmm, you say that darling Dom has been unusually lovey-dovey of late. That's often a sign of guilt, in my humble opinion. And you've said many times you don't feel the same way about him anymore. Now, is that solely because of his dalliance with the French tart, or because you have feelings for Jürgen?'

Charlotte hesitated before answering. The two were intertwined, but in a chicken-and-egg way. Which had come first? Her misgivings about Dom, or those feelings she had tried and failed to push away?

'Charlotte, how long have we known each other? I can read you like a bloody book, woman, and my epilogue demands a happy ever after. With whom remains to be seen, but when you mention Dom your face does this.' Ruth tugged the corners of her mouth down. 'Jürgen, on the other hand — well, it's like you've been plugged into the National Grid. I'd fly over right now and give you a kick up the arse, but no airline would take me and I can barely see my feet these days.'

Desperate to change the subject, Charlotte related a funny story from their Christmas Day visit to the Montreux Palace. 'So, Alastair heads off to the pasta section, his heart set on a mountain of spaghetti carbonara. Two minutes later he's back, proudly places the plate on the table, and ... we all stare at it.'

'Go on,' urged Ruth. 'Did it look disgusting, or something?'

Charlotte shook her head. 'There was nothing on the plate except some residual steam. Alastair looked totally baffled until we heard a scream and a loud bang a few feet away.'

'Oh God, he'd dropped the pasta?' said Ruth, clamping her hand to her mouth.

'Yup. And a poor waitress stepped right in it and fell on her arse. It was bedlam, with staff rushing around making sure she was OK and mopping up the mess. I half-expected someone to point the finger at us and sue us for her injuries.'

Both Charlotte and Ruth convulsed into giggles, once Charlotte explained that the only injury was to the waitress's pride. 'Needless to say, Alastair decided against pasta and settled for a less slippery helping of turkey with all the trimmings.'

'And speaking of slippery, you need to decide what to do about your snake of a husband. Don't be one of those women who sticks it out for the sake of the kids while her own happiness dribbles down the toilet.'

Ruth was right, but Charlotte felt like the cowardly lion in *The Wizard of Oz*. She desperately needed courage, but didn't know how to find it.

CHAPTER 46

THE DOORBELL DISTURBED CHARLOTTE'S ATTEMPTS TO REMOVE the hard water stains in the bathroom sink. Cursing under her breath, she squirted more product on to the stubborn rings and dried her hands.

As she wasn't expecting any visitors, Charlotte sported ancient jogging pants and a vest top with a bleach stain. She quickly retied her unwashed hair with a bobble and checked the mirror in case her face was smeared with muck.

Whoever it was, they were persistent. 'I'm coming!' yelled Charlotte, clumping down the stairs that were next on her list for a mopping.

Opening the door, Charlotte gasped. Of all the people she might have imagined, the vision of wintry loveliness before her was right at the bottom of the list.

'Hello, Charlotte,' said Amelie. 'I hope I haven't disturbed you.' She looked Charlotte up and down, her pert nose wrinkling in disdain at Charlotte's house-cleaning ensemble. By contrast, Amelie looked like she'd stepped off the set of a *Dr Zhivago* remake. She wore an enormous furry hat, coupled with a deep purple military-style coat and a thick woollen scarf in shades of blue that emphasised her heavily mascaraed eyes.

'Just doing a bit of cleaning,' said Charlotte. 'I'm afraid Dom's not here. He's at the office if you need to see him urgently.' She kept the door ajar, unwilling to let Amelie inside.

'Yes, he's in back-to-back meetings all day,' said Amelie, tugging off her hat. Her glossy blonde hair cascaded over her shoulders like a shampoo advert, and Charlotte's dislike of the younger woman rose another notch. Whenever Charlotte took off a hat, her hair remained flattened to her skull. 'It's you I want to talk to.'

Despite the queasy feeling in the pit of her stomach, Charlotte gestured for Amelie to come in. This obviously wasn't a social call, and if it ended in a cat fight, she would prefer the neighbours not to witness it.

'Can I get you a tea or a coffee?' *Or a mug of hemlock?* Charlotte led Amelie through to the kitchen and filled the kettle.

'Nothing for me, thank you.' Amelie took a seat, undoing her coat and crossing her legs demurely at the ankle. 'I'll get to the point, Charlotte. I know you've had suspicions for a while, and I think it's time you heard the truth. Dom and I... We're in a relationship.' She tossed the sentence across the room as casually as a child throwing a ball to a friend, but there was nothing playful about her demeanour. Amelie's countenance screamed smugness and jubilation.

Needles of anger stabbed at Charlotte, and she switched off the part-boiled kettle. 'And you thought I needed to hear it directly from you? How incredibly thoughtful of you, Amelie. Do you make a habit of screwing other women's husbands and then popping around to put them in the picture?' The needles of anger gathered strength, and Charlotte banged the table with her fist. 'Does he know you're here?'

Amelie's defiant look wilted at Charlotte's words. 'No, he doesn't. He's been — how shall I say — avoiding me recently. Not replying to my texts, and keeping his distance at the office. But I know it's only because he's afraid of losing his children. He's told me many times that he only stays with you for their sake.'

'How very noble of him,' retorted Charlotte. 'So what you're saying is that Dom's broken up with you, and you're here out of sheer vindictiveness. What a lovely person you are, Amelie.'

Her nemesis scowled, tapping her immaculately polished nails on the table. 'He just needs time to work things out. He says he loves me and he wants to be with me. You can't cling on to a man who doesn't want you any more.'

That, to Charlotte, sounded exactly what Amelie was trying to do. And it was what she herself had tried to do from the start, knowing deep down that their marriage was falling apart. But she felt little sympathy for Amelie.

'My darling husband assured me not so long ago that you'd done nothing more than kiss, and that it was all a mistake. I'm assuming he was lying through his back teeth?'

Amelie's top lip curled in a sneer worthy of Elvis at his finest. 'I can assure you that we've done *much* more than kiss. Your naivety is surprising, Charlotte. Although Dom did say — ah, such a funny English expression — you are not the sharpest tool in the box.' She gave a tinkling laugh which made Charlotte want to hunt out Dom's toolbox and select the sharpest object she could find.

'You really are a poisonous bitch, Amelie, and I sincerely hope that karma bites you hard on your bony little arse one day. Now get out of my house, before I do something I might regret.' Charlotte waited as Amelie took an eternity to button up her coat, put on her hat and get to her feet. A huge part of her wanted to grab the twisted cow by her scarf and drag her to the door, but an assault charge wasn't something Charlotte needed right now.

Amelie paused in the hallway, her pretty features distorted into a mask of malevolence. 'One day you'll thank me. Because Dom will come to his senses and realise that what we have is special.'

Charlotte recalled Amelie's words after the party. 'I thought he was too old for you. Or was that just a smoke-screen designed to steer poor dumb Charlotte down a blind alley?' Amelie had been toying with Charlotte, a kitten with pointy claws dead set on getting what she wanted.

'What he lacks in youth he makes up in energy,' said Amelie, hastily backing through the door and slamming it behind her.

Amelie drove off, her brakes squealing as she negotiated the sharp bend at the bottom of the driveway. Charlotte imagined her misjudging the turn and her horror as the car careened towards the neighbouring vineyards, flipping over and exploding in a ball of flame. 'Oh, your mistress?' Charlotte would say casually when Dom returned home. 'She's toast, darling. Came around for a cosy chat, but ended up burned to a frazzle. Tragic. Now, can you pack your bags and get out of my fucking sight?'

That thought made Charlotte laugh; a hollow, bitter laugh as she replayed the entire surreal encounter. She considered ringing Dom, but if he was in meetings, he'd be unlikely to answer. Was Amelie on her way to the office now, ready to tell her lover that the whole messy charade was over?

Mopping forgotten, Charlotte took a hot shower to wash away the dirt of her labours. What she couldn't eradicate so easily was the riot of emotions ricocheting around her head.

He only stays with you for the children's sake.

You can't cling on to a man who doesn't want you any more.

Towelling herself dry, Charlotte put the pieces of the whole sorry affair together. Dom had been lying throughout, if Amelie was telling the truth, but recently he appeared to have developed cold feet. That was hardly surprising, if Amelie had behaved in the calculating, controlling way she'd just witnessed. Did that mean it was all over between them, even if Amelie didn't see it that way? And did that make a difference to *her*? Dragging a comb through her hair, Charlotte looked in the mirror and didn't like what she saw. A bitter, defeated woman who'd thrown all her vitriol at Amelie when — truth be told — Dom was hardly the hapless victim. *He* was the one who'd consistently lied, putting his family life in jeopardy. Amelie might be a shit-stirring piece of work, but she at least was single.

Charlotte sat up straighter. Was she going to remain a doormat forever, or was now the time to act? *Not the sharpest tool in the box?* Dom was about to discover that his wife's days of being a blunt object were over.

CHAPTER 47

THE DAY BEFORE THE BOYS' SKI TRIP, AND CHARLOTTE'S stomach felt tighter than a drum skin. She'd been so, so tempted to boot Dom's cheating arse out immediately, but decided to play it out a little longer.

Ruth had finally given birth to a baby boy, weighing in at a whopping ten pounds. 'Jeez, hon, now I know what they mean when giving birth is described as being like squeezing a bowling ball out of your nostril!' she said, pulling an agonised face. 'I was sucking on that gas like a madwoman, and poor Simon got a mouthful of abuse every time he tried to say something encouraging.'

After cooing over pink-faced, hairless Jacob — 'he looks like an alien, bless him,' Ruth said adoringly as she dangled him in front of the camera — Charlotte related the Amelie incident.

'And you still haven't spoken to him?' said Ruth. 'It must be like living with a ticking time bomb.'

'The boys go on their ski trip tomorrow,' said Charlotte. 'I need them out of the way before I can talk to Dom. But what

I don't get is why he hasn't cracked by now. Surely Amelie would have told him she'd been here — or is it really all over between them?' Charlotte doubted Amelie would quit without a fight. She struck Charlotte as someone used to getting her own way.

'Even if it is over, do you want to stay with him?' Ruth grimaced as Jacob latched on to her breast. 'Who's to say he won't cheat again, or be worn down by that bloody bitch? I mean, if they're still working at the same place, he can't avoid her all the time. Ouch, you little bugger, that hurts!'

The next day Charlotte stood with the rest of the mums and dads, waiting to wave off the coachloads of excited children. Alastair and Robson had proudly packed their own boot bags and suitcases, Charlotte assisting with a school-supplied list of essentials.

'They'll have a fantastic time,' said Sadie, double-checking Miranda's backpack for sunscreen. 'The food's great at the hostel, and they do loads of fun activities in the evenings. Mind you, the younger ones are usually knackered by 9pm after a full day on the slopes.'

Charlotte blew kisses at the boys as their coach started up. Alastair returned the gesture, but Robson had his back to the window. She turned to leave and almost collided with Jürgen.

'Hello, stranger,' he said. Sadness filled his eyes, and Charlotte felt awful for not replying to his recent texts. Filled with kindness and concern for her well-being, without directly asking about Dom. Humiliation still coursed through her when she remembered the kiss, and her reaction to it.

'Hi, Jürgen.' She moved a few steps away from Sadie, now chatting to another mum, and he followed. 'Listen, I'm so sorry for everything. What happened, and for ignoring you. I've just … well, it hasn't been an easy time.'

Jürgen raised a hand to wave at Marcus as the senior students' bus pulled out of the courtyard. Charlotte waved too, smiling at the young man's enthusiastic response.

'You don't have to tell me anything,' said Jürgen. 'I just hope we are still friends, Charlotte. I've missed you.'

'I've missed you too,' she whispered. Her dread of the conversation with Dom that lay ahead, and the contrast of Jürgen's constant kindness, brought unwanted tears to her eyes.

'Coffee?' Jürgen took Charlotte's arm and steered her towards the parking area. 'Or something stronger? I have a very fine brandy at my apartment, if you prefer to go somewhere private.'

Charlotte smiled, wiping away a stray tear. 'It's nine thirty in the morning, Jürgen. A little early to hit the booze, but a coffee would be lovely.'

Agreeing to follow him in her own car, Charlotte noticed Pamela giving them the evil eye. Out of sheer devilment, Charlotte hooked her arm through Jürgen's. Pamela's eyebrows rocketed north, and she stomped off in the other direction.

Jürgen's apartment was warm and homely, and much smaller than Charlotte had pictured. He gave her a quick tour, and Charlotte was pleased to see a well-stocked bookcase and a gleaming kitchen. After Jürgen had made coffee with a high-tech machine that boggled Charlotte's mind, they moved into the lounge. Settled on a comfy sofa, she hesitated for a second when Jürgen produced a bottle of Rémy Martin. He poured two small measures, and Charlotte took a grateful sip.

'Now, I am guessing that something has happened regarding your husband. You said before that you were at a crossroads. Do you know now which way to go?'

Jürgen's turn of phrase often amused Charlotte. Not in a funny ha-ha way, more that he said things differently. Probably because he wasn't a native English speaker, but it was just one of the endearing things about him. One of the *many* reasons to like him.

'Yes, I do.' Charlotte swirled the brandy round the crystal balloon glass. 'It's over.' She hadn't said the words before, out loud or in her head, but saying them now felt right. Saying them to Dom… Well, she'd cross that bridge this evening.

'I'm sorry. We seem to say that a lot to each other, don't we?' Jürgen raised his glass, and Charlotte clinked hers against it.

'To the end of a marriage.' She shook her head. 'Not exactly a cause for celebration, is it? Ten years down the drain, because my husband slept with another woman.' She filled Jürgen in as quickly as she could on Amelie's visit, her revelation — hardly a shocker — that they'd been sleeping together, and Dom's recently altered behaviour. Charlotte omitted the cruel comment about her own intelligence. She might not be a candidate for Mensa, but she didn't care. She was taking charge.

'To the future.' Jürgen raised his glass again, his voice strong and filling Charlotte with positivity. She would need that by the bucketload to get through the coming hours, weeks and months. 'Change is hard, because it requires a strength we do not always believe we have. But you have that strength, Charlotte. I knew it from the first moment I met you. I know you don't believe it, but it's true.'

'But what if I let him talk me round? What if Dom falls to his knees and begs for a second chance?' Charlotte's voice quavered, her steely determination side-swiped by the image of a contrite Dom pleading for forgiveness.

Jürgen gathered up the untouched coffees and left the room. When he returned, he sat next to Charlotte on the sofa. He was close enough for her to feel the heat from his body, yet far enough away that an outsider would suspect nothing amiss. Nevertheless, her head was spinning, and she couldn't blame two mouthfuls of brandy.

'Charlotte.' Her name hung in the air, his emphasis on the second syllable sending goosebumps up and down her arms. 'I cannot interfere in your life. You are one of the most engaging, attractive women I have ever met. But I cannot influence what you do. I do not condone infidelity, but sometimes the heart wants what it shouldn't.'

Hours from telling her husband that their marriage was over, Charlotte couldn't deny the attraction between herself and Jürgen any longer. It shimmered in the air, an electrical charge of pent-up emotions. But they couldn't act upon it, even though Charlotte saw her longing reflected in Jürgen's eyes.

'I have to go.' She got unsteadily to her feet, the shakiness down to what lay ahead and what she knew she had to walk away from.

'Charlotte.' Before she could take a step, Jürgen rose and wrapped his arms around her. She stiffened for a moment, then accepted the steadying embrace. She inhaled his musky aftershave and buried her face in his chest. The rhythmic thump-thump of his heartbeat helped her own to find a calmer pace. They stood like that for what seemed an eternity, but could only have been a few minutes.

Finally, Jürgen released Charlotte, planting a tender kiss on the top of her head. 'You will be OK.' It wasn't a question. 'I'm here if you need me. At the end of the phone, ready to fetch you if you need to escape. With no strings, Charlotte.'

He walked her to the apartment door, and she paused. A huge part of her wanted to stay, and not have to face the ordeal ahead. Then Charlotte looked at Jürgen. Her very own

Wizard of Oz, giving her — no, *showing* her — that she had all the courage she needed.

'You're smiling again.' Jürgen ran the back of his hand gently across her cheek. 'That is good. Keep smiling, Charlotte. And be brave.'

Five minutes later, driving home, Charlotte realised she was still smiling.

CHAPTER 48

'Honey, I'm home!' Dom's recent attempts to sound like a jocular husband from some excruciating fifties American sitcom set Charlotte's teeth on edge. She imagined removing her starched gingham apron and drawing the strings tight around his neck, his last vision a pyramid of lovingly baked cupcakes.

'Did you have a good day?' Charlotte dribbled virgin olive oil and balsamic vinegar over the salad she'd prepared.

'Not bad. We're looking at opening up two new stores in Switzerland. Early days, but profits are on the up in the existing ones.' Dom nabbed a cherry tomato and popped it into his mouth. 'Any word from the boys?'

Charlotte shook her head. Although several of their classmates had mobile phones, she and Dom didn't see the need yet. There was plenty of time for them to get sucked into the black hole of social media, selfies and one-upmanship.

'I had a visitor the other day.' Charlotte tossed a handful of toasted pine nuts into the salad. Dom looked at her quizzically, but a telltale twitch beneath his right eye told her what she needed to know. 'It was Amelie. What a delightful young woman she is, Dom. I can see why you'd be attracted to her. Want to kiss her, in fact. Except you did a lot more than that, didn't you?'

Dom's twitch intensified. Charlotte took a vegetable knife from the rack and chopped half a cucumber with deadly precision. With each slice, she pictured parts of her husband's anatomy tumbling to the floor in a bloody heap.

'She told me she came here,' Dom stammered, watching Charlotte's rhythmic slicing. 'I'd said it was over between us — me and Amelie — not that it was ever more than a stupid infatuation on my part. The stupid cow only did it to force my hand, sweetheart. Please believe me. I got carried away and I'll regret it for the rest of my life.'

Charlotte scattered the cucumber slices over the salad. Poached salmon with a tarragon sauce was resting in the fridge to complete the meal. The Last Supper. Complete with Judas, the man who'd vowed to forsake all others but betrayed his wife repeatedly.

'You've lied to me right from the start.' Charlotte set the food out on the table. 'It's been going on since before we moved here, hasn't it? And I swallowed every word like the idiot I am.' Before Dom could interrupt, Charlotte raised a silencing hand. 'Amelie said you'd described me as not the sharpest tool in the box. That stung like hell. But she was right, in a way. It's taken me far too long to face the fact our marriage is over. Because it is, Dom.'

'Sweetheart, don't say that. Please. We can fix this, I know we can.' Panic swamped Dom's features, his eyes wide with disbelief.

Charlotte almost laughed at his reaction. Did he really expect her to carry on as if nothing had happened? She only had his word that the affair was over. For all Charlotte knew, his avoidance of Amelie was only temporary. Given time, she'd lure him back with the promise of magical sex, and Dom would revert to his old cheating ways.

'Do you still love me?' She blurted out the question, knowing the answer would change nothing.

For a moment Dom didn't reply. He gave a tiny shrug, as if Charlotte had asked whether he would prefer red or white wine with dinner. 'Of course I do. We've had a bumpy patch, but we'll get through it. Splitting up isn't an option, not least because of the boys.'

Charlotte looked at the man she'd thought she'd grow old with, and the tension she'd borne over recent months melted away. Starting afresh as a single mother scared her, but staying unhappily married terrified her even more.

'Children aren't glue, Dom.' She looked at the untouched food, her appetite gone but her resolve rock solid. 'Alastair and Robson will still have parents who love them. Even if they live in different countries.'

'Charlotte, please don't do this.' Dom's eyes shone with tears. He hardly ever cried. She recalled him welling up at both the boys births, and once during a silly movie, but that was it. 'Let's talk some more and figure this out.'

Charlotte picked up her plate of salmon, covered it in clingfilm, and placed it in the fridge. 'Enjoy your dinner; I'll be in the lounge watching TV. When you've finished, I'd appreciate it if you'd pack some things and go as soon as possible.'

* * *

CHARLOTTE HAD no idea what she was watching, but it involved lots of swearing, weeping and door banging. She stuffed handfuls of paprika crisps into her mouth, hunger dictating that she ate something. Upstairs, Dom clattered around. He'd popped in three times begging to talk, but Charlotte waved him away.

'Where am I supposed to go?' His earlier contrition now carried an edge of wounded bitterness.

'To Amelie. To Zurich. To the moon. I really don't care.' Charlotte licked crisp crumbs off her fingers. Her phone lay next to her on the couch. A message from Jürgen had arrived minutes before: *Are you OK?* She hadn't replied yet.

'When did you turn into such a cold-hearted bitch?' Dom loomed over Charlotte, the face she'd once adored distorted with anger.

'Oh, around the time I realised you were a philandering git. Now leave me alone before I call your parents. I'm sure they'd *love* to know what their darling boy's been up to.'

Charlotte knew that Torquil and Jean would side with Dom, and blame her for driving him into another woman's arms. She'd leave it up to Dom to break the news. Her own parents would be upset, but they'd support Charlotte and the boys one hundred per cent. Financially, too, if necessary. Charlotte had no idea whether Dom would make life difficult for her in that respect, but she'd deal with whatever he threw at her.

For the next two hours, Dom swung from begging for forgiveness to accusing Charlotte of judging him too harshly. She wanted to stick her fingers in her ears and shout, 'Not listening'. Eventually he left her alone, and reappeared half an hour later with a wheeled suitcase. 'Right, I'm off. I'll let you sleep on it, and hopefully you'll see sense in the morning.' Dom hopped from foot to foot, convinced he had the upper hand.

'I've already seen sense,' said Charlotte. 'A night's sleep won't change anything.'

Dom banged the front door shut with such force that the windows rattled. Charlotte waited till his car drove away, then made herself a gin and tonic with considerably more gin than tonic. She returned to the sofa, pulling a plaid throw over her legs. Taking a restorative mouthful, she fired off a text to Ruth.

Sent Dom packing, although he doesn't believe I'm serious. A bit shaky (a large gin's helping) but there's no going back. Lots to sort out, obviously, but the first step feels good. Big hugs xxxx

Ruth's reply came within minutes.

Go girl! Don't let the bastard wear you down. Here whenever you need me, any time of day or night. Nights are actually great because Jacob isn't a big fan of sleeping more than an hour at a time. Have another gin for me (bloody bollocking breastfeeding) xxxx

Charlotte chuckled and stretched out with her feet on the coffee table. So much to think about— not least telling the boys — but she allowed herself to imagine a shiny new future. Well, not *entirely* new. She hoped they could return to the old family home, at least for now, and prayed that the boys' school would have places for them. She'd look for a job too; something that fitted around school hours.

A huge yawn took Charlotte by surprise. She finished her drink and took the empty glass to the kitchen. Before she headed upstairs, she picked up her phone again. She opened the message from Jürgen, and typed:

Yes, I'm OK x

CHAPTER 49

'It's a cryin' shame,' said Hugh, loading up his dispenser with another roll of tape.

'It is that,' replied Des, bubble-wrapping a pile of dinner plates and soup bowls. 'Barely been here five minutes, and they're off again.'

'Well, the missus is off again. The boss said — on the quiet, like — they'd split up because the husband did the dirty on her. Jeez, and with two young boys and all. Some blokes don't know what side their bread's buttered on.'

'True, true.' Des finished the wrapping and moved on to serving platters and random pieces of china. 'She's a real looker, I'll say that. I wouldn't kick her out of bed for eating crisps—'

'Thanks for the compliment.' Charlotte gave a mock-stern look at Dump It. He blushed like a teenager caught looking at a porn channel, and grunted an apology.

'No offence taken. Now, I've hung up most of our clothes on the wardrobe thingies, shoved lots of stuff in the boxes you gave me, and stuck stickies on everything that stays. So please don't dismantle kitchen blinds, or take down curtains that belong to the house.'

Charlotte swept out of the room with all the grace she could muster. Inside, she didn't know whether to laugh or cry. She'd done a lot of the latter recently. Less than a year after moving to Switzerland, she was homeward bound. Except this time, four had become three.

Moving to the master bedroom, she perched on the edge of the marital bed. It was freshly made, with her favourite seersucker duvet cover and pristine Egyptian cotton sheets that had cost a fortune. Not that it had been the marital bed for a while; not since Dom had moved out. And Charlotte had resisted all his pleas for a second chance, accompanied by lavish bouquets of flowers, handwritten notes begging for forgiveness and late-night texts filled with vomit-inducing emojis.

Charlotte opened the bedside cabinet drawer. Dom's side, with a fine film of dust coating its surface. He'd cleared out most of his stuff over the past two weeks, while Charlotte hid at Sadie's with the boys.

Nestled inside the drawer was one of his collections of cufflinks, most of which had been gifts from Charlotte. She flipped open the small leather case and touched each pair. Miniature golf clubs — not that he'd played since moving to Switzerland; *I ♥ You Daddy* enamel ones gifted by the boys one birthday, and personalised wooden ones with the initials C and D, which Charlotte had bought him for their fifth wedding anniversary. She bit back a laugh which was half sob. Wood to symbolise solidity and durability. What a pathetic joke that was now. Charlotte took the box downstairs and stuffed it in her handbag, lest Hump It or Dump it pack it away with the other bedroom items.

'Fancy a brew?' she called out to the dynamic duo. Hearing affirmative grunts, Charlotte boiled the kettle and popped tea bags into three mugs. She dreaded picking up Alastair and Robson later, on what was their last day at school. Charlotte expected tears, mainly from herself and Sadie. While undoubtedly sad to say goodbye to their new friends, the boys were excited to return to their old school.

For now, they were moving back into the family home, until she and Dom figured out the divorce details and financial settlement. They'd found replacement tenants for the Swiss house to avoid being hit with rent for the rest of the contract, and fortuitously, their UK tenants had found a place to buy and had moved out two weeks ago. The entire divorce process made Charlotte feel physically sick, but Ruth had counselled her not to rush into agreeing to anything. 'Simon's got a hotshot lawyer friend who's happy to check things over when you get to that point,' she said. 'Dom's not exactly strapped for cash, and after ten years and two kids you deserve more than your fair share, hon.'

Delivering the tea and a packet of Ginger Nuts to Hugh and Des, Charlotte wandered outside. She shivered, glad of her cardigan and thick socks. A dusting of snow still topped the Alps, achingly beautiful with a blanket of low-lying clouds hugging their jagged peaks. At least the boys had got a ski season in, and their ski trip to Morzine in France. As they were both smitten with the sport, Charlotte had done some research and found a dry ski slope complex half an hour away in the UK. Alastair and Robson needn't hang up their skis and poles just yet, and Charlotte even contemplated giving it another go herself. *Be brave*; that's what Jürgen had said. Her heart lurched at the realisation she'd probably never see him again, unless she bumped into him at school today. Charlotte hoped she didn't. Some things were never meant to be, but she'd always treasure their friendship. Damn it, she knew that what they had went further than friendship. That kiss remained etched on her soul, as did the regret of how she'd misjudged and falsely accused him.

In two days, Dom would drive Charlotte and the boys to Geneva Airport to make the journey home. The prospect didn't thrill Charlotte, but she couldn't deny the boys the chance to say goodbye to their dad. He'd visit them, and they'd fly back to Switzerland during school breaks. Charlotte or Dom would have to accompany them because of their ages, but Sadie had offered her a bed whenever she wanted. As long as Charlotte didn't have to see Amelie — or as little of her as possible — she could cope. Knowing that woman would be part of the boys' lives made her sick to the core, but relationship break-ups came with complications. Charlotte didn't want Alastair and Robson to hate Amelie, but not really liking her would suffice. Anyway, a long-lasting relationship between Dom and Amelie didn't seem all that likely.

Checking that Hump It and Dump It had everything under control, Charlotte grabbed her coat from a peg in the hallway. She needed some space before the school pickup, time to psyche herself up for what lay ahead.

As Charlotte walked by the lake, her breath puffed out in icy plumes. The weather could turn dramatically here, with early signs of spring already appearing. Tentative buds were peeping out on tree branches, and crocuses and daffodils were nudging their way through the earth. She took a few photos, promising that one day, when she felt strong enough, she'd create an album of memories for Alastair and Robson.

After treating herself to a hot chocolate and a cinnamon-dusted waffle, Charlotte set off for the school. A heavy weight lay in her stomach, and she drove slowly, trying to focus on the positives ahead. For one, she couldn't wait to be close to Ruth again. Then she could hold Jacob in her arms and inhale his newly minted scent, all talcum powder and milk and those other unidentifiable baby smells.

'Simon changes nappies!' Ruth's patent disbelief that a man — *anyone* — could muster the courage to remove a steaming pile of baby poo was only matched by her adoration of someone willing to give up the TV remote. 'And he lets me watch *my* stuff. No arguing if the footie's on, or whatever bollocks most men are glued to. Nope, he strolls off with Jacob strapped to his divinely hairy chest while I lie back and channel-hop to my heart's content.'

Funny how both Charlotte and Ruth's lives had changed so dramatically in a short space of time. Who would have guessed a year ago that Charlotte would be heading back to the UK minus her husband, while Ruth was totally loved-up with a new man and an even newer baby?

Thankfully, the boys had taken the split in their stride. Charlotte's biggest fear of inflicting lasting damage on them seemed unfounded.

'You don't cuddle like you used to,' said Robson, when Charlotte and Dom sat them down to break the news.

'Does it mean you don't love each other?' added Alastair, his adorable face scrunched up in confusion.

His question ripped at Charlotte's heart. Before she could reply, Dom took her hand — now stripped of engagement and wedding rings — and squeezed it.

'We'll always love each other, because we'll always share you two. That will never change, no matter what happens.' He looked at Charlotte with eyes that held a multitude of emotions. Sadness, regret, guilt, and perhaps a tinge of relief. Now that it was all out in the open, Dom could get on with his new life. Whether that included Amelie in the long-term remained to be seen. He'd moved in with her, albeit reluctantly, but a little bird had told Charlotte that the love nest was lined with thorns.

'I don't want to speak out of turn,' said Juliette when she called Charlotte unexpectedly one day. 'We all figured out what was going on — I'm so sorry — but Amelie is a force to be reckoned with. She is not my favourite person, and I hoped Dom would see sense. I think he tried, but she is very persuasive.'

Assuring Juliette that she didn't blame her — although an earlier heads up would have been nice — Charlotte ended the call. She'd liked most of Dom's colleagues — with one notable exception — and understood their reluctance to interfere.

Pulling into the school gates, Charlotte smiled at the memory of her first encounter with Jürgen. OK, not with the man himself, but his Ferrari. A flash car was a flash car. What counted was the person behind the steering wheel. *Dickhead,* she'd thought. How wrong she'd been. Bracing herself, Charlotte parked, inhaled deeply and marched purposefully towards the chalet.

CHAPTER 50

'I can't believe you're leaving!' Sadie flung her arms around Charlotte. 'Although I still haven't forgiven you for keeping schtum about Dom.'

Charlotte returned the hug, Alastair and Robson settling for fist bumps and high-fives with their friends. They'd emerged weighed down with artwork, jotters, and a selection of goodbye gifts from classmates.

'I know, Sadie. I'm sorry, but it took me a long time to process it myself, and then I didn't want to dump my woes on you. But thank you for being such a great friend.'

Pamela sidled up next to them, and Charlotte gave her a less enthusiastic hug.

'It's been nice knowing you,' Pamela said. 'I wish you all the best for the future.'

'You will keep in touch, won't you?' Sadie added, as Miranda and Louise skipped into view. 'I want to know all about your new life back in England, particularly' — she leaned over and whispered in Charlotte's ear — 'when you meet a gorgeous new man.'

Before she could reply that meeting a new man was the

last thing she needed, Charlotte's stomach did an involuntary cartwheel. Jürgen was metres away, chatting to another dad. Snatching up the boys' bags with one hand, she waved in the general direction of other parents she'd got to know in the past year. To shouts of 'good luck' and 'take care', she ushered Alastair and Robson down the path towards her car.

'Mummy, look what Jodie gave us!' Robson delved into a bag and produced a book entitled *The Everyday Vegan.*

'And our teachers gave us these.' Alastair rummaged in another bag, forcing Charlotte to put down the cumbersome load. 'We made them in secret last week.'

Charlotte swallowed hard as she looked at the two tea towels, each bearing hand-drawn pictures of their respective classmates, complete with names and scrawled messages.

'That's so lovely, and a great reminder of your time at La Montagne. Now, we need to hurry and get the car back home.' A local dealer was collecting it in an hour, payment in cash.

'Charlotte, wait!'

She turned, that achingly familiar voice inducing another internal belly flop. 'Hi, Jürgen. It's good to see you.' And it was, it really was. Charlotte took in his immaculate appearance, at least clothing-wise. His face told a different story: tiredness mixed with sadness oozed from every pore.

'And you, Charlotte. I wasn't sure if I would see you. But I'm glad I didn't miss you.'

Charlotte smiled, although she knew it was a feeble effort. 'I'm glad too. I'm just sorry we have to rush off, but at least we get the chance to say goodbye.'

Jürgen's intense eyes probed Charlotte's. 'Indeed, although I prefer the German or French versions, auf wiedersehen and au revoir, because they speak of meeting again.'

Charlotte had called Jürgen to tell him of their plans once

she and Dom had hammered out the details. He'd replied with a simple: *I wish you only good things, Charlotte. Always in my heart x*

'Thank you for everything. For listening, for being there for me, for helping me find the courage to...' Charlotte's voice wobbled. She glanced around for the boys, spotting them heading back to the chalet surrounded by more friends.

'I did very little, Charlotte. And do not forget, you helped me too. To realise my heart is still open to finding true love again. When I meet the right woman...'

Charlotte saw the sad longing in his eyes, and wanted nothing more than to leap into his strong, supportive arms and cling on for eternity. Instead, she stepped back and collided with Marcus.

'Oops!' Marcus grimaced in fake pain. 'I hope a hospital visit will not be necessary.' He rubbed his left foot, winking at Charlotte.

'Marcus!' Alastair and Robson bowled down the path, grinding to a halt in front of their much-loved babysitter.

'Ah, I will miss you two.' Marcus shook each of their hands formally, before drawing them in for a group hug. 'Now, remember to be good for your mum and work hard at school. In fact, I would very much like to be your pen pal.'

'What's a pen pal?' Robson looked at Charlotte for an explanation.

'It's someone you write to with all your news. It's a nice way to stay in touch, although most people use email these days.'

'I am old-fashioned, and prefer to write proper letters,' said Marcus. 'There is something special about a letter arriving by post.'

Jürgen laughed. 'I sometimes think my son belongs in a different era. He'd be happier if we still travelled using coaches and horses!'

The light-hearted conversation helped ease Charlotte's raw emotions. As Marcus continued to chat to the boys, she looked at Jürgen. She saw her sadness reflected in his eyes, mirrored in the dip of his generous mouth.

'Please may I have your address, Mrs Egerton?' Though she had corrected him several times, Marcus never called her Charlotte. Jürgen was right; Marcus had an air of bygone days about him. He was unfailingly polite, chivalrous and charming. The apple hadn't fallen far from the tree.

'Here you go.' Charlotte scribbled the address on a scrap of paper and handed it to Marcus. 'Now we really have to leave.'

Jürgen and Marcus walked them to the car. Popping open the boot, Charlotte dumped all the bags, then strapped the boys into the back seats. 'Bye Marcus, bye Jürgen,' they chirruped in unison before Charlotte closed the door.

Marcus gave Charlotte a half-bow, before pecking her on the cheek, his own cheeks reddening as he did so. 'Dad, I left some files in my locker. I'll be back in a few minutes.'

Left alone with Jürgen, Charlotte didn't know what to say or do. Her arms drooped at her sides, one hand clutching the car key, the other digging her nails into her palm. She should leap into the driver's seat, speed through the gates, and not look back. But Jürgen's presence was a magnetic force field she struggled to escape from.

'Charlotte.' He reached out as if to hold her, then stepped back. The line they couldn't cross, the place they couldn't go, was marked out in invisible chalk.

'I'm glad Marcus will keep in touch with the boys. That's such a sweet thing to do. I'll help them reply, of course.'

'May I keep in touch too?' Jürgen kept his distance, but the energy between them was palpable.

'I don't know — I'll be so busy getting the boys back to school and sorting out the house and… things.' The excuses dried up, none of them a valid reason for not staying in contact. Charlotte just felt the pain of not seeing Jürgen would be very hard to bear.

'I'll leave it with you. Please take care.' With a last smile that didn't reach his eyes, Jürgen turned and walked away. Back to his own car, his son and his life, and out of Charlotte's for ever.

CHAPTER 51

CHARLOTTE SAT BACK WITH A SATISFIED SIGH. A MERE THREE hours, and she'd self-assembled a bookshelf and a desk. Remarkably, there'd been no missing screws, and she'd only sworn half a dozen times.

Getting to her feet — her knees were definitely getting creakier — she headed to the kitchen for a well-earned cup of tea. Waiting for the kettle to boil, she flicked through her beloved wall calendar, pleased she'd found one with three columns instead of four. She'd headed each with their names: Charlotte, Alastair and Robson. Dom was excised from the day-to-day activities, although not from their lives. He called or FaceTimed the boys regularly. Charlotte joked with Ruth that he had more contact with them now than when they lived under the same roof.

Adding some appointments to next month's page, including a job interview for a medical receptionist's position, Charlotte paused, pen in hand. *June 29.* That was exactly a year since the Elton John concert. So much had happened in between, and memories of both the good times and the bad flooded her mind.

Dropping a tea bag into one of the boys' hand-painted mugs, Charlotte circled the first of August. That was the day the boys broke up for the summer holidays. She'd agreed that Dom could fly over — on his own — the day after, and take them to Switzerland for two weeks. He'd visited a month ago, staying at a local B & B, and taking Alastair and Robson out in the evenings for pizza and movies.

'How are you?' he'd asked Charlotte when he arrived on the Friday evening. He looked thinner, with bluish shadows under his eyes and decidedly crumpled clothes.

'I'm good. Great, in fact,' she'd replied. Tempted as she was to comment on his appearance, Charlotte had said nothing. Perhaps Amelie demanded all-night sex which left them both too exhausted to tackle the ironing.

'That's, erm, good.' Dom had shuffled awkwardly on the doorstep. Charlotte hadn't invited him in. At some point soon they'd need to discuss the divorce and settlement, but for now Dom was covering the mortgage and paying a reasonable monthly amount into Charlotte's bank account. Then the boys had appeared, launching themselves at their dad like heat-seeking missiles. Charlotte had waved from the window as they drove off in Dom's hire car, before settling down with a book and some soothing background music.

Now, sipping her tea, Charlotte looked forward to seeing Ruth, Simon and Jacob later. Her best friend and partner had been total rocks since her return, helping with everything from unpacking to setting up new phone and internet packages and shopping around for a decent second-hand car. Seven years old, with low mileage, the red Nissan Juke now took pride of place on the driveway. Alastair and Robson loved its quirky look and insisted on sending a photo to Marcus. Jürgen's son had been as good as his word, his first letter arriving in the post a week after they left Switzerland. Charlotte helped the boys to draft a reply: two pages of around ten sentences written in a mix of coloured pencils.

'I can't believe you haven't sent him a single text!' Ruth gave Charlotte a disbelieving look as they prepped nibbles together in the kitchen. 'Who are you torturing the most, yourself or poor Jürgen?'

'What's the point?' Charlotte upended a pot of mixed olives and feta cheese chunks into a bowl. 'He lives there, I live here, and never the twain shall meet. Anyway, it's far too soon to think about another relationship. I'm not even bloody divorced yet.'

Ruth rolled her eyes. 'Hon, when you meet someone who makes your insides melt faster than a Magnum in a heat-wave, you don't let a little thing like geography get in the way. Isn't that right, Simon?'

Jiggling a contented Jacob on his knee at the table, Simon shrugged. 'Ruth, we only lived a few miles apart, so our situation was rather different. Stop haranguing poor Charlotte and let her decide what's right and what's not.'

Charlotte high-fived Simon just as Jacob let rip with an explosive nappy-filling noise.

'Oh, good God,' exclaimed Ruth. She went to take him, but Simon gathered up their stinky son and the changing bag they'd plonked in the corner.

'You two carry on nattering, and I'll deal with our darling super-shitter. Seriously, considering how little goes in, it amazes me how much comes out.'

'He's a keeper, that one.' Charlotte topped up their wine glasses, smiling at Ruth's contented expression. 'Dom dodged nappy changing; he said he was no good at it. As if women relished the prospect of wiping away yellow-green poo multiple times a day. And when the solids started...'

They clinked their glasses together, united in mother-hood, albeit at different stages of the process.

'I love him — I love *them* — to bits. Oh crap, now I'm getting all maudlin.' Ruth dabbed at her eyes with a piece of kitchen roll. 'Who'd have thought, your commitment-phobic bestie going mushy over a man and a baby.'

'At least it's not *two* men and a baby. Or, perish the thought, three,' said Charlotte. 'Ooh, I think Jacob's fan club have got in on the act.' From upstairs she heard screams of delight from Alastair and Robson. They adored Jacob, treating him like a baby brother and even relishing the chance to help change his nappies. Charlotte had picked up a second-hand changing table and set it up in the spare bedroom for when Ruth visited. The boys squabbled good-naturedly about who got the first cuddle, and the odd time they got to help bath Jacob filled them with joy.

'Mummy!' Robson tore into the kitchen, breathless with glee. 'Jacob just did a wee all over the bedroom curtains!'

Ruth burst out laughing, pulling a 'forgive me' face. 'That lad's willy's like a mini fire hose. You never know what it'll spray next. He got Simon square in the face the other day.'

Robson scrunched up in a fit of giggles at the word 'willy', then hearing Alastair calling to him, he took off again at breakneck speed.

'I'll pay for the dry cleaning,' said Ruth.

'You bloody won't. Those curtains belonged to the previous owners, and hideous doesn't describe them. Jacob's done me a favour; they're something I'll be glad to replace.'

'Like Dom?' Ruth adjusted a pad in her bra, prodding her boobs like a baker testing his dough.

'I'm not replacing Dom any time soon.' Charlotte stabbed at a chunk of feta with a cocktail stick. 'I'm happy with it just being me and the boys. Stop meddling, Ruth, and go feed that eating machine before those puppies cause an explosion.'

Lovely as it was to have Ruth, Simon and Jacob around, Charlotte closed the door behind them after a couple of hours with a contented sigh. This was *her* space now, and she relished every precious square foot of it. Not for ever — she'd have to downsize at some point — but right now, Charlotte was queen of her mid-sized suburban home.

A quick squint around their bedroom door revealed Alastair and Robson adrift on a sea of innocent slumber. Charlotte envied their ready acceptance of the changes thrust upon them. They were so capable of adapting, of absorbing everything thrown at them, good and bad. She hoped life would treat them kindly, but life didn't come with shiny warranties or guarantees. You tried your best, and if it didn't work, you tried again.

It was only ten pm, yet Charlotte craved her bed. She tidied up the kitchen and folded a pile of laundry still warm from the tumble dryer. Double-checking that she'd locked the front and back doors, she placed a foot on the bottom stair, and—

The sound of a car pulling into the driveway made her stop. Had Ruth and Simon forgotten something? Not Jacob; she'd definitely have noticed *his* lingering presence.

Peering through the front window, Charlotte frowned at the unfamiliar car. A taxi, its sign unlit. She watched as someone clambered out, turning back to pay the driver. Her breath caught in her throat as the passenger straightened up. *It can't be.* She hurried to the door, twisting the lock open with fumbling fingers. The figure stood before her, his face in shadow, but Charlotte knew exactly who it was.

'Charlotte.' That voice catapulted her back in time, stirring up emotions she'd tried to repress. She'd convinced herself there could be no future between them. And now he was here.

'Jürgen.' She opened the door wider, and he stepped in.

CHAPTER 52

'I WAS JUST PASSING.'

Charlotte looked at the man whom she'd initially despised, then become friends with, and latterly, grown close to. *Very* close to. Someone she'd leaned on when the going got tough. In a funny way, they'd propped each other up. Both damaged, both in need of a sounding board.

'Just passing? I live in a cul-de-sac in a sleepy English village miles away from the nearest motorway. Or airport.'

Jürgen massaged his left wrist with his right hand. Charlotte sensed his nerves, which weren't something she'd normally associate with his air of Germanic togetherness.

'OK, I am lying. I had a business trip to London, and I wanted to see you. I'm sorry, I'll leave if you want me to.'

Charlotte shook her head. 'Of course I don't want you to leave. I'm just — surprised to see you. How did you know I'd be home?'

Surprised didn't cover it. Gobsmacked, stunned and more than a bit thrilled went some way towards describing her mood. A mood she needed to douse pronto. Jürgen couldn't be part of her life; to imagine otherwise was insanity. Still, he was here, and Charlotte's inbred good manners meant she had to invite him in.

'I took a chance that you would be. If not, I planned to leave a note.' Jürgen touched the top pocket of his jacket, a sliver of paper just visible.

'Please, come in.' She gestured upstairs, pressing a finger to her lips to signal keeping their voices down.

Jürgen nodded and followed Charlotte into the lounge. 'You have a lovely home,' he said, his gaze taking in her efforts to create order from chaos in the past few weeks.

'Thank you. Now, can I get you something to drink? Tea, coffee or something stronger?' The latter seemed a good idea to Charlotte, to help her deal with a situation she'd never envisaged.

'A glass of wine of any colour would be lovely.' Jürgen smiled as he admired a series of photos lining the mantelpiece: the boys at different stages of their young lives, and one family portrait with Dom and Charlotte in the middle.

Returning from the kitchen with a bottle of red and two glasses, Charlotte poured two generous measures. Jürgen took one, and they toasted one another. His eyes never left Charlotte's face, and a hot tingle coursed through her body.

'Alastair and Robson, they are doing well? Marcus enjoys writing to them, I think. He became very fond of them during their time together.'

'They're great,' said Charlotte. 'They've settled back into their old school as if they'd never been away, which isn't surprising as we weren't in Switzerland very long.'

'And you? You are happy to be back?' Jürgen swirled the liquid round his glass, his penetrating gaze still fixed on Charlotte.

'I am. It's familiar here, easy to fit in again, and I don't have to worry about speaking French or navigating those twisty mountain roads!'

They sat down on opposite sides of the room. Charlotte wanted to ask Jürgen why he was here, but the words welded themselves to the roof of her mouth. *You know why he's here*, an inner voice screamed in her ear. She just wasn't ready to hear it, and afraid of her reaction to an impossible situation.

'Charlotte, I haven't stopped thinking about you since the day you left. You are the first thing on my mind when I wake up, and the last before I go to sleep. I've tried to bury the thoughts, but—' He ran a hand through his silver-streaked hair. 'You are like a beautiful ghost who haunts me.'

Charlotte swallowed her mouthful of wine. She wanted to make light of Jürgen's remark and joke about being a hundred per cent alive and kicking, but she couldn't. She felt the same. This warm, compassionate and desperately attractive man had occupied her thoughts every single day.

'Jürgen, I… I know we have feelings for one another. I tried to deny them while my marriage was falling apart, and I didn't want to cheat on Dom — not even in my head — because that would make me as bad as him. But how can we possibly act on those feelings? We can't, we just can't.'

For a mad moment, Charlotte pictured Jürgen upping sticks and moving to England. The two of them, dipping their toes into a fledgling relationship, figuring out if their mutual attraction was solid or destined to fizzle out. She blinked rapidly, erasing the unlikely scenario.

'I could move to England.' Charlotte gasped, wondering if Jürgen had mind-reading powers. 'Marcus wants to study here, perhaps at York or Durham University. He is in his last year at La Montagne, and I can work anywhere in the world. It sounds crazy, but being closer to you, just knowing I might see you sometimes, would feel like the sun coming out on a winter's day.'

Coming from anyone else, Jürgen's words might seem overly flowery, like a wannabe poet's attempt to woo a reluctant partner. For Charlotte, they typified everything she loved about him. *Did I just use the L word?*

'Jürgen, I need to process all of this. You appearing out of the blue, saying the things you're saying. I'm still legally married. I need to think about the boys, I need to build a new life here, and—'

'Mummy, I had a bad dream! A monster snuck into my bed and did an enormous poo. Oh, hello!' Alastair stood awkwardly by the door, sucking on the neckline of his pyjama top.

'You remember Jürgen?' *Of course he does, you idiot.* Charlotte's memory had the occasional Swiss-cheese-style hole, but her boys' memories were laser-sharp. As they should be, at such a tender age.

'Alastair.' Jürgen rose and offered his hand. Alastair looked at Charlotte, confused and uncertain how to react.

Charlotte leapt to her feet and wrapped her arms around her precious son. 'Sweetie, Jürgen's in town on business and he dropped in to say hi. Isn't that a lovely thing to do?'

Alastair accepted the handshake. 'It's nice to see you. Are you going to have a sleepover?'

Jürgen, to his credit, kept a straight face. 'No, sadly I have a taxi booked to come in' — he looked at his watch — 'ten minutes. And I must return to Switzerland the day after tomorrow.'

So soon? Charlotte massaged Alastair's shoulders, feeling his bones through the delicate skin. *Stay,* she wanted to scream. *Go,* her rational side shouted. 'Alastair, take yourself back to bed and I'll be there in a minute to check for monster poo.'

As Alastair's footsteps receded, Charlotte remained motionless. She wanted another drink; she wanted Jürgen to stay; she wanted life to be less bloody complicated. She wanted a happily ever after that delivered, instead of collapsing in a heap of acrimony and doubt.

'Charlotte, my taxi is here.' Sure enough, a sweep of head-lights and the toot of a horn signalled Jürgen's time to leave.

'Is this goodbye? A proper goodbye? None of that, "I'll see you again stuff"?' Charlotte trembled, pain swelling inside her chest.

Jürgen took her hand as he'd done before, and Charlotte rested her head against his chest. The taxi tooted again, and she silently cursed its unwelcome presence.

'If you want to see me again, text me tomorrow.' Jürgen stroked the nape of her neck. Charlotte tingled at his touch, before stepping away. 'If I don't hear from you, I will under-stand. I will never forget, but I will understand.'

For several moments, Charlotte stood by the window as the taxi pulled away. She wanted to bang her head repeatedly on the glass, to knock some sense into herself. Why couldn't they be together? Was she creating obstacles that didn't exist?

After reassuring Alastair that no monsters had left unde-sirable objects in his bed, Charlotte kissed him goodnight and went downstairs. As the clock's hands moved to midnight, she threw herself down on the sofa and reached for Jürgen's wine glass, fingering the stem as if she could connect with his earlier touch. *He was here.* Her tears fell with ferocity until sleep pulled her into oblivion.

CHAPTER 53

'You're telling me that a man who clearly worships the ground you walk on turned up out of the blue and poured his heart out, and you sent him packing?' An incredulous Ruth twirled her finger at the side of her head. 'You've got a screw loose.'

'I did *not* send him packing. He had a taxi booked.' Charlotte honked into a tissue, last night's crying fit threatening to start up again.

'Hon, that is one of the most romantic things I've ever heard. He comes all this way to see you, says he thinks of you night and day, and doesn't even go in for a snog? Crikey, it sounds like something out of a Hugh Grant romcom. I mean a younger Hugh Grant, obviously.'

'I'm no bloody Julia Roberts,' retorted Charlotte. 'Anyway, in the movies they always find a way around seemingly impossible scenarios. This is real life, not a fairy tale created in LaLa Land. It's hopeless.'

Ruth ducked away from the camera, cooing 'who's a clever boy, then?' before popping up again. 'Sorry, Jacob's become an expert at batting the toys on his play mat. It's like watching a mini Roger Federer in action. Sorry, where were we?'

'You were accusing me of insanity and comparing Jürgen to a floppy-haired Brit,' said Charlotte. 'And I told you it was hopeless.'

'The only thing that's hopeless is *you*. Hunky Germans aren't like meter readers; they don't appear on your doorstep regularly. Hon, you two have something special going on. Surely it's worth at least talking about it together?'

Picking at a lunchtime tuna sandwich, Charlotte stared at her phone. She'd started writing a text several times, but deleted them all. What could she say? *Come back and let's give it a go.* Or was it better to leave well alone, and keep the memories of an almost-romance?

Gathering up a pile of the boys' dirty laundry, Charlotte stuffed it into the washing machine and measured out the powder. Switching the machine on, she sank to the floor in front of the rotating drum. Round and round it went, in tandem with her swirling thoughts. Mesmerised by the motion, she jolted at the clatter of the letterbox flap. Strange — the postman had already been.

Reaching the door, Charlotte picked up a folded piece of paper.

Dear Charlotte.

I don't want to trouble you any more. Seeing you last night meant the world to me, but on reflection, it is unfair to put you under pressure. As I once said, sometimes the heart wants what it shouldn't. I will never forget you, and I wish you and your wonderful boys every happiness in the future.

Yours always,

Jürgen x

Charlotte clasped the note to her thumping chest. He was leaving. She didn't *want* him to leave. Not like this, not with so many things left unsaid. Wrenching the door open, she saw Jürgen standing by the kerb next to the waiting taxi.

'Wait!' Charlotte ran towards him, cursing the fact that she sported an unflattering combo of faded black leggings and an oversized T-shirt with a hole in it.

'Charlotte.' Jürgen hesitated, his hand on the taxi door handle. 'I'm sorry, it was cowardly to leave a note. When you didn't text, I decided it was best not to see you. You need to build your new life, and I must let you do that without causing you any pain.'

As the taxi driver tapped his fingers on the steering wheel in time to an 80s disco song, Charlotte wrapped her arms around her trembling body. 'You know, I'm done with you apologising all the time, Jürgen. And I'm angry with myself for being a spineless wimp. I vowed to be brave in ending my marriage, and you helped me find the strength.'

Jürgen blinked in surprise at Charlotte's forceful tone. The taxi driver turned the music off and looked in their direction.

'And I know I have the courage now to take a chance on something scary and new and exciting. Because if I don't, I'll spend the rest of my life regretting it.' Charlotte pictured Ruth punching the air, cheering her on. *Go girl!*

'Mate, fascinating as your Romeo and Juliet routine is, the meter's ticking. Are you getting in or not?' The driver leaned out of the window, giving Charlotte a salacious wink.

'He's not.' Charlotte tightened her grip around her chest, aware she wasn't wearing a bra. 'He's coming with me.'

Jürgen handed a tenner to the driver, whose face lit up like the Blackpool illuminations. 'Cheers, mate. Don't do anything I wouldn't do.'

Left on the pavement, Charlotte and Jürgen stood silent. Charlotte noticed a neighbour's curtain twitching, and a curious stare from a dog-walker. Yes, a barefoot woman with mad hair next to an immaculately clad man might attract attention.

'Inside. Now.' Aware that she sounded like an undercover cop hustling a suspect away from prying eyes, Charlotte led the way towards her house. Once inside, she marched into the living room. 'Ow!' She looked down and spied a piece of rogue Lego.

'Are you OK?' Jürgen watched her hop to the sofa.

Massaging her stinging foot, Charlotte patted the cushion next to her. 'Sit.' Great, now she was addressing Jürgen like a belligerent puppy in the throes of training.

'Jürgen. I'm fine. Better than fine. You're here, and I can't quite believe it. If you really want us to make a go of this, I'm in.' Charlotte sighed as Jürgen moved closer and tentatively lifted her throbbing foot into his lap.

'Does it hurt ... here?' He worked his thumb in gentle circles around the sole, and the throbbing subsided.

Charlotte collapsed into a fit of giggles. 'Aargh, stop!' Jürgen laughed too, releasing her foot and taking her hand instead. He raised it to his lips, kissing it with such tenderness that Charlotte's insides liquefied.

'We have a difficult road ahead, Charlotte. I can visit perhaps once a month, and spend some days here. In a hotel, of course. What is the English saying — baby feet?'

'Baby steps.' Charlotte smiled. Sometimes things got lost in translation, but she and Jürgen spoke the same language, were on the same page. Both had been kicked in the teeth by life, both were willing to grab a chance at happiness. To finally 'seize the day'.

'So would one of those baby steps be a kiss? A proper kiss before I go?' Jürgen's look of naked longing sent shock waves through every fibre of Charlotte's being.

'Just a kiss,' she whispered. 'For now.'

They shuffled closer. Charlotte closed her eyes, resting her head on the back of the sofa.

'Open your eyes, please.' Jürgen's voice made her look at him, and lose herself in the abyss of adoration radiating from his face. Then they kissed. And it was magical.

CHAPTER 54

CHARLOTTE CHECKED HER WATCH FOR THE UMPTEENTH TIME.
He'd be here soon. She grinned, grappling with a stray strand
of hair that had escaped her casual up-do. Not that Jürgen
cared about whether her hair was up or down. He loved her
exactly as she was.

'Mummy, why is Jürgen not here yet?' said Robson.

'He's on his way, sweetie.' Charlotte ruffled Robson's hair.
He huffed, obsessed as he was with styling it into a quiff.
How her boys had grown in a mere six months.

'When Gran and Grandad come, can we go to Thorpe
Park?'

Charlotte nodded, although she didn't know how keen
her parents would be to take the boys to a place full of scary
rides. Not that they were tall enough to go on most of them,
but every time she measured them they'd sprouted a little.
Her parents were arriving in a week's time for a two-week
stay.

Alastair appeared, sweaty and dishevelled after a bike ride
round the estate with friends. 'I'm starving. When are we
eating?' He tugged off his helmet and filled a glass of water

from the tap.

'When Jürgen arrives.' Charlotte gave the lamb casserole a stir. 'Go and have a shower, stinky boy.'

Alastair sloped off, leaving Charlotte alone with Robson. He sat at the table, flicking through a pile of Panini football stickers. 'I like Jürgen,' he said as he sorted a handful of stickers into team colours. 'Better than I like Amelie.'

Charlotte sat down opposite him. She knew the boys attempted to get along with their father's new partner, but both complained that Amelie talked to them as if they were babies. 'And she hardly eats anything and spends hours and hours in the bathroom,' grumbled Alastair after one of their stays in Switzerland.

'Maybe she's constipated?' quipped Charlotte naughtily.

Alastair sniggered. 'No, Mummy, she just spends *ages* putting on smelly lotions and fixing her face.'

Charlotte had heard through Juliette that no one in the office believed the relationship would last. 'Dom is not happy,' she said, during one of their occasional chats. 'He has lost the sparkle he once had, as if Amelie has sucked the life force from him. She is so controlling, always checking where he is and what he is doing.'

Poacher turned gamekeeper, thought Charlotte. Perhaps Amelie feared that Dom would find someone else. Either way, Charlotte didn't really care.

Dom hadn't been happy when Charlotte revealed she was seeing Jürgen, either. 'Don't you think it's a bit soon after our break-up to dive into a new relationship?' he'd snapped down the phone one evening.

'At least I waited till the existing one was over *before* diving in,' Charlotte had retorted. That shut him up.

Over the past six months, Jürgen had visited several times. He always stayed at hotels in the area, where they could meet in privacy. Fearful of upsetting the boys, Charlotte had waited some time before breaking the news.

'Are you going to get married?' asked Robson.

'Of course not!' Charlotte bit down a laugh. 'Jürgen's a … a friend. A good friend.'

'He was always nice to us in Switzerland,' Robson added. 'Marcus, too.'

To both Jürgen and Charlotte's delight, Marcus had received almost top marks in his International Baccalaureate exams, which secured him a place at Durham University to study Environmental Geoscience. He'd start his course later that month, his accommodation in halls of residence already sorted.

'You must be so proud,' Charlotte had said to Jürgen over dinner shortly after the results came out.

'Of course, Charlotte. Good exam results are a cause to celebrate, but my pride is mainly for the fine young man he has become.' He'd grasped her hand across the table, his touch filling her with that sense of rightness she'd fought against for so long.

Now, with divorce proceedings underway, Charlotte's world felt good. Different, scary, but *good*. She worked three days a week at a medical centre, volunteered at an old folks' home once a fortnight, and spent as much time as possible with Ruth, Simon and Jacob.

She still kept in touch with Sadie, the font of all knowledge concerning the goings-on at La Montagne. 'Alicia's bagged herself a new man!' Sadie had announced with glee. 'Even more minted than Derek, if that's possible. Mind you, he must be kicking on for eighty. She's probably hoping for a quickie marriage and an early expiry date.'

Charlotte had laughed at Sadie's rapid round-up of all the gossip. The news that Pamela and Martin were on a break took her by surprise. She'd told Sadie about Pamela coming on to Jürgen — and of her fledgling relationship with him — which had made Sadie whoop with delight.

'I don't think Pamela ever forgave him for getting his leg over with the au pair. Martin's moved to Dubai on a contract, and now she's lost a stone in weight and skips around like a bloody spring lamb. Do you remember how weird she was in Divonne? I reckon she's got her eye on someone else, or she's ready to pounce on another unsuspecting man. All that bullshit about Jürgen... Ooh, how's *that* going, by the way?'

Charlotte had played it down. What she and Jürgen shared was wonderful, their time together limited but made all the more precious for it. *Absence makes the heart grow fonder.* They'd agreed to take things slowly: an old-fashioned courtship. Albeit one spiced with delicious kisses, and the first time they made love... Charlotte tingled at the memory.

'He's here!' Robson dashed to the front door just as Alastair headed downstairs rubbing his head with a towel.

'Hello, boys.' Jürgen's solid frame filled the doorway, a carrier bag in one hand and a small holdall in the other. After much discussion, they had decided that he would stay the night, but in the guest bedroom. Jürgen had argued that he was happy to stay in a hotel, but Charlotte countered that the boys knew him well enough.

'So Jürgen's having a sleepover?' said Robson, when Charlotte broached the subject. 'Cool!'

After dishing out much-missed sweet and savoury Swiss treats, Jürgen took his bag to the guest room, accompanied by a chattering Robson. 'The bathroom's here, our bedroom's there, and that's Mummy's. Don't worry, she doesn't snore *too* loudly.'

Listening to Robson's faint but audible directions, Charlotte turned to Alastair. 'I do *not* snore,' she said indignantly.

'Well, maybe once in a while. Now let's get the table laid before the casserole sets like cement.'

Over dinner they swapped silly stories, tucked into the food, and finished up with a feast of chocolate bars and a game of Mouse Trap. Jürgen helped Charlotte wash up, and the boys were despatched to get into their pyjamas and brush their teeth.

'I don't recall you snoring,' said Jürgen with a teasing look. 'Perhaps a little snuffle, that is all.'

Charlotte whacked him with the dishcloth. 'You'll be safe from my snuffles tonight, unless—'

'I can tiptoe into your room for a goodnight cuddle?'

Charlotte waggled her finger in mock disapproval. 'Only if you're very, very quiet. Now come here and kiss me.'

Lost in Jürgen's embrace, a comforting feeling spread through Charlotte's body. She took a moment to analyse it. It felt like … coming home.

ACKNOWLEDGMENTS

My fourth book! Who would have thought it. I'm thrilled — and terrified — to send this baby out into the world. A bit different to my previous works, but I really hope you enjoyed it.

A huge thanks again to the talented Lisa Firth at Oliphant Author Services for the stunning cover. It completely captured what I was looking for in every way.

Editing is vital to ensure a book emerges into the world in the best possible shape. Liz Hedgecock took on board my rough manuscript and kicked it into shape, in the nicest possible way. Any errors that remain are entirely down to me.

I'd like to thank so many Facebook groups and Twitter friends for supporting and helping me along the way. There's no such thing as a daft question when it comes to writing (and I ask a **lot** of questions). A special mention to fellow author Mark Pearson for coming up with the cover tagline and fellow Scottish writer Alix Kelso for reading an early draft and providing invaluable feedback. Also, thanks to my friend Emma Vijayaratnam for coming up with the Swiss school name.

Finally (are you still awake)? can I just say thank you for reading this. When it's five o'clock in the morning and I'm clattering away at the keyboard, staring at the screen through tired eyes, it's you who keeps me going. Knowing that someone enjoys these stories I make up is a wonderful feeling, and I appreciate it more than you know.

If you have just a moment more, I really need your help. Today's blockbuster authors have publishers who don't mind spending millions promoting their books, but I have something better. I have you! If you enjoy what I write, you can play a huge part in keeping these stories flowing, simply by sharing.

Readers trust other readers. Would you please leave a review on Amazon? (Reviews are the lifeblood of today's authors). Here's the link — Lost In Translation. After that, if you're a social media user, please help to spread the word. Tell your friends, share your review, mention me over a cup of coffee. Whether it's Facebook, Twitter, Pinterest, Instagram or down the pub, I'd be eternally grateful if you'd be part of my team and help get the word out.

Thank you! ♥♥ Audrey

ABOUT THE AUTHOR

Audrey Davis published her first romantic comedy novel *A Clean Sweep* in 2017, followed by a short prequel, *A Clean Break.* She originally released her second book *The Haunting of Hattie Hastings* as a novella trilogy, before combining it into a standalone novel. Her third — *A Wish For Jinnie* — released in June 2020.

Audrey lives in Switzerland with her husband and enjoys shopping, cooking, eating and drinking red wine. And — of course — reading and writing. She is a social media addict, so please get in touch through FB, Twitter or Instagram. Or, you can sign up to her newsletter where she babbles on about books, hair and other exciting subjects. audreydavis-newsletter

For a **free** short prequel to *The Haunting of Hattie Hastings,* just pop over to audreydavisauthor.com to sign up for your copy of *When Hattie Met Gary.*

Finally, authors love to be followed on Bookbub, as it helps raise our profile and offers us more promo opportunities. Plus, you'll hear from them when the next book is out! Just click on the wee BB icon.

Printed in Great Britain
by Amazon

77259018R00188